1934   *Ten Lyric Poems*
1935   *12 Ethical Sonnets*
1936   *15 Poems with Time Expressions*
1937   *Homecoming & Departure*
1938   *Childish Jokes: Crying Backstage*
1939   *A Warning at My Leisure*
1941   *Five Young American Poets: Second Series* (with Jeanne McGahey, Clark Mills, David Schubert, and Karl Shapiro)
1941   *Stop-Light: 5 Dance Poems*
1942   *The Grand Piano: or, The Almanac of Alienation*
1942   *Pieces of Three* (with Meyer Liben and Edouard Roditi)
1945   *The Facts of Life*
1946   *Art and Social Nature*
1946   *The State of Nature*
1946   *The Copernican Revolution*
1947   *The Copernican Revolution* (expanded edition)
1947   *Kafka's Prayer*
1947   *Communitas: Means of Livelihood and Ways of Life* (with Percival Goodman)
1949   *The Break-Up of Our Camp and Other Stories*
1950   *The Dead of Spring*
1951   *Gestalt Therapy: Excitement and Growth in the Human Personality* (with Frederick S. Perls and Ralph F. Hefferline)
1951   *Parents' Day*
1954   *Day and Other Poems*
1954   *The Structure of Literature*
1955   *Red Jacket*
1957   *The Well of Bethlehem*
1959   *The Empire City*
1960   *Growing Up Absurd: Problems of Youth in the Organized System*
1960   *Our Visit to Niagara*
1961   *Ten Poems*
1962   *The Lordly Hudson: Collected Poems*
1962   *Drawing the Line*
1962   *The Community of Scholars*
1962   *Utopian Essays and Practical Proposals*
1962   *The Society I Live In Is Mine*
1963   *Making Do*
1964   *Compulsory Mis-education*

PAUL GOODMAN

THE BREAK-UP OF OUR CAMP

STORIES 1932-1935

VOLUME I
of the
COLLECTED
STORIES
EDITED BY
TAYLOR STOEHR

BLACK SPARROW PRESS - SANTA BARBARA - 1978

"The Propriety of St. Francis" is reprinted by permission of Sigmund Koch, founder and editor of *Mosaic* magazine.

LIBRARY OF CONGRESS CATALOGING IN PUBLICATION DATA

Goodman, Paul, 1911-1972.
  The break-up of our camp.
  (The collected stories and sketches of Paul Goodman; vol. 1)
  Bibliography: p.

  I. Title.
PZ3.G6235Co vol. 1   [PS3513.0527]   813'.5.'2s   [813'.5'2]
                                                    78-941
ISBN 0187685-329-7 (paper edition)
ISBN 0-87685-330-0 (trade cloth edition)
ISBN 0-87685-331-9 (deluxe edition)

I often wish that I were old, had done
the work within me to which I owe my days,
the hundred stories and the twenty plays,
and what I have to add to thought, and one
good deed, at least, before the time is gone;
to know as a whole my art's bypaths and ways,
and what is latent in the present phase
(which I can hardly guess), this would be fun!
what joy to know that I have said enough
before I am by death or vice cut off!—
for I am dubious about my mode
of life—unnerved by augmenting fears—
and where I stand today upon the road,
see little pleasure in the coming years.

Paul Goodman
New York City 1935

Contents

Introduction

Paul Goodman lived just short of 61 years. He began writing stories in high school (poems much earlier), and produced a book a year for the rest of his life—fiction, drama, poetry, social criticism, literary analysis, psychoanalytic theory, etc. He called himself "a man of letters" to account for the range of his interests, but he valued his poems and stories above all his other work. They would last.

He composed in pencil and always had some stub in his pocket, along with the scraps and used envelopes on which he wrote most of his poems. His stories were written in longhand on the cheapest newsprint, now brown and crumbling; he used every inch right to the edge of the paper. The second draft was typed, expertly, and he sometimes made further corrections in pencil before sending it to an editor. After publication he sometimes revised again, on the printed pages, whether or not there was any likelihood of a new edition. Manuscripts were discarded like husks, so that there was rarely more than one version, always in process, alive, the cambium layer of his imagination.

Eager as he was for publication, he did not work for the sake of final products. A few stories like "Martin," part of the *Johnson* studies, he was still retouching a full generation after writing; readers complained that he spoiled their favorites, "The Lordly Hudson" and *The Grand Piano*, with second thoughts. All this goes to show a passion for writing itself, the act rather than the result. It was, as he frequently bragged, his vice, or more affirmatively, his "way of being in the world."

During different periods in his life he fell into different habits; up to the age of about 35 he was a night-owl, and told people he did his best work between two and four A.M. But morning, afternoon, or night he had one inviolable rule of thumb: write at least a page a day. This was enough to become involved with the material, so that on good days he might continue working well beyond that minimum. Since he threw very little away, this means that his average output should have been about a book a year—just as it was.

One is reminded of the stories about Trollope, writing by the clock and breaking off for luncheon in the middle of a sentence. In Goodman's case however the crucial factor was not discipline but method—or better, rhythm. That is to say, it was not the daily stint that produced so much, but the daily temptation to do what he loved to do, to lose himself in his work. There was something almost physiological about it. In his style, in his very character, there was a flow that fed this rhythm, so that if the first page went well, he was likely to complete an entire section in a sitting. His typical unit of composition was just that long—what he could write in a sitting. It was like breathing to him, second-nature.

The enormous advantage of such a combination of habits and intentions is obvious. The act of authorship is thereby rescued from the tediousness and drudgery of all long-term, open-ended pursuits, where the moment of completion lies at some ultimate point, not known till it suddenly arrives, little solace for the pleasures and frustrations buried along the way. Perhaps especially for a writer like Goodman, who never quite let go of his works but kept on tinkering with them even after they were printed, this potential for daily achievement and closure was indispensable. I think it was the secret of his productivity.

Very rarely did he attempt anything that required a slow swelling development. The average episode in his magnum opus *The Empire City* is perhaps two or three pages long; in *Communitas* and *The Structure of Literature*

10

history and analysis fall into the same measure. The exception is *Making Do*, probably his least successful, and certainly his least characteristic novel. (He once explained that he had written it according to a blueprint prepared in advance.) Otherwise all of his longer works move along at a sprightly pace, in part determined simply by the parade of small units, full of variety and motion.

Goodman's prose rhythm developed during his long devotion to the short story. In that genre he could always work with episodes that might be finished in a sitting. The manuscripts that survive are scarcely smudged or interlined, and many of them have a rhapsodic quality, almost chanted, with little trace of any pause longer than the time it might take to whittle a pencil sharp. These episodes were easily accumulated into larger wholes, loose structures of emotion and event that often seem like prose poems.

Although from the beginning he favored the rhapsodic episode, he also wrote "scenes," somewhat in the manner of Maupassant. Much of his juvenilia struggles in this straitjacket, and one can watch the progressive releasing of his powers as he discovered models that encouraged him to follow his bent. His creative writing teacher at City College accused him of imitating Joyce, but he had darker corners to explore: Ring Lardner and Sherwood Anderson, Cocteau and the obscure surrealist Pierre MacOrlan. Most of all, he learned from Hawthorne, who taught him that a story was like a dream.

Hawthorne was Goodman's favorite writer of stories, and he borrowed so heavily from him, and was in some ways so similar, that it helps to keep him in mind while considering Goodman's career. Like Hawthorne, he wrote an undergraduate novel which he then suppressed, turning instead to the short story, a genre that allowed for youthful experiment at less risk. When Hawthorne finally returned to the novel, after 20 years, he did so more or less by accident, and he never really abandoned the episodic method. Goodman did not wait so long to try out the possibilities of the novel-in-stories; he began his first, *Johnson*, soon after he graduated, and his second, *The*

11

Break-Up of Our Camp, followed in a few years. These books were experimental, for Goodman never stopped trying out different forms and genres, but though more complex and ambitious than his stories, the same raw materials went into them, and they were composed according to the same pattern of small units. A number of their chapters were published in magazines as separate stories—obviously part of the plan, another idea he may have gotten from Hawthorne.

Like most of his early fiction, these books were based on Goodman's own experience. *Johnson* was written as part of the campaign to win the affections of the "black-blond sea-lion" who inspired its fantasies, and some of the adventures really happened, like Johnson's visit to the camp where Leonard was swimming counselor—though the happy outcome of that trip, Leonard's acceptance of Johnson's love, was just Goodman's chagrined invention. The actual trip was a fiasco; art improved on life.

The Break-Up of Our Camp was also written in the midst of its scenes—the Jewish boys' camp where Goodman himself worked, as dramatics counselor during the summers of 1934, 1935, and 1936. Its opening, the arrival out of the night of the canoeist, occurred during Goodman's first weeks there, and the book was still in process the following summer when for the second time he mounted his own children's-version of *Macbeth* as a Saturday night show for the campers. He seems often to have preferred to write about the things going on around him, as if they might still be soft to the impress of the imagination. The history of love poetry is full of precedent for the conversion of sexual longing into art; but *The Break-Up of Our Camp* is not about love at all. By the time he wrote it, Goodman was so confirmed in his art that, through a curious twist of the usual order, all experience had been potentially eroticized for him. He was not an ambulance-chaser, looking for stories to tell, but everything that happened to him was doubly quickened, like living at risk or under a vow; if it came to nothing in life, it might in art.

This was not all to the good. Consider "Martin, or The

12

Work of Art." Life could become too artful, while art stared and ogled shamelessly. One result was a strong tendency toward symbolism, of the self-examining sort found in those tales of Hawthorne that deal with the temptations of the imagination, "Young Goodman Brown," "Wakefield," or *The Scarlet Letter*. All through the *Johnson* stories Goodman plays with these possibilities of watching the self from the perspective of its other avatars, like Chillingworth gazing rapt into the soul of Dimmesdale. But for Hawthorne it was the unpardonable sin, while for Goodman it was simply a fact of life for the artist, to make the self an object of contemplation.

The short story format lends itself to such interests by not setting up complex narrative expectations; one is alone with the author and his thoughts. Dedicating his last book of stories in 1968, Goodman acknowledged his debt not only to Hawthorne's tales but also to Beethoven's piano sonatas, a model that suggests something of the almost abstract self-communing that his stories facilitate with their harmonies of tone, symmetries, formal rhythms independent of any threads of plot. More like dreams than anything else, these patterns are only partially in the control of the artist—which is why in his best work they seem to express character rather than mere attitude or tone. It was to this level of the self that he wanted to dive. Sometimes, as in most of the *Johnson* stories, he merely arranges his motifs without finding this stronger current—but then he will strike upon it in the midst of formal exercises, in the breath-taking surges of "The Tennis-Game" or "Out of Love." It cannot be an accident that these are occasions when Johnson himself is suddenly translated out of his ordinary consciousness to a new state of awareness, where everything is luminous. One begins to understand Goodman's addiction to writing, and its reciprocation with his daily life.

Perhaps even more extraordinary is "Iddings Clark," a story that rivals its inspiration "The Minister's Black Veil," in its slow accretion of everyday scenes, more and more oddly skewed, to achieve an eerie symbolic impact. Yet it is a different sort of success. Goodman obviously set out to write a prize-winner. By and large he was not a writer of set-pieces; he could produce such things, just as he could write Elizabethan sonnets and *ballades*, but after he had proved he could do it—"The Wandering Boys" won an honorable mention in O'Brien's *Best Short Stories* for 1933— he lost interest. Notice too that neither "Iddings Clark" nor "The Wandering Boys" came from Goodman's own experience. The former was imitation, the latter was based on an anecdote his mother brought back from one of her excursions to the West Coast. In a sense these stories were nothing but exercises in structural possibilities. Goodman was fascinated by form, but usually more tempted to try out something new than to perfect what had become easy for him. There was more chance that his hand would be seized, and he would write something beyond his reach. Nor was this likely to happen unless he wrote from the heart, for only there lay the truths that mattered, and the beauty that could make you cry.

In some ways *The Break-Up of Our Camp* is both a formal *tour de force* and in touch with these sources of feeling. Not that there is anything flashy or even very dramatic in it. The surreal automobile ride in chapter V is a feat of pace and emphasis, but most of the moments one remembers come in passages of quiet prose: the survey of the crowded mess-hall, when the dramatics counselor's eye falls on the camper, "Winkie, who did not yet know— but I knew—that he was going to be Macbeth"; or the comical departure of the camp owner, "Huffski Puffski Ben Tumpowski," just a hop-skip-and-jump ahead of the sheriff; or the laconic exchange between the narrator and a Vermont farmer looting the premises before the last occupants have left:

> "There are some good bulbs in the footlights on my stage," I said to Wells. "You can get in the back way by forcing the latch."
> "Got 'em," he said.

One by one these little unveilings have a mild, almost picturesque turn, but their lasting effect is disturbing rather than calming. For one thing, these are merely odd moments, unimportant events, not the hinges of action. Why remember them? And after all, what *are* the important events? It is a vision of the last days, collapse, decay, and the saving remnant. Again comparison to Hawthorne is hard to resist, for the shadowy unease engendered is precisely that of *The House of the Seven Gables.*

It is difficult to put one's finger on the essential quality or singularity that underlies these effects. It is not really a question of subject matter, for that might have led in many directions, nor is it only in this book that the pulse is to be felt—though perhaps one does get the best sense of it at the end of *The Break-Up of Our Camp,* in the chapter called "A Memorial Synagogue." That story was written more than a decade after the others, and the shift in manner is decided enough to throw the earlier chapters in strong relief—not so much by any new tone or intent as by the sudden falling away of all literary amenities, leaving the deeper meanings stark and impatient. This, of course, is not something one finds much of in Hawthorne—unless perhaps in the unfinished romances of his decline, when he could no longer muster a plot to make his obsessions presentable—but in Goodman's case it is his strength and not his weakness that is revealed in the change; it is his characteristic style that has been, as it were, incubating in *The Break-Up of Our Camp* and all the other stories of the Thirties. What Hawthorne was reduced to, by infirmity, Goodman has all along been girding himself for, the abjuring of every pretense at a realistic façade. If stories were like dreams, let them be just like that, let the images float to the surface, let impulse guide the dialogue—until someone says what you are afraid to hear, and the characters make their own fate. He might have read it all in Hawthorne's notebooks, a fancy of his youth that old age literally brought to pass:

> A person to be writing a tale, and to find that it shapes itself against his intentions; that characters act otherwise than he thought; that unforeseen events occur; and a catastrophe comes which he strives in vain to avert. It might

15

shadow forth his own fate,—he having made himself one of the personages.

But Goodman did not fight it, he courted it. If not to this end, where else were all his habits and pleasures leading him?—the rhapsodic method, the toying with experience, the addiction to risks, the incessant experimenting, and the drift away from realism into symbolism. It was all part of a general decision to follow impulse at any cost.

Lose yourself of thoughts and fears.
Your face will fade out of the looking-glass.
You breathe a mist of sighs, they slowly pass,
your heart is empty when the mirror clears.
What's *in* there? what's to come? what of art?
—this void no natural animal can breathe.
Stifle the clouds that from your nostrils wreathe
now eagerly.
           Ah! the light-curtains part,
appears the Unicorn with his light step
and the breath of roses curling from his teeth.
He wants to speak. *"I am not fed on corn*
but on the chance of being." His white horn
silently shatters the barrier with its tip
and he emerges between life and death.

T.S.

THE BREAK-UP
OF OUR
CAMP

VOLUME
1

JOHNSON
(1932 - 1933)

A Study of Johnson

Johnson searched thru the multitudes in the city to find those he might love. In the tens he met professionally, in the threes and fives who sat near him at the theatre, in the score of his remembered school-fellows, in the single faces that struck him on the thorofares, he looked for a sign. This was the absorbing study basic to all other contemplations. The agony of his soul was the peril of unbefriending, tho there were many with whom he laughed, exchanged ideas, quarreled, and drank.

What he desired was a human sympathy from those he might love, that his own nature might have a pasture not only to graze, but to lie down in. To be an object not only of interest, for he was that to many, but in some degree of concern to somebody. For his part, he threw himself willingly into the wells of other personalities and tried to plumb those depths, to offer assuageal for the trouble of those waters. He wanted to know and love—if only, also, some one might want to know and love him.

It broke his heart when in conversation he could not strike at once to depths of understanding, but was rebuffed to a plane of small talk—so that his heart was often broken, for everybody cannot always lay bare his soul. He desired three things of lovers: that they be candid, that they have spiritual purposes, and that they pity the miseries of the world. Envy, self-satisfaction, cruelty or callousness, he feared. It thrilled him to find one who could comprehend the sober poetry of the *Georgics* of Virgil, and perceive the dignified grief in the poet's heart when he writes:

> But if you do not assiduously rake the weeds,
> frighten off the birds, prune the tree, and pray for rain,
> alas! in vain shall you look at your neighbor's heaped-up store
> and, shaking trees in the woods, console your hunger with acorns.

Johnson at this time found two lovers, of whom one was a young girl named Mildred, the other a young man named Leonard. Both of them respected and loved him sincerely. Being with either, he felt that he was at peace, and yet nourished, and this was an additional joy and tonic for himself. For he knew that he might benefit those he loved—not because of any powers he himself might possess (tho these were not negligible) but just because of love. A neoplatonist mystic might thus liken love to the fertile wedding of the one and the indefinite dyad. Johnson, however, was rather humane than mystical.

Being a man of considerable powers, temperamental complexity, cultural breadth, and physical well-being, he could be fervently enamored of two different people at the same time, and in very different modes. Mildred and Leonard each mirrored, and gave back enriched, a different face of his individuality. Mildred's relatedness to him, a certain passivity pervaded, with a corresponding expansiveness on his part towards her. This is the vegetativeness which characterizes a true sexual concordance, making it a rationale of restoration and growth. He was not chivalric or deferential towards her, for this sonneteering way of displaying superiority was beneath them. Nor was he masterful in that male and selfish crudity that D. H. Lawrence has neurotically immortalized. In any case she was not unintelligent herself, she had her own interests, and a career to make in a laboratory science.

Between Leonard and Johnson was the hard shock and somewhat hot cauterization of hyperlogical characters.

22

A Study of Johnson

They were both inveterate scholastics: ingrown, tough, frank, quick, and tortured. They were not active or passive to each other, but were peers (except that Leonard was younger). This strengthened their mutual respect, their moral fibre; and it favored their utility to one another. They had not, of course, any interests apart, as Johnson and Mildred had, since what they meant to each other was precisely not any vague energy or intention, but the details and formality of arts and sciences. Leonard could play Chopin as no other person that Johnson knew. No woman can play Chopin; most men brutalize this music: what is needed is a courageous hardness of intellect, forthrightness—very different from in Brahms, or other vague piano-music—but likewise a certain unassertiveness of temper.

Mildred was small, dark, olive-skinned, soft-skinned, like a little girl. Leonard and Johnson both were big and blond. I mention this to illustrate an erratic theory of Johnson's: that a person like himself must love only a dark girl, only a blond boy. He attributed to colors of the complexion not so much traits of character, as entities of metaphysics! But he did not always act in accordance with his generalization . . . Checkered in Johnson's golden hair were patches of brown.

Being honorable, proud, and confiding as he was, he did not fail to tell Leonard about Mildred, and Mildred about Leonard. He made no attempt ever to conceal anything in his private life, except what he was ashamed of. Leonard was not displeased that he should be in love with this girl, for he understood that it must lend completion and manliness to Johnson's character. Mildred, on the other hand, was made angry by the disclosure. She was surprised and resentful that Johnson should be in love with a man. She was not in any sense jealous of Leonard, but she told Johnson, frankly, as was her custom, that she must consider this sentiment as a debilitation, even a perversion, of his manhood. She did not for the moment consider that his delicacy and his comprehension of what was best in her own mind, qualities which were his whole superiority, to

23

her thinking, over other men, were alike due (perhaps) to this double mask of his nature. Piqued, for a long time she refused to meet Leonard. This refusal, this dissension, made Johnson altogether miserable.

This meeting when it did occur, however, was calculated to make him even more miserable. For from it began a fascination between Leonard and Mildred which was to result in their flaming towards each other, their rapid cooling towards him, and his being left alone. To begin with, they were more nearly alike in age than he and Mildred were. Perhaps they were even simpler in personality and therefore felt even easier with each other than they had with Johnson. Their respect and love for Johnson furnished a powerful initial tie between them, yet could not serve as an obstacle, since a new passion creeps up unawares. And Mildred did not carry over into her attitude towards Leonard her recent suspicions of Johnson, either because he was a blinding picture in her eyesight, whom she did not know intimately; or that his desires were really more single, with a less defined cleavage, than Johnson's.

They both had open countenances and eyes wide apart. They did not hesitate to inform Johnson of their state of feeling (which in any case he ought easily to have surmised). They loved him yet, yet could not be his lovers. At this, Johnson had a stroke of black and bilious rage: that they should be so frank and, as he wildly fancied, brutal! It was as if those qualities of candor and kindliness which he loved most dearly of anything should now seem hateful to him; and as if a deception of affection could have endured in an atmosphere most designed to make it putrid, as well as dead! But he was struck to the heart especially by this fact: that they were so grateful to him for having unselfishly brought them together.

In the end it was this wound that cured him: for by it he got to see a philosophical lesson in the episode; and insight, as Aristotle promises, leads to catharsis. What more natural, he cried, than for that boy and that girl to suit each other, inasmuch as they both suited me! And I suited them both. I am the affection they have in common, and the unity of my taste is their love. I am a tuning fork, I am the law of Selection! And might, by merely continuing my career, set up a marriage bureau.

[New York City]
[1932]

Johnson and the Total Good

As a young man, Johnson had a moral sense strongly developed, and was able to see more clearly than is possible the division between *fas* and *nefas*. This made a great difference in his actions. Furthermore, there was a Kantian distinction which he understood, between the highest good and the total good: the highest good being what it is one's duty, as he sees it, to do; the total good what would be the superlative condition of affairs if only the world were equitably regulated. Now Johnson, as I say, took the first very seriously, and he did his duty with might and main. But he took the second seriously, too, and he tried to regulate the world more equitably. That is what this sketch is about. For instance, riding on a New York 'bus-top, he would suddenly feel impelled to sing out, awe-struck, "Oh look at the high houses!"—for this was a source of innocent pleasure to everybody, and was therefore good to do. When a mother passed with a child, "What a pretty baby!" said he.

My heart
breaks with the weight of selfishness these days—

he wrote in a sonnet, for he was a poet, too. "So far as I can give of myself," he swore, "I shall never allow anybody to suffer some of the bitter, unfulfilled desires that I have suffered."

Now at this time he was bitterly disappointed in love. He fell in love with a young man named Leonard (for he

27

had bisexual tendencies) and his hopes of this relation did not prosper, but sickened and died. It was not that Leonard was indifferent towards him, but that he mistrusted him, feared him, and hated himself for being attracted to him. In a sense, with Leonard, it was a question of pride: he wanted, as he thought, to be an individual, self-sufficient, free; whereas if he became the love of Johnson, he would be absorbed and lost. "My God, how wrong he is!" thought Johnson, "when it is the very opposite that is occurring." Another grievance of Leonard's was that Johnson's care-freedom, his unconventionality in social matters, was immature, a kind of childishness; whereas he (they were equally young men) desired to grow up. Johnson agreed, he agreed; but he stalwartly denied that the charge of child-ishness involved any stigma. "Unless ye be as little children," he quoted, "ye shall not enter the kingdom of Heaven. Remember that the philosopher Heraclitus used to sit in front of the temple and play with the little children: that was because he knew a good thing. To grow up," he summarized, "is to become involved. Death is the condition of being so tied up that one cannot proceed to the next step. But it is not the loss of freedom that is so terrible in becoming adult, but the loss of truth, which is attainable only by a naïve person."

What Johnson thought he perceived in Leonard, was a certain fine-grained quality. This inner delicacy, this ex-quisite subconscious discipline, or whatever it was, he tried to define and explain to other people, but he could find no words for the unique quality, so that everybody assured him that he was crazy. The only other character in all history, besides the boy he loved, to whom he felt he could surely attribute this mysterious attribute, was the philosopher Plato! . . . In any case, feeling that he himself was coarse, an ordinary person, he could not bear to see this precious animal slip away from his fingers; he pur-sued desperately; in pursuing, he frightened the deer further; and he made himself quite ridiculous. "The bother with you," said Leonard to him, "is that you're not a symphony, you have only one tune. A symphony has to have more than one tune." "My God!" cried Johnson in

agony, "can't he understand?—" All these emotions he
wrote down in a poem:

> I love him more because he loves not me:
> If he could stoop to me I'd love him less,
> for he is more than I and love must be
> equal; but do we not also bless
> Charity?—I mean love without degree.
>
> I've lost him, the one fine-woven soul I know.
> I am in need, so coarse—he is like rare wood,
> I cannot find words to tell it—Plato was so,
> Socrates not; it is not being good,
> wise, even disciplined; aloof? no—no—
>
> Oh how *could* he? how could Leonard savagely
> as he did, cry at me for drumming, drumming only
> on one theme—"you are not a symphony!"
> My God, must I be musical, being lonely?
> to be so little sensitive, being he!

This poem was called "Lines" . . . But into the endless
variations of vagaries on both sides, in such an affair, it is
unprofitable to follow. It is enough to say that toward the
end of Spring Leonard suddenly went off to the Orange
Mountains without so much as a good-bye; and there was
Johnson left suspended in mid-air, in a pit of disillusion. "I
am cured," he swore.

Now likewise at this time, Johnson was loved by a girl
named Rosalind; but tho he thought her amiable, he was
at heart indifferent whether she was a nigger or a China-
man. She made many efforts to be near him, and kept
performing services to attract him. They won only his
gratitude, however, and made him uneasy. He could not
understand why she should devote herself particularly to
him: "She must be generally amiable," he assumed. He
expressed this opinion again and again; and when it was
reported to her by kindly friends, how much he admired
her, she saw at once heaven and death. She tried to give to
him of herself what she could; but it was generally only

books from the library. One night, because she wanted to see him, she bought tickets for a play and telephoned to him that the manager, who was her friend, had surprised her with a pair of seats; but he could not go. She was a slight, blonde girl, who was pretty when the sunlight set her hair afloat like a stack of hay in a picture by Renoir or Pissarro. It was a pity that Johnson did not ever look at her.

But suddenly, in June, when he had altogether despaired of Leonard, it dawned on him that Rosalind might be in love. This revelation struck him to the core: he felt like a cad. It dawned on him seated, overlooking the River where the sun had just set and the sky was full of brown clouds and orange clouds. It was at this moment that, elevated by enthusiasm for the Total Good, he undertook to regulate the world more equitably.

"How callous of me, how cruel!" thought he indignantly. "I have caused her to suffer in just the same way I have. I am acting exactly like a Leonard, just as if I did not know how terrible a thing it is to love and not be loved. In a sense it is my moral duty to fall in love with Rosalind, at least to try. For altho I cannot blame Leonard for not responding to my affections, since every one has the right to live his own life as he will (and I used to love him more because he loved not me)—I have a different, perhaps a nicer, perhaps only a more quixotic perception of these matters, and what is right for him, for me is not so. Furthermore, I understand more clearly than he can the torment of a hopeless attachment (it being not so much the unsatisfied desire of a lover that counts, for this is the kind of ordeal by fire that every lover must expect, but the hopelessness of some such desires). In the third place, Rosalind is a very pretty, amiable girl."

Thus, and because he was lonely and his vanity a little flattered, Johnson began to pay some attention to Rosalind. Many reasons could be offered to explain his sudden interest in her and perhaps all were operative to a degree; but one of the reasons, it remains, was that he felt it was his duty to increase the sum total of good in the world.

When she telephoned: "How amusing!" he sang out, "I

Johnson and the Total Good

was just about to lift the receiver from the hook to call you." He knew that this would make her happy—just as on the 'bus-top. Likewise he sent her a night letter dated Midnight and which, delivered at one o'clock in the morning, sent her tumbling from bed in a cold sweat, until she read that Johnson was thinking of her. He dutifully attended her on the excursion and to the theatre. Everything he did, he did dutifully. He put his hands and his mouth in the proper places. And did not spit when wisps of her wind-blown fine hair straggled into his mouth. In a short while he became really fond of Rosalind, for he was not such a fool as to believe that we have no voluntary control over our affections, where propinquity and habit are half the game.

Rosalind, at this time, was in a condition of such ecstatic satisfaction that she sat quiet; everywhere they went, she sat quiet, and merely looked about with large eyes.

Certain extrusions of his basic indifference to her, however, Johnson could not suppress; they came up like igneous rock, hot and clear. There was especially a disposition to be late at every appointment that he made with her, and try as he would he could not cure this. One time it would be fifteen minutes, another, half an hour. On one occasion he swore to himself that he would not be late for an appointment at 11 o'clock in the morning, and the result was that, having relegated to the conscious the time-keeping that is properly the function of the unconscious, he could not fall asleep all that night. He got out of bed so irritable.

"But the appointment was for 10 o'clock, not for 11!" said Rosalind cheerfully to him when he arrived, on the dot, where she had been waiting for more than an hour, in the sun, in front of the Aquarium.

At first he thought she was mistaken. Then he became very furious and excited.

"It's all right," said Rosalind. "I didn't mind in the least."

"Oh you don't understand the point at issue!" he cried. "It's that I haven't any control over my mind. I wanted to remember and I wanted to be on time. But something

31

betrayed me. I'm not a free man!"

"But since I tell you that I don't mind—"

"Oh Christ!"

They walked along a little ways. "I was just thinking, waiting there—" said Rosalind.

"What were you thinking about, dearest?" asked Johnson, ashamed of his petulance.

"I was just wondering whether you had heard from your friend Leonard lately."

"Leonard! For God's sake, why on earth should I hear from him?"

"I thought that you two were such good friends; he might drop you a line—"

"Oh, shut up . . . I suppose we've missed the boat," said Johnson bad-humoredly.

"There'll be another soon," said Rosalind.

The truth is that, at bottom, Rosalind, so easily satisfied, was a quite impossible kind of girl for Johnson. She was, as I have described her, blonde and slight, and with a southern voice. She liked to ride back and forth on the same ferry. She liked to eat apples. She liked to dangle her feet, to croon, to wade. She almost liked to sit under a tree and read poetesses. During adagio movements, she shut her eyes. Now this kind of girl is invariably amiable; but Johnson is too high-strung. He is too hard, neurotic, petulant, critical—which is only the dark side of his moral scrupulosity. What Rosalind sees in him is only one side of him: his boyishness, his unconstraint (that Leonard objected to). She likes him best in a brown open shirt, and with tousled hair. She has a distant admiration for the spontaneity of boys . . . One time they passed a circle of boys shooting craps furiously. "Oh, see how he snaps his fingers! How spontaneous!" . . . But it was not Johnson.

Yet Johnson was sincerely fond of Rosalind; perhaps even more so because he was less so. There was a deep moral consideration here, which he understood, the element of expiation. "The reason I have been so miserable," he conjectured, "is that I have been ill-controlled. I gave way to an unbounded passion, and therefore could not hope for anything. In this new way, at least, I can discip-

32

line my desire to seek its possible and fitting object. This is a relevant expiation." He felt sorry for Rosalind because he did not love her; feeling sorry for her, he began to love her. But the cause of it all was that, in the beginning, he had been himself so deeply wounded.

His fondness endured for more than a month.

Then the beginning of August came and out of a blue sky, as the phrase is, a postcard from Leonard. "Again you have disappeared," began this curious message, "this time without return or unambiguous explanation. To be sulky is the prerogative of every child, but I did not think you took your immaturity so seriously. Lack of consideration is one kind of bad heart; you above all should know this. But why this sudden cleavage?—" While he was reading this message—curious one to write on a postcard— Johnson's heart boiled with indignation at the injustice of it, and his imaginary pen began to sputter recriminations; but as soon as he had finished it, realizing that such quarrels are endless, he went off after the author himself, leaving Rosalind, so to speak, holding the bag. "For," he reasoned, "in just the same way that my most hopeless situation has suddenly burst into sunlight, so may hers— some day. It is not the unsatisfied desire of a lover that counts, for this is the kind of ordeal by fire that every lover must expect, you know." That is, he reasoned that his moral responsibility was at an end.

[New York City]
[1932]

The Mirrors

Johnson and the other walked in the wood on the red dead pineneedles. A half moon was up. Looking in each other's countenances, they saw that they were mirrors. The moonlight shone as in a pair of mirrors. But she, in the mirror of Johnson, saw herself; while he, looking at her, saw another, Leonard. For her mirror, not flat, but many-dimensioned, let thru this other image.

She pushed him against a tree and pushed against him, frontwise. First she rested both her palms on his hips, but a little to the front, on the knobs of the pelvic girdle; and then she raised them to his cheekbones, which seem to have the same shape, only smaller. In this way she touched herself more and more woundingly. When she laid a finger on him, she burned herself in the same part. For he was a wondrous mirror, in which she not only saw, but heard and hugged herself, and licked herself—as if she put her tongue in his mouth, but herself felt it coming in—and in all the dimensions she felt it, external and internal; but especially inside all the dimensions, in the transcendental reflection of her unitary being, something not sensuous. A mirror that withdraws from light to geometry, then to thought.

But if this were all—whereby being with Johnson, she was with herself—it would be easy to describe. More was involved than this: he was not a simple reflection, but an operation, a wilful act, somehow; a mirror not passive (or impassive, as we say) but acting. I find this very difficult to describe. For instance, whenever, thru him, she touched

35

herself, it was traumatic, like a wound. Again, her ideas, when they came from him, were at once *beliefs*. Looking into him was not like looking at the glassy black surface of a lake, but like being obliged at once to plunge in and drown. Or when you fall on your back and see birds fall into the sky. She loved him—only in so far as he gave back herself—but in a way that you could not love a dead mirror.

The reflection-part alone was more complicated than you would imagine. Johnson did not look like her, but like her brother. But therefore he had the same mother, and the same blood coursing in his veins, which she could lick and smell at his pulse, almost bite. He loved a legion of children, in the country, in New York, in Britanny, little boys and little girls, grey-eyed and violet-eyed. He spoke of them all the time. But what he loved was the natural intelligence and the singular purity of their minds, so that he said:

> I felt if I could look in the eyes of a child
> without flinching, my heart were still whole, unspoiled;
> and I did, and the untried-one's eyes were like an amber
> gem.
> With elders I could not, ashamed for myself and them.

What she loved was their bodies, to touch and kiss them. She felt that this was the same. In general when he referred to science and education, she felt this in her as generation and thus assimilated two things which are nearly the farthest apart of all, fatherhood and motherhood. Johnson loved men and women: and the former with passion, and the latter with heat. To her it was all a warm lust, or domination. But she felt that it was a mirroring. "How like me he is," she thought, when he disclosed to her that he was bisexual. She loved him, further, because he could give strong arguments for his, and her, unmoral notions. She could not see that all his notions—each one was like a mirror—were on a different level . . . There is a painting by Giotto at Harvard, of St. Francis receiving the stigmata. He is kneeling and the spirit of Christ hovers above him. Now from the bleeding hands and feet and breast of the Savior, go forth, across the panel, right hand to right hand, left to left, heart to heart, occult red lines of force (action at a distance) impressing the miracle on the body of the Saint. Yet one is still God and one only a man.

She forced her tongue between his lips. Their heads together formed a full moon. In the dark wood their blond hair was like the golden shadows about the full moon. (Johnson's hair was checkered brown and blond.) She could not see his eyes. The mirrors, as their faces came together, became obscured in a cloud of breath.

I find it very difficult to describe in what manner the other loved Johnson only in so far as she found herself in him, and at the same time he was not a passive reflection, but traumatic. But I shall try to illustrate this by an analogy. In East Africa, up towards Abyssinia, the warring negro tribes still traffic for slaves, selling off those captured in war, or perhaps even those unwanted at home. Now the more beautiful youths are made eunuchs for the households of petty chiefs. The form of castration is this: the genitals are rather torn out than cut off, and in the terrible cavity, to prevent its closing, which would of course be fatal, a peg dipped in hot butter is inserted. Every day the peg is removed to allow the victim, prostrate and spread-eagle on his back with his hands and feet bound, the opportunity to pass water. Then the peg, dipped anew in hot butter, is reinserted. This lasts for up to thirty days. The flesh heals smooth and firm. Now it is not to be doubted that, with this unexampled probing of his entrails, amid the very heat and torture a new desire is born in the youth. In a basic lust of his nature, he becomes effeminate, that is, passive. He is then assumed as a new concubine by the chieftain. But the excuse for this brutal illustration is this: change around the sexes, make the other, who was in the forest with Johnson, acquire manhood just as this unfortunate negro boy takes on effeminancy; except that she finds her manhood in herself only in a *mirror image* of herself, tho she feels it with the burning trauma of the hot peg. Mirrors! mirrors! the forest cast black shadows across the moonlight like sticks bent in a translucent pail of milk. One black shadow fell across the mirrors; which at a deeper level were crossed not by shadow and moonlight but by pain and peace.

Suddenly, as she pushed his head back against the rough bark and her swollen tongue was in his mouth, his eyes were cut across by the half-moon; and then suddenly he understood that she did not love *him* at all; he played no part in her satisfaction, but only as a bulwark and reflection of herself. How he suddenly came to see this, I do not know. Perhaps it was that, his eyelids going up, he suddenly perceived that the moon was exactly half, alone in the sky.

He pushed her away roughly, into the shadow, and he brutally said, "Why do you keep at it? Aren't you ashamed?"

For already for a long time he knew that to her he did not exist in himself, but only as a mirror. He knew it by the fact that, when she disagreed with him, when he said something she did not like or acted in a manner she considered exasperating, she always turned away in a contemptuous way and full of hate. She was not wounded at the fact of difference; you could not see any hurt in her eyes. And she did not try to correct him, which would require a ground of mutual sympathy. She did not sympathize with his faults, that is, but only hated him for them. If she had loved *him*, she would feel sorry for the faults and be kind to them as, so to speak, to the accidents in a substance. This is the meaning of Charity. But she turned to him with love only when he said what she was thinking, or wished she could think.

"I know you are not sympathetic to me," he said. All this happened in the moonlit thickets.

"No." She felt, somehow, trapped, and she began to cry.

At this Johnson felt coldly cruel. He leaned against the tree-trunk and said nothing, but listened to her sobbing in the shadow where he could not see her.

"I can't help it, I cannot!" she said. "But I cannot think of any one but myself. Nothing else seems interesting to me. And I am afraid that, if I fell in love *elsewhere*, I should *lose* myself. I would not be myself, any more. But I am so

38

much in love with you, sometimes. I touch you and am burned everywhere, like a man and a woman."

It was the most degrading plight Johnson had ever experienced.

"It is an honorable situation for me!" he said coldly. "To be the pool for a narcissist."

For an instant, he thought that he would burst in anger. Then he laughed and thought: "To be a mirror, a mirror—it is a new role!"

But how like Leonard she is! he thought. It is the same voice. It is the same lisping in the forest, so that, amid all the dark trees, it might be Leonard, instead of she, standing. But if it were he, even in the shadow one could see his presence, for he stood in the air in a special way; the light, refracted all about him, seemed to be golden in the daytime, and even darker in the darkness, like velvet. But she sounded like him among the trees.

I cannot think of any one but myself. If I fell in love elsewhere, I should lose myself. How like Leonard it was, he thought, because he had said, "I am afraid that I shall be absorbed." But what a difference there was, also! For when Leonard thought only of himself, it was not, like the other, in pride, satisfaction, and even lust. But it was that he felt himself so divided, so desperately at war. He was like all who are suicidally cleft at the very bottom of their personalities, and must struggle for their values and their unity, because that unity and assuredness and *self-satisfaction*, is not given to them in the first place, but they must fight towards it. All these people are like St. Paul, thought Johnson. But it is not conceit, to be thus concerned with one's-self, but the very opposite: humility and fear. "Oh, Leonard! Leonard!" said Johnson aloud.

"Come," he said to her, in the wood. He put his hands on her shoulders and drew her from the shadows. She came into the moonlight. Johnson, staring, tilted back her chin with his right hand so that the moon flooded her face.

"What is there in this boy!" he cried, "that I am so struck. That I love him beyond the law. First, he is beautiful. Black-blond, his hair is more delicate than milkweed-plumes. His eyes are blue and clear as water, and cold as glass with anxiety. He is on edge—this is why I love him! His body lean moves with erratic grace.

"And I love him because he loveth children, and is loved by them. I have seen them come to him to touch his cheek (which I cannot do). Once I heard him speak to them at night, by candlelight. So full of irony, he was, yet very humble, so bitter, eager, sarcastic with himself, and full of love. This is how I know him—whom of myself I could not ever know: he is a stranger when he talks to me.

"And he is manly and responsible (except when I perplex him). He is not cast into confusion by his curious personality, and does not suddenly, as I sometimes do, give way and let all work die. Thus he, this summer, cold and sick, afraid of water, yet watched on shore and saved ten people from drowning. Oh I am in love with that blond sea-lion! . . . I have loved him more than poetry and more than science. I had hoped, once, to find my one truth, I ask only one, in Leonard . . . I ask only one, for given one truth, we can demonstrate the existence of God, as Augustine has pointed out; but his own demonstration does not sufficiently succeed, for his elementary 'truth' is not of an adequate scope."

During this rhapsodic outburst, Johnson held the girl by the shoulders in the silent thicket, her face tilted back into the moonlight. He passed his fingers thru her gossamer hair. He touched her cheek. He spoke in a low, impassioned tone, and as if every word were charged with unspeakable certitude, a private oracle from the Beyond. She, for her part, said nothing.

"A mirror, a looking-glass!" he said, rather sadly than bitterly. Having her by the shoulders, he shook her. "How could you be so heartless, girl? I know that you are not sympathetic with me, but you ought not therefore to use me merely as an *instrument*. I am a person, after all. . . . I confess it is a new role for me, to be looked at and thought about only that you may see yourself again. It is a new kind of admiration!"

"But I can see all my loves on her face," thought Johnson, as he shook her back and forth. "They flicker by, come and go." It seemed eerie to him, standing in the

The Mirrors

middle of the forest, to recognize so many, so many—the half-formed smiles, the lifted eyebrows; the closed eyelids, the lips opening to sob. It was like many slabs of time, in a close stratification (I borrow old Whitehead's jargon), that we suddenly cut across from another time-system altogether, and see, all together, the pictures hidden in each layer. But there is a passage, a $'\rho\upsilon\sigma\iota\varsigma$, a fluxion, a flowing pervading them all. They are in time, gone and bygone. All on her face. As if, with each one in turn, he had fallen in love only because of the reflection, on that face, of the one before, of the two before, of the three before. It was the saddest thing: he was no longer free to hear a simple tune, but always a chord—all of whose notes were ancient. But in them all there was one harmony and one type; Leonard. This was the *Recherche du Temps Perdu*.

He looked up and beheld the half-moon, alone overhead. And then suddenly, this also seemed to him like a mirror in which was reflected a face. So desirous was he of seeing his boy everywhere, that he saw him as even the Man in the Moon.

[New York City]
1932

41

The Moon

During the month of June, Johnson at last was not alone; but he was with his dear friend. In his ease and joy, he began to contemplate the moon, which was new on the 2nd, and then started to grow, night after night—as he watched it grow—thru the 4 quarters.

1. He said:

> At my door in the green gold
> the first monthly edge of the moon, sharp as ice,
> I saw twice,
> during which time I grew not old,
>
> but quietly as fell the changing moons
> rose and worked and went to bed
> and 28 days fled.
>
> I raised up my arms to feel the passage of time
> and I felt Him both outside and inside;
> I bowed my head,
> for He is a great god.

2. "Now that I am not alone, but at last with my dear friend," he explained, by way of gloss, "it is evident that time does no damage: for what could be lost? Only broken things can possibly decay; all that is made whole endures of its own nature forever and ever, unless of its own nature (time playing no hand) it breaks down. In this way the month is exculpated of all responsibility for dissolution,

43

disease, and death, which instability is in ourselves, not in
the medium. Is that clear? I mean, for instance, if the law
of Entropy were a true law, that fact in itself would prove
that the world is evil—otherwise it would not inevitably
break. But we, now, as we are, shall continue forever and
ever; therefore I have begun to count the moons."

Leonard, to whom he said this, agreed that it was probably so.

3. "None of the moons is broken, falling thru the
skies!" cried Johnson one night, alone, standing on a white
boulder by the side of the Delaware River. "The moon was
new on the 2nd; but even then I saw it full. On the 12th it
was half-opened, but I saw it perfectly rounded. Tonight
the moon is full indeed; but even when it begins to wane,
tomorrow or the next day, I shall still behold it, more and
more full. This is how we understand the great moon, as it
is said:

> the broken moon is falling thru the skies—
> but I have made her whole with Thales' eyes
> and in the top of heaven pinned her face!

See her! the round round moon forever pinned in the top of
heaven, while time and nights slowly turn about her and
fade. Thales was the Greek who first made theorems about
circles."

4. He said:

> Time! time! good liquid, pure act—
> we have drunk fresh quarts of him these 30 days.
> He is also a light wind.

> Our canoes drawn up on the beach!
> Our canoes drawn up on the beach!
> yet moving with holy motion thru the waves.

> Time is not lack of being, but spins out
> the being of our houses, their floors, their rooms

44

into more being.

It is a receptacle, a womb,
a mother-presence, whom I (though no hero)
know erotically.

5. "What does that mean?" asked Leonard, who, hearing speaking on the shore, had come out of the lean-to to stand on the gravel beneath the white boulder. Opposite, the full moon was just rising, yellow, pasted above the River like a lawyer's seal.

"Why, I don't know exactly," said Johnson uneasily.

" 'Our canoes drawn up on the beach—' " he said, "you see, that is the same as the full moon forever pinned in the top of heaven. Even when the canoe is in the waves, or the moon broken and falling—they are both *there*, I mean . . . the moon has often been compared to a ship or canoe. The Manichees thought it was a ship transporting the good light to heaven. Conversely, Hendrick Hudson's boat was called *Half-Moon.*—

"It is not very clear, but consider the end part: 'It is a receptacle—a mother presence whom I (though no hero)—.' That is obviously nothing newer than Plato, where he says that the Receptacle is 'the foster-mother of all becoming.' The hero, full of formal action, is he who can make that mother germinate or, as we say, 'bring forth' events."

6. "But is not time the same mother," asked the younger man, "whether we are whole or broken? the same today, when we are so pleased together in Pennsylvania, my dear lover, as yesterday—or tomorrow—"

"She is always the same good mother!" cried Johnson bravely. "But we do not always know her. When we were broken, we could not perceive the true passage of time; it is not every day that we get a clear and whole glimpse of the past, present, and future. For instead of the past, we have had memory; instead of the future we have had hope; instead of the present, pain. The sentiments of hope and

memory are diseases of true perception, and all the broken
people suffer chronically from them. By God, Leonard, you
have made me sick enough this way!—

>—but the sudden recollection of unfinished
>hopes, of loves by failure abased.
>With which my courage constantly diminished . . .
>oh April is the cruellest month for memories.

Or,

>—Just now I, clad in brown,
>have emptied old poems round me, a large yield,
>on the rug, and knelt among them staring down,
>like a Memphian colossus on a snowy field.

Or,

>l ong and white, evening lies
>e legant as T. S. Eliot
>o n a lecture platform, and dies
>n ow is it close to being not.
>a s the words of the tired poet go,
>r ounds and squares of light below
>d ecay in Inwood.

>. . . Sleep and Thought are likewise thick and pied
>with pictures of Leonard,
>more than a cinema, and random calls . . .

>I have no heart again to hunt and build:
>a cardiac betrayed before I start.

>. . . Oh the great insolence of loving unrequited
>for which I am punished again and again!
>as all the still-born children of unhealthy mothers
>must be registered and put in the grave.

And I do not mention 'A Journey to Flatbrookville'! . . .

The Moon

Attar said: 'He who would tread this Path must have a hundred thousand living hearts, so that with every breath he may cast away a hundred of them.' "

Now Leonard, hearing of the past this way, felt just awful (more than I can describe). He turned his back to the white boulder and looked at the River. Over his left shoulder, the one turned away from Johnson, he said, "I did not act well. Please do not mention it."

7. But Johnson, on the white boulder, in the radiant moonlight where every one walked like a ghost, thought on in a rising rapture and said, "Now there is neither memory nor prospect! no fear, no love, no pain. Together, together, we have a true perception of time (which is beyond time of course, not colored by any sentiment of time). Standing apart—standing apart—she is the same good mother, and we know her as she is—" He began to say everything double, as if he were drunk on gin. "None of the moons falling thru the sky is broken to him who knows geometry. The one round moon stands in the sky always lighted in full (except during eclipses)—if we transcend an accidental point of view. . . ."

They spent more than a month along the River Delaware. On the 24th, when the moon was entering its last quarter (altho to Johnson's eyes it still shone round and full in the sky), the 2 set out on a canoe-trip over several nights. They left one canoe drawn up on the beach (turned up on its side to keep the rain out) at their old camp near the white boulder; but went upstream in the other.

8. "Look," said Johnson from the stern, "the Delaware is full of turnings. As we round each little wooded peninsula, we come into a new land in the moonlight. In this the river is like an affair of love, that discloses a new view of everything at each turning. Constantly evolving. I once read this in a story called 'The Rivers'—it was all told there."

"Where was that story?" asked Leonard.

"Oh!" said Johnson, putting his hand over his mouth, as if he should not have spoken. "There is no such story yet. I see now, suddenly, that the events of that story have not yet all occurred; they are occurring even now. I see that we are in his story. I do not know what the end is. . . .

"But look," he said, lifting his paddle, dripping in the moonlight, "the Delaware is indeed like an affair of love, full of novel turnings—but we, this month, are not like either. We are outside both those streams. There is no change, no evolution. We are like the enduring moon, always at the full. As our canoe rounds each peninsula, we are offered a new landscape—cliffs, the Water Gap, many orchards—for there is a great variety in both Pennsylvania and New Jersey; but all are printed with the same golden sign; we are at home with all; have no pain of novelty; but merely the joy of becoming richer and richer; nothing is mysterious; everything is real and complete. This is because tonight," he said to himself dreamily, "I have a whole view at last. Love completed—each thing comes with a sure guarantee; I have no occasion to doubt of its existence."

9. Oh the Golden View is an act of creation:
   the Moon and Stars were not, now they became!

   As each tree grew to be gold as Leonard,
   it came to be, and the world was peopled . . .

Johnson began to sing a song he had made up:

   When I am so filled with uncertainty
   whether the Moon be real or a dream
   that I am dreaming in the sky—
   so fanciful does its slow traffic seem
   and so like the night-images that teem:

   then if I behold in its bright rim
   the face of Leonard like the Man who lives there,
   my eyes confess it real and grow dim,
   as they do always when they look on him.

10. What he meant by this was that, in proportion as each thing grew to be like that which he knew full well—

the Man in the Moon like Leonard, or each tree gold as Leonard—he *recognized* it: "it came to be and the world was peopled." By "Leonard," he did not mean, altogether, the man in front of him paddling the canoe—but the happy love they had—what we have chosen to call their "completed love"; and of this, he himself was a part, about a half. In the end, what he "knew full well," was what he was. But therefore everything in the world was printed with the golden sign, for that was how he perceived everything—for instance, all the cliffs, beaches, and woods that kept swinging into view along the Delaware. The moon was always round because his love was . . . This is a very ancient augustinian doctrine, and nothing new, that I am using here to explain how Johnson felt. *Verum est id quod est:* the truth is that which is; whereby we know the truth by being it—and this works both ways.

11. But now Johnson risked becoming altogether fatuous. For he was ready to believe that what he now saw of things, was what they were entirely (as if he *were* everything). As if this little affair of love of which he was a part, with a person whom he had known for a few minutes of a few years, were an equivalent of all the kinds of love that there were in heaven and earth. The Delaware River (and the Moon) had had a hundred true forms before, and would have again; but Johnson fell into the vanity that, just because he felt so good now, he knew what there was to know. . . . This is a very ancient risk, and nothing new that I have invented to trap Johnson in, to make him seem a fool. For though, except by printing things with this sentiment of integrity and perfection, this "golden view" which comes by *being* whole and perfect, there is indeed no other way of knowing any truth; yet this very view also, that seems so whole, is only part—or better, it is an analogue of whole.

Falling in and out of love: like climbing up a hill and tumbling down again, heels over head.

"My joy is so stable," thought Johnson, "up to this golden month, I seem to have been dreaming. But now I am awake."

In the same way, in every previous vicissitude, he thought that *before* he had been dreaming; but he was always in error, for he had always been more or less awake. If only he could realize that his love for the Leonards and the Mildreds, the Margerys, Bobbys, and Dorothys, would never be enough to show him all of the Delaware—tho he became each one in turn and got to know more and more. But he would better have fallen in love with God right off: forsaken all the analogues and metaphors for very Love. This way, instead, his consciousness became more and more thronged with former dreams, as he thought; each thing, he looked at thru a dozen flickering memories—a smile with other smiles hovering round it, a gesture with other hands and fingers flashing near. He never saw anything quite right, I think. . . . But the cure for this confused and multiple love was a process of rigorous *Abstraction:* which would have disclosed to him love itself; but our Johnson was too proud and sensual (as I hope by now to have shown) for any such Abstraction.

12. It was the more the pity that Johnson should now risk becoming so fatuous with happiness, because previously he had understood more clearly than a good many that in excitement, fear, jealousy, in temporary callousness, or hurt love—the world appeared always anew, one could become extremely wise in interpretations. "It is by sadness we perceive delicate relations," as he said. In this way he became wise in interpreting the Hudson and Delaware Rivers, and in construing the meaning of Chess Game and Tennis Game. He had also learned intimate details about the Moon, as when he said:

How often to the Moon I bow:
O Empress of Heaven, recklessly virgin Queen!
tonight in more refined perception, I
bowed to her waning.
This law is nobler than her silver beauty:
it is by sadness we perceive delicate relations.

But now, even when she waned, the Moon seemed to him to be grinning with a foolish round face forever.

13. And finally, this fatuousness can likewise be described by the metaphor of the Relation of the Sun and the Moon; for the point here is that, if the moon were always full, we should not guess that its light was borrowed from the sun.

> —so, if the Moon
> would never wane, but round and full all night,
> all month, glowed in the sky, and moved across
> the sky undiminished, round and full I say,
> (surrounded by the violet and blue stars)—
> we should not think its light was borrowed from
> the yellow Day God, but that by a natural
> heat she radiated, like a pale stove;
> and all the moonstruck people would not think
> of the Sun, but sleep by day.

14. I came upon the 2 of them sleeping on the shore, clasped in each other's arms. It was the night of the 16th of June, lit by a full moon. Their faces gleamed, together, like the 2 halves of a moon. They were asleep and breathed against each other.

Meantime, the edge of the River rasped on the gravelly shore. Their breathing against each other's face, must have seemed like the roaring of the sea. Their moonlike faces were surrounded by golden hair that seemed black blond in the night—all like a full moon in a cloud; and it was this sight that brought me to write this story. They were not like each other, nor mirror images of each other, but together, they formed a round and perfect moon.

"It would be possible," I thought suddenly, "for them, sleeping there, always breathing in each other's breaths and no other air, to die of asphyxiation. But what a death—full of the other's breathing!"

"Leonard! Johnson!" I cried, shaking them by the shoulders, "wake up, else you die, sleeping there together!"

15. In these 9 studies of Johnson, I shall have written

only about love, or about Johnson in love; and I think this demands an explanation. For, like every one else, he was political, domestic, mechanical, artistic as well. Yet I haven't passed over these simply because one cannot tell everything, nor because I did not want to make Johnson completely known—but because love of somebody is one kind of perfect action, and it is sufficient to describe one such.

Aristotle distinguished between action and contemplation; and St. Thomas Aquinas, holding that the proper life must include both, found in teaching the noblest possible career. (He was a famous professor himself, of course.) But an affair of love, too, calls in play all the faculties, of passion, and contemplation of form, and the chase. What is more, their play is not conventional, but free and creative: every moment the love-affair assumes a new and evolving shape. Habit is no rein; lovers do and say, spontaneously, at any moment, things that overturn everything established and conventional.

It is true likewise (but to a lesser degree) of shipbuilding, of working in an iron-foundry, of teaching, of preaching, of agriculture: each could be perfect action and sufficient, if I described it with good rhetoric, to make Johnson perfectly known.

16. During those 28 days, Johnson likewise studied theorems about circles.

Out of Euclid, for instance, he studied the theorem,

If a circle is divided into any number of equal arcs, the chords joining the successive points of division form a regular inscribed polygon; and the tangents drawn at the points of division form a regular circumscribed polygon.

Given a circle divided into equal arcs by A, B, C, D, and E, AB, BC, CD, and EA being chords, and PQ, QR, RS, ST, and TP being tangents at B, C, D, E, and A respectively:—

52

The Moon

Prove that: ABCDE is a regular polygon; PQRST is a regular polygon.

I. Since the arcs are equal by hypothesis, then AB= BC = CD= DE= EA, for equal arcs are subtended by equal chords.

Then, ABCDE is a regular polygon, for an equilateral polygon inscribed in a circle is a regular polygon.

II. ∠ P = ∠ Q =∠ R = ∠ S = ∠ T, for an ∠ formed by two tangents is measured by half the difference of the intercepted arcs (which are equal by hypothesis).

Then, PQRST is a regular polygon, for an equiangular polygon circumscribed about a circle is a regular polygon.

As a corollary to this it can be shown that:

The perimeter of a regular inscribed polygon is less than that of a regular inscribed polygon of double the number of sides; and the perimeter of a regular circumscribed polygon is greater than that of a regular circumscribed polygon of double the number of sides.

He studied the theorem that,

An arc of a circle is less than a line of any kind that envelops it on the convex side and has the same extremities.

Given BCA an arc of a circle, AB being its chord.

To prove that the arc BCA is less than a line of any kind that envelops this arc and terminates at A and B.

Of all the lines that can be drawn, each to include the area ABC between itself and the chord AB, there must be at least one shortest line, for all the lines are not equal.

Let BDA be any kind of line enveloping ABC as stated.

53

The enveloping line BDA cannot be the shortest; for drawing ECF tangent to the arc BCA at any point C, the line BFCEA < BFDEA, since FCE < FDE (a straight line being the shortest distance between two points).

In like manner it can be shown that no other enveloping line can be the shortest; and therefore BCA is shorter than any enveloping line.

Q. E. D.

But after this it can be assumed that,

The circle is the limit which the perimeters of regular inscribed polygons and of similar circumscribed polygons approach, if the number of sides of the polygons is indefinitely increased.

Out of the calculus, among other interesting theorems, he studied the one identifying the so-called Osculating Circle and the Circle of Curvature.

17. But in all the theorems that he stopped at, he discovered (for he did not read them systematically, but here and there—each one as it seemed imaginative or elegant), there was really the idea of the circle as a *limit*, of the *growth* of the circle, its "formal growth," if one might use such a phrase, to perfection. He saw that to him, as to so many others, circles typified all kinds of things moving towards their goals.

He thought of many Pictures of Things Moving Toward Their Goals, as: a person or group gradually becoming clarified in an idea; a dagger that has stabbed some one to death is becoming stuck fast in the congealing flesh; an affair of love; a little fat girl greedily gobbling lumps of sugar:—he saw that to him all these could be typified by the symbol of a developing circle.

18. Spinoza, somewhere, has pointed out that in defining the circle, it is better to do so as the trace of one end of a

54

freely moving straight line whose other end is fixed—than as a locus of points equidistant from a fixed point, or something like that. For in the first case, both the essence and the *generation* are described, not only the essence; the essence implies the generation. One morning this notion forcibly recurred to Johnson—like a shot of scotch whiskey—becoming sharply defined out of a haze of memory: "What an exalted world," he thought, "full of necessity, in which everything need only to be possible in order to have to be!" He saw that in *such* a world (as indeed it seemed to him now, tho he watched her fading at the end of the month) the Moon would be round for ever and ever.

19. At the end of the month, the 2 returned to Philadelphia, since (for Leonard) the beginning of a new term of the law-courts was in the offing; and Johnson, a radical politician, had been consigned to organize certain miners near Wilkes-Barre.

[New York City]
[1933]

Dialogue of the Clock and Cat

Tick tick tick tick, said the clock.
   The cat was asleep.
   Johnson said:

> Gray-dressed day, O day
> of 100 voices, ma-
> trix of clock-ticks—speak
> to, and guide to me, the one I seek.
>
> If I, all night for this
> hour, at the window (whis-
> pering many times that
> thing I most wish) have sat
>
> waiting, to greet thee first
> palely coming, yet uncurst
> by acts, therefore yet free
> to hear and grant: O grant it me.
>
> Guide him to me; not
> by force, but—O polyglot
> Dawn! for many whisper thru the burning
> night—by ghosts and yearning.

This story occurred before the dawn, which Johnson
was at the window waiting for. In his hand, also, he held a
square alarm clock; and on his lap lay a black cat, asleep.
   The clock, electrified and throbbing, had a large second

hand that kept sweeping over the whole surface in constant, visible circularity. The angle that the pointer, extended, made in turn with each side of the square frame, grew larger and larger, from 45° to 60 to 90 to 135—and then, it was cut off, started again at 45, growing larger. "It is always cut off! it will never become full! . . . " cried Johnson. "The growth of that angle (the intersection of pointer and side) is a function of the progress of time and could easily be analyzed by the calculus." By every sweep of the pointer round the face the minute hand was slowly pushed ahead one space; and the hour hand also moved, invisibly. The second pointer swept past the minute and hour like a boy on a bicycle past pedestrians. The small hand was like a woman dying in childbirth, always more tired.

"Suppose a spider," he thought, "spun its web from the hour hand to the minute hand. Then the minute hand moves on, and the web would break. The spider could try again—as they are said to do—and then it would break. The perseverance of the clock is stronger than the animal; soon the spider has spun out all its belly. You could see it, emaciated and dying. The clock-hands would henceforth trail around wisps of moist thread.

"By God," he cried, "if I had a blue coat, yellow pants, and top-boots, I should be Werther!"

Tock tock, said the clock. "Not stopping, I hope," thought Johnson.

Closing his eyes he at once fell asleep, altho he did not mean to. Then, on the black screen of his eyelids, he saw, very large, like a cinema close-up, a picture of the square clock; but now the hands were bound with a spiderweb so strong that they couldn't move. The clock was stopped at a quarter past seven, and, in the middle of his web (over the number 5) sat the spider.

He awoke and began right where he had left off. He was perfectly clear-headed, but he just kept dropping off to sleep, as a boy, balancing on the kerb, sometimes steps off. "There is no Werther in our day. Yet we did not have to give up the philosophy of Sensibility so lightly as we did. It was not refuted, it merely became ridiculous; but the fashions in comedy change every day. Werther! Werther! who treated his heart like a sick baby. That was what he *had*, a sick heart. The immoral thing would have been for him not to follow what that heart so surely told him was good, to act according to only second-best intuitions; not to walk over the countryside reading Homer, nor love children. Notice what love of children . . . Not a way of life for healthy people, but there are many sick people, even today."

At this Johnson fell asleep. (Nothing was finished; everything began over and over.) He dreamed a dream about the summer before. He was in a dance-hall, somewhere in the country, at night; looking out the window he could see a round moon over a lake. A noisy band played jazz-music and there were 100 couples. He wanted to dance, but did not know any one. So he sat at a table building a house of sugar-cubes.

> —and I love him because he loveth children
> and is loved by them: therefore is twice blest—

he awoke with this couplet in his ears. "Who is it? Who is it?" he called. He noticed that it was four-thirty. The sky outside seemed to be getting gray; but this was false-morning, for in a few minutes it would be blacker than ever.

"I know the one I mean," he said.

The whole air was full of voices. He could hear Leonard's voice so near, and he began to die with longing. It was a lisp that was ridiculous and beautiful in a young lawyer standing before a judge. Also there were certain words that Leonard habitually mispronounced, such as *misled*, which he always called "misl'd," as from a verb "to misle"; or *mishap*, which he pronounced "mish-ip" (deriving it from *misshapen*, which he therefore spelled with one s). Now every time that Johnson heard one of these words mispronounced by another, or even correctly pronounced, he thought of Leonard and trembled. Then he tried, by steering the conversation, to make the other use the word again and again. "What did you say?" he asked, or

59

"Repeat your train of thought in as nearly the same words as possible; I think I see where the error is." He himself used the words again and again and sometimes, wilfully, mispronounced them. Then, becoming ashamed, he at once corrected himself, and you could often hear him say, "misl'd, that is misled."

Tick tock tick tock, said the clock, in the still room.

Johnson looked from the clock in his hand to the cat on his lap, trying to ascertain a connection between them—why these two, of all the world of things?—but he could not think of any way to bring them together.

"Every time I listen for it, the clock seems to have a different sound—

> My piano has a different tone tonight:
> nothing is changed, except I have seen Leonard.—

"Among the *Characters* of Theophrastus," thought Johnson impatiently at four thirty in the morning, "is the Flatterer, who runs before his patron in the marketplace, spreads his witticisms about the town, and says, when his patron is being fitted at the shoe-store, 'the foot has more style than the shoe.' But in the end, the fellow he has described might as well pass for the lover as for the Flatterer. Act for act, they act the same, except that the lover is sincere (not always, at that). If one wants to write an amusing 'character' . . . the lover—imitates his mispronunciations, sees him as the Man in the Moon, falls in love with the girl who looks like him when she smiles, and trembles when a stranger at the grocer's, speaking of coffee, says 'blended,' because he hears it as 'Leonard.' He uses him as a simile on all, even uncomplimentary, occasions, just to keep talking about him; and constructs an anthropology proving the superiority of blondes, because he is a blond . . . .

"But why do we call *Werther* a great, a successful work of art except just that it is a closed world which, according to its own rules, is real. This is just what we mean by an artistic perception, a sense of unity and reality in the arrangement, according to its own rules. It is a judgment of

60

fitness. How dare you say that there is something extravagant in the character of Werther? We have judged it a work of art!—"

At this moment Johnson began to address, aloud, a silent interlocutor inside his head.

"How dare you say something is wanting to his way of life?—when we admit that all his actions are adequate to his world. The boy who loved the children and gave them pennies, shot himself in misery thru the head; but it is all a *unity*, how can we judge against him. Men die every day. You cannot judge a way of life by the length or pleasure of it. Werther! Werther! what they deny is that his dream is the real world, or that his disease is a disease of the people. *But they cannot deny* THAT!—"

This exclamation rang out smartly in the night. The whole room was full of sound.

He recalled the brief snatches of his two dreams.

"Sometimes I want to dance, or build architecture, and I sit at a table and pile up sugar-cubes. Sitting, playing with sugar, in the midst of a jazz-band—" this naïve metaphor nevertheless struck Johnson with such a weight of desolation that he began to sob bitterly and became incoherent. "The satisfaction is never commensurate with the longing; no, not once. But how long can that continue without something dying in one? Sometimes to be active, to be passive—but you go for a quiet walk thru the streets looking in the faces of all the people. Sometimes unable not to be with the boy Leonard, and then write letters (that go unanswered) and this is all the gratification, all the gratification. Tear them up, too—like pushing the sugar-cubes onto the floor where, crushed, they become gritty and noisy underfoot.

"It is always cut off! it will never become full! it is stopped! it never *has* begun.

"Ah! ah! the spiderweb hung between the hands has stopped the clock. Then it was dead and covered with dust. Before that the web again and again broke, exhausting the poison glue in the vitals of the arachnid; then everything was beginning over and over, and this was the worst of all. The desire is like a poison glue spinning out of my breast.

Then there was none left and I was dead as the clock. This was better than beginning over and over.

"Now I comprehend the symbol of the clock and the cat. Both have movement. Under my fingertips I can feel the breath and blood of the animal trembling. But the clock is beginning over and over, without inward development or creative life. It is nervously dead, unable to lie still. The only life of a clock is in the time, external to it, that it measures and that goes on endlessly creative. But a cat is alive and has the time inside himself, as well as outside. There is a sense in which he is not beginning over and over. Somehow my brain has gotten like a clock—without force, but nervously reacting to a thousand signs from outside.

"Natural motion is that whose principal is within the subject; violent motion is when it is *pushed*: Aristotle.

"The desire does not come in a full, steady, and growing flood (like the moon), as if fed by a real impulse, a deep spring; but in shocks, like the heart-attacks of a cardiac, every hour for a few days. It is not pleasant to have a mind like a frog's galvanized leg, that jumps but is under no living control.

"I cannot think why I do not go to bed."

At this he again nodded and fell asleep.

A loud prolonged ring of the alarm brought him awake, wild-eyed and with shrinking organs. The clock dropped out of his hand onto the floor. At the same time the cat bounded from his lap. The dawn, at five o'clock, was just breaking, as he sat, terrified, at the window. His organs inside him seemed to shrink from contact with his flesh. I myself have had a similar terrible experience when walking once, alone, on the dark River Drive, amid many couples going each way. I came opposite a small empty police-booth where, suddenly, in quick plaintive bursts, a 'phone began to ring. Nothing was so terrible as the quiet jerks of noise, calling, calling. At the same moment the moon rose. Weakly I clung to the rough wall of the booth, and for a long time stared at the metal lattice of the great Bridge tower, 200 yards distant, far below. . . . At

Dialogue of the Clock and Cat

Johnson's feet, the square clock, on its side, ticked.

But as the cat had leapt from his lap, so a new energy welled in Johnson, enabling him, of his own will, to move and act. He leapt thru the window into the dawn, onto the green lawn. As he sped across the grass, and it was cold and moist to his soles and between his toes, he flung his lounging-robe from him. He disclosed his naked golden body in the gray light, for it was scarcely dawn—fleeing across the grass, like a wonderful upright animal. Then he came to the lake, sped out on the dock, and dove; and the water encased him more warmly than the air. As he struck out, the axis of his body, in the stroke he used, moved straight and horizontal thru the gray foam beat by his elbows and cutting edge of hands; but on that axis, regularly at every third stroke, his body rolled and up above came his golden right shoulder and his face. Behind, his well-timed legs threshed the water in a six-beat. He came across in a few hundred strokes; the lake was 1700 yards, about a mile, across. His mind, now, was much clearer and more vigorous. As he paused a moment, in the water, after this efficient exhaustion, he was much less a fool than he had been. "It's damned cold," he thought, "and the sun isn't up." The whole sky was violet and foggy and light. The water, too, began to take on color, like a convalescent boy. Johnson drew himself into a rowboat moored offshore and began to row, at random, hard, hard. Looking back at the long triangle of wake (of his swimming), which seemed more dark and glassy and still than the other water, he imagined he saw the golden triangle of his shoulder rising in a parallel series, a hundred times, over the course, and his body a continuous beast beneath, surging thru the foam. "One time—" he thought—his thought and his breath both being punctuated by hard thrusts of rowing—"Leonard—on the River Delaware—" thrust, thrust, "—swam till he was faint. —But he came back because of certain responsibilities."

He rested. "There is no Werther in our day," he thought. He was like a certain subtile, powerful philosopher whom I know (from a distance), who holds that every age should have a good Platonist and a good Aristotelian among its scientists; but since, in the person of Whitehead, we *have* the Platonist, he feels it his duty to be the Aristotelian.

[*New York City*]
1933

The Rivers

Sometimes Johnson, walking in the evening, bowed to the moon. If a black poplar detached itself from the skyline and sent a chill to his heart, he nodded to that. In the daytime also he saw many meanings all about him to be reverent to. He nodded to white clouds, to the advent of spring, to the flags of many nations, to the sound of distant music or the name of Haydn, to kindly people, to beautiful dogs. And when he beheld the sun for the first time each morning, he raised his right arm in an imperial salute, as if to greet Augustus passing in a golden ship. In this way he acknowledged the power and activity of the great sun, or of those other things. Not that he saw the world *peopled*, full of mythical personalities, but that he saw it full of objects with meanings, and to every object that we clearly understand in itself, he felt, we owe a measure of love and, therefore, respect. (This was also, to be sure, a kind of lunacy.) And there was an intimate connection between his feelings and behavior in this respect and his moral life. For, the whole world round-about thronging with values, was a constant witness, and judge, of his own desires. He was ashamed to think certain thoughts before the moon, or a cow. When he felt particularly despicable in the morning, he did not dare lift his palm toward the sun. And conversely (and this is the motive of this whole story), in accordance with his own spiritual adventures, he saw the world more or less clearly, this way or that, so that one night, for instance, returning from a long row on the placid River Delaware, he wrote:

65

How often to the Moon I bow:
O Empress of Heaven, recklessly virgin Queen!
Tonight in more refined perception I
bowed to her waning.
This law is nobler than her silver beauty—
it is by sadness we perceive delicate relations. . . .

Now among the Objects to which Johnson paid his respects, none more than the Hudson River aroused in him the sentiment of Awe *(Achtung)*. His heart spun round like a top when he saw it. It was either that he had known it a long time and it was naturally splendid, or that he felt for it that active sympathy everybody feels toward the ideal that he himself would like to be. And he himself desired to be severe, self-sufficient, forthright. Every day he came down to look at the Hudson River. He could likewise spy the river from his window in the heights of the city. It exerted a perpetual influence on him, comparable to that of the sea on those who live nearby; except that, unlike the sea, the river was soundless.

When the sun was in the west, in late afternoon, and the red streak of its reflection burned across the water towards him, Johnson was struck by majesty and power; he nodded as deeply toward the water as if it had been the light. Where it flows past New York City, the Hudson River is a mile-wide plane between a cliff wall and a city. That is its form: the eye is borne onward and abruptly stopped.

The cliff, the Palisades, is how the river has ploughed down 400 feet into the bedrock. But once Johnson, blotted against the sheer face, found himself crossing a fault-line from a layer of gray granite to one of green felspar; and suddenly, as in a dream, he imagined that he was some Devonian monster imbedded there, coming to life; and he could hear at the same time the rush of the centuries of water ploughing through the strata.

His mind was jarred by the sound of waters; in the swirl he almost perceived the gray atmosphere of a less ancient dream, of childhood memories unconscious but suffusing his thoughts. On all sides rose ponderous heaps of rock, and there was a terrible flat line, like a cutlass, coming to slash across his eyes . . . Snatching at the tail of his vision, a fleeting animal, he almost perceived that when he beheld the flat grandeur and the uncompromising rockiness of the river, the power and size, what he was really beholding was the time when, as a boy, swimming naked in the water, he had seen it spread out from the eye-level of a swimmer, or his childish figure had clung to immense rocks in a way that a grown-up would not have to—amid the clamor of a train and a pall of coal-gas. His soft child lips had learned its feel and taste, a soft compound of salt and oil. The boys swam from craggy rocks piled as an embankment for the railway. Clamorously the occasional train rushed by, trailing a sweet lethal odor of coal-gas, while the passengers leaned out to look at the white figures of the boys on the gray crags.

An unvintaged plain! full only of eels and crabs. At the end of a line he had pulled up one fat, squirming eel, and one hard crab in a wire box-net. Then, half disappointed, half frightened, he had left off fishing.

When he was 10 years old, a great wooden steamer, the *Indian Point*, set afire at one of the piers; the pier itself burned; the blaze lasted through the night; and one of the images that he could not forget (so that later, without knowing it, he used to speak about it) was the white furnace of the ship coiled round with black oil smoke, like the sun in the midst of a pall of ashes—roaring against the night.

The sunburnt cliff—on which Johnson was all this time hanging like a red berry—was severe but not forbidding, for it was grown here and there, and all along the river-bank, with woods. There was the undeviating length of the cliff. The surface of the water was either slate gray or white, like pottery, and one mile wide.

This was the spiritual quality of the river: it was severe but not forbidding. It was broad but strictly bounded by high banks, not like the indeterminate sea. It had a military dignity rather than any other, powerful and silent. Stern, broad, abrupt, soundless, not boundless, military.

One day, when they had hung a great suspension bridge

across the river, seeing its five or six slender lines from far off and all the water in the foreground silver and glittering like a school of fish, Johnson thought that this was the most beautiful sight in the world. The blood rushing from his head, for he was lying on a hillside—he suddenly began to hear a hundred voices coming from everywhere; and the River spoke out:

"Bear up, Johnson!"

"How do you mean, River?"

"I mean that the most important thing in the world is to be an Object."

This oracular utterance, though it did nothing to enlighten Johnson, had at least the effect of increasing a thousandfold his respect for so gifted a river.

Across the river (from the cliff) was the architecture of the city, and Johnson hated it because it was all either brutal or ornate, or both, which is to say, barbaric. Yet this also, viewed from the river, under the special quality of the river, became absorbed almost into a kind of severe beauty. Its brutality became dignity, its ornateness could not be seen. As Johnson cruised up the river in a motor-launch, the prodigal heaps of buildings in the south, although neither proportioned nor useful, became impressive at least as heaps, particularly at night, when they loomed vaguely a thousand feet overhead, with 50,000 lights blinking, here and there. He cruised further north and the city, like the river, became broad and quiet. There were occasional large buildings along the shore: a granite mausoleum, a white cylindrical memorial, a tall steeple whose tip had been touched by lightning. And at the tip end of Manhattan was a tulip tree more than 300 years old, under which Hendrick Hudson treated with the natives, and about which are scattered the shells and fireplaces of an Indian village.

He likewise sought to learn about the Hudson River through names, almost by tasting them—as if, to learn to know a statue, he should not only walk all about it and view it from above and below, but should feel himself inside its fingertips, and its loins, and its mouth. Hackensack, Hoboken, Weehawken. Englewood, Tenafly, Fort

The Rivers

Lee. These names to Johnson, as he more and more tried to imbue himself with the *being* of this admirable river, seemed to have either a warlike sound or a certain purity . . .When it thundered and the echo went along the cliff, Johnson knew, this was because Hendrick Hudson and his men were playing bowls among the Catskill hills in the north. Henry Hudson, an English Mariner out of Amsterdam—so Protestant a name!

"In the end this is what it comes to!" cried Johnson to himself, just as if he at last understood. "The Hudson is a *Protestant* river. It is rigorous in power, bare in appearance. This is what I mean when I say that it is military, I mean that it is Cromwellian. And if, looking at these cliffs, I were obliged to sing a hymn, what other could I sing but this: *Ein feste Burg ist unser Gott!*

"Other rivers may have other qualities," he went on, "but for better or worse I shall never love any other as I do this, with its bare brown walls without stained glass!"

As for himself, at this time, what Johnson desired was to be self-sufficient, to stand on his own legs, as the phrase is. What he loved in art was large form and rough directness of statement, and poetry that sounded like prose. And the virtues of character that he loved were these: frankness, decision, dauntlessness, and wholeness, and independence, and all such other qualities as go to make us morally soldier-like.

2.

Now when Johnson fell in love for the first time, many of his most heartfelt ideals underwent a complete change, and this was true of rivers as well as aspirations. He did not become conscious of these changes until a long time after they occurred. First, for 6 months, he was in too much of a misery of unrequited and rebuffed passion to notice anything, and his life altogether went along on such a bumpy road that he could truthfully exclaim with Antiochus in *Berenice:*

69

Tous mes moments ne sont qu'un éternel passage
de la crainte à l'espoir, de l'espoir à la rage!
et je respire encore . . .

"All my moments are but an eternal passing from fear to hope, from hope to rage."

Then, in the month of August, in the heart of summer, his beloved went off to the Orange or Kittatinny Mountains of New Jersey, and he followed there; and it was under these circumstances that he came to view the River Delaware.

But quite the contrary of his acquaintance with the Hudson River, he met the Delaware not where it is sweeping broadly into the sea, but near its source, at Water Gap, where it is first breaking loose from the barrier of the mountains and is becoming a river at all. The direction of its flow has not yet been determined at this point; no tons of water have ploughed a course down into the rock. But it slowly goes with great windings, often turning almost back on itself, creating knobby peninsulas, and sometimes making wooded islands which it quite surrounds with its pliable arms—wherever there is a way. It is docile, like anything in its beginnings. This does not mean that it is weak, for there is a strength of water that will somehow get to the ocean, and if there were absolutely no path past the mountain, one would be cut through the rock. But the river is content to have that path chosen for it and, if one may employ such a phrase, to fulfill itself by another's will.

The quality of its flow, for the same reasons, has not yet been determined, but it goes a ragged, bumpy road. At Flatbrookville the stream widens out to be a round lake; its motion is imperceptible; Johnson could watch the water for an hour and not tell which way it was flowing, except that his boat had drifted. But at Bushkill, further down, the stream has gathered momentum; it is shallower, quite narrow, straight. And still further down, a few miles, it is a spitting rapids, never more than a foot deep, and rather foam than water. There is a place where it threatens to disappear altogether among the rocks; in dry weather you would not suspect that it was there, unless

70

you reached down your arm between 2 rocks and felt the frigid water. But Johnson could not drive from his mind, as he did so, a picture, like a double-exposed film, of the lordly progress of the Hudson.

He was astonished, when he came to think of it, that any river should measure so few score yards across. To get to the other bank was so easy a swim that you would not think of taking a boat—unless you wanted to keep your clothes dry. The land extended out into the water in reeds and overhanging boughs, as if they were used to living together, and the Delaware no foreigner in the territory.

Thus, when Johnson first came to the river, he did not even see it. Here and there were round yellow hills, and planted among them, a dark, thick avenue of trees and growth. In the midst of this was hid the Delaware, not visible through the luxuriance, except that ahead, below, it could be seen rounding a bend. The Hudson, Johnson recalled, was salty—a few willows on the bank. But this river obviously watered the land.

And drew from it. For the river was not yet so out of all proportion to the country roundabout but that a large creek (like the Bush Kill) still seemed to contribute something appreciable to its flow when it spilled into it. The whole network of rivulets and brooks, of creeks and kills, the outlets of lakes and ponds 20 miles away, was an intimate marriage of the country and the river. The Delaware wet the roots of orchard-trees that extended, in their alignment, down to the bank.

It was all a region of farms and cattle. Nobody could maintain here, as they might of the lower Hudson, that the dominant element of the landscape was the river, for it was patently the land. "But the proposition is more subtle than that," thought Johnson. "If the river is obviously subordinate, this is because it is really dominant, as the whole is obviously less than the parts (being nothing apart from them) but really greater. Supposing we were to say that the relationship here between the land and water were as intimate as that of body and soul: then the water would be the active or spiritual principle of the union, and the land the bodily or massive. In the growth of an apple,

71

for instance (since such is the fruit of this fluvial marriage), the swelling of the pulp, the distending of the skin, the red coloration of it, would all belong to the watery virtue; the cambium would belong to the water! the stiffness, the ossification of the trunk, to the land—or something *like* that, anyway. . . . But the Hudson, on the other hand, would be rather a stiff-necked, ascetic spirit, struggling to quit a rocky, hateful body—so Protestant!"

He threw himself under a pear-tree near the river and began to think of the great subject of Analogies. By analogy alone, it was evident, can we try to guess at the details of categories of existence about which we have no direct evidence. (Whether this is ever permissible is another question.) A good analogue, says Suarez, is one that can be substituted in the second term of a syllogism. It is the Catholics and Platonists who have most exploited the analogical method of philosophizing; for in this way, and this is the only way, they feel, they can at last connect finite and infinite, man and God. Man is not thus left, a stranger in the whole world, but all about him in the world are signs, printed with the nature of Eternity. In all things. The 3-leaf clover and the 3-fold division of philosophy, equally indicate the divine Trinity. And so profound a mystery as the Emanation and the Incarnation of the One, is easily understood as the history of a man on a cross.

"But what an analogy," cried Johnson, "can be seen between Love and the River Delaware!"—

A sickle-pear dropped down near him and he automatically bit into it.

—"Like Love, the river is a fluid power, and it seeks to concentrate itself and progress. But it is not self-sufficient and it needs, for its channel, another element. It has no will of its own, but follows, without struggle, where it is led. It nourishes the land and receives nourishment from it. The whole region is full of fruit. The path of the Delaware is adventurous; it is now calm and deep, now bickering and flat. There is intimacy between the land and the river; they are not averse; the river serpentines back on itself as if it wished to embrace from all sides each plot, or as if the land wished to draw it closer, enfolding it around.

And in a sense, the river is stretched among the hills as at somebody's feet.

"Every view on this river is various; in this it is like Love. As you go forth along it, each turning is a discovery and creates new ways of understanding. It is for this reason that it is so rich in analogies—like a Cathedral which offers a different view from under every pier, but is so concentratedly ornamented only in order that there may be, in one place, many analogues of the beauty of the living God. . . . Delaware—de la Ware: so French, so Catholic a name! and this is the river that is like Love."

Johnson bit into the pear, but, though warm from the sun, it was still unripe and filled his mouth with fuzz.

3.

Johnson came back to New York bitter and disappointed. The passing of his moments, having once more gone from fear to hope, had again landed him in rage. Now was the time when he could practice being self-sufficient, soldier-like, full of fortitude, and virtuous in all those other ways that he used so to admire. But precisely what, with his whole heart, he just now did *not* want, was to be alone, to be left alone, to rely upon himself.

"How can *I* be an Object, by myself?" he asked.

He beheld the Hudson River, and he was physically wounded by the brutality of its flood and the bare, beautiful cliff. He could not, having been away, understand it any more, as an object, and therefore worthy of love. His ideal having changed, he could not sympathize; without sympathy, he couldn't *see*. "Oh, the severe, murderous river!" he said, "what peace or pleasure could there be in paddling on such a river! If you do not maintain an eternal vigilance, you may be run down by some enormous liner coming up the river, or buffeted about in the wake of even a ferryboat! And if a strong wind were suddenly to blow and the chop to capsize the canoe, who knows but that you may drown, caught far off from land in the middle of the flat water? The Hudson is too big for us; it is independent of us; it is out of proportion; where is there love in that? But when I paddled on the Delaware, even if my eyes were full of tears, the river was not *hard* to look at, and seemed even to have a measure of sympathy."

[*New York City*]
1932

The Tennis-Game

The process of Johnson's falling out of love was like fever and a quick death; and during the course of it his mind so thronged with a delirium of pictures that the most ordinary actions became impossible.

Striking the ground smartly, a tennis-ball bounded toward the level of his eye, while he raised his racket to strike.

Then he saw that the white ball, and his action, were in an infinite Receptacle of possibilities. He might strike it or not strike it, and fair or foul. There were many other things he might do with the ball. He might throw it into a field, or watch it bob on the waves of the sea (traveling there for that purpose), or skin it, or explode it by heating, or place it before a colored lantern; or he might think of it, as he was now, or think about thinking of it. He could annoy sleepers with it at night by tossing it against their windows; or write on it a rendezvous; or use the white sphere as an element in a mobile abstract-design; or with a sharp knife cut in the rubber a grinning face. And all of these to any degree or quality. . . . From the Receptacle was it all drawn. In the midst of a lake of relation he felt himself swimming—like a little beetle. . . . The ball began to emanate a halo of light such as painters place round a figure in the foreground to make it stand out from the canvas; and in this way, being a center of attention, the ball ceased to have relational existence at all, and became art. Or, on the other hand, it became all relations and altogether invisible, like the bundle of moves in the mind of a good

75

blindfold-chess player who does not *visualize* the board as a plaid, sat on by wooden pieces with names, nor even geometrically, but as a complex of moving formulæ in a world of 64 units.

Bounding past him, the ball sang against the wire-net backstop. The player looked around, smiling a little shamefacedly at being so preoccupied in the midst of a game. The play continued with astonishing rapidity, he thought. A ball sped on a line into his service-box: he smartly sent it back up the alley for a placement-shot. But he had been caught almost altogether unprepared; and before he could really draw back his racket, crossed in front of his body from the drive he had just made, the game was again on. The reason everything seemed so fast to him was that he had lost quick control of his muscles and limbs; before he could bring them to any appropriate action—they were so heavy—everything had passed on.

From another point of view, however, the time of the game passed with incredible slowness, like a river so sluggish you can hardly tell whether it is flowing forward or backward. This was from the point of view of the speed of his thoughts. For his inner activity was so accelerated and so various that everything else, by comparison, seemed stopped dead. He saw images with the profusion of a nightmare. Among the troops of ideas that marched across his mind, the end one could always be that of returning the ball to the other side, and it would always arrive with time to spare; and there would still be an infinite number of thoughts between that one and the one that was really the last before hitting the ball, in which he could always make up his mind like Achilles catching the tortoise. "Thus," he thought, "I do not prepare to swing at the ball because it is never time; but when my arm moves to execute the swing, the ball is already flown by."

While he was deciding this, another ball sped by and sang against the wire net. He stabbed at it more than a second too late. Everybody laughed and the umpire said, "Game!"

"It really will not do," said Johnson, "to be so distracted.

The Tennis-Game

I really must keep a firmer grip on my thoughts, and keep my thoughts on the game. I cannot understand what has gotten into me; I am not feverish." This resolution to keep rein on his wandering thoughts was made with the perfectly lackadaisical manner of one already embarked on another day-dream. And it was a day-dream itself, for if his thoughts could really be gotten under control, as he wished, he would never think about it, any more than he would think about falling asleep. "I am not feverish," thought Johnson; "I used to be in love. I once knew a philosopher who said that if falling in love is blind, falling out of love is dizzy; for we are even more unfair now to the person we used to love, than we were partial at first. But it seems to be dizzy in a very literal sense as well, if it is what is happening to me now; if indeed I ever did love."

It was his service-game. But far from botching it, as he would any other situation—the hyperæsthesia that had possession of him gave him such accuracy of control as to terrify as well as exalt him. From a high place he seemed to dominate each little square of the field, so that if it were laid out with lady's-handkerchiefs, he could without difficulty hit any one of them and stain it with brown dust—for each one seemed big as a tennis-court to him. And he spun out like a rapid line in the air, in that graceful glittering curve that is only like itself, the flight of the ball to where it shot from an inside white line two feet from the corner, untouchable. He had more space to aim at than players ordinarily have. He served the balls deliberately; but they sped away with astonishing speed, for it was not the power of his muscles, but their synchronization, that was erratic. One time he missed altogether and dropped his racquet. This was because his eyes, following the ball he had tossed upward, were magnetized by the sight of many boy-children on some benches on the side, or seated on the ground. Many boy-children together, so that their combined gestures and scores of expressions formed a whole pageant of childhood, simple and fresh, yet because of their very numbers, various and interesting. For a single child is like a single beautiful note; there is a moment's pure joy and then you cannot listen any more, but must turn to an adult, corrupt, not nearly so radiant, but at least complex. But a group of children is a whole symphony, without sacrifice of purity. There were two in particular who caught his eye, 8-year-olds, bare-kneed, dressed in grey shorts and roll-down grey woollen stockings and heavy grey sweaters with enormous collars that curled up over their chins and ears. They were seated on the ground leaning against the legs of a man whom Johnson at once took to be their father, and he began to seek out the family resemblance in their features and expressions. "What a projection into Time a face is that we see in both the son and father!" thought he. "A certain modern french romancer—Pierre Villetard?—has deplored the passing away of the old family-portrait, for it was, as he thinks, the fugue-form of painting; there was an inner rhythm of meaning, richer than a rhythm of form, in the 8 or 9 heads subtilely resembling each other thru 4 generations. But in life this rhythm recurs in language, manners, gestures, in the inheritance of furniture and dress; in the Hapsburg lip and in the Bourbon mind; it is a whole chorale!—as well as in the grey-blue eyes of these boys and of their father. . . . But what am I thinking of? it is my friend Cleveland and not their father at all." At this, Johnson missed the service-ball he had tossed up.

He served a fourth ace, the ball seeming to be at the same time above his head and hitting a white corner many yards distant, as though there were a continuous glittering wire gracefully poised over the field; while everybody applauded, including his opponents. Several dozen people had come out to watch the practice. "What desirable children the two grey boys are!" he thought. "I am envious of Cleveland sitting above them, talking to them, instructing them in what is a good play, watching their teeth when they look up, he looking down reversed, into their eyes upside down. He is touching the hair of one: how dare he! . . . It is curious enough," he stopped to think, leaning on his racquet, "that among all the children these two seem so especially attractive to me that I am about to insult a lifelong friend on their account. . . . So, given any group of

The Tennis-Game

10, of children, or of the girls or nuns who live next door in the convent-school, there is always one with whom, immediately, I am in love. It is only later, when I have watched at my window for one to return home, or perhaps have even called out a name at night, in bed; when I have been undeceived a dozen times, by callousness, avarice, cruelty, mendacity—and still unwilling to learn; that I at last concede that there is nothing extraordinary about *this* one. (And even so, he or she is never just anybody, after.) For, what is it? it is perhaps only a dress or an outfit that catches my eye, or a certain ash-blonde color of hair, or a surly, unhappy face that may really be due to a toothache, or the fact that in a large group there are twins"—as a matter of fact, the boys in grey were not even brothers, but were dressed alike by the imitation natural to some friends—"or that one girl, when first I met them all, smiled at me more sympathetically than the others, because she was thinking of something else. . . .

"Then have I been truly in love these past two years, or has it been one of these?" Johnson asked himself anxiously. For he was in the peculiar position that, the first time in the past two years he could think coherently and without effort on this important question, it was beginning to make no difference whether he ever thought about it or not. He understood this himself. "The fact that I can doubt, proves I no longer love. For while actually I was seeing the great value, the qualities, of that person, this perception was so self-evident to me that, to deny it, I should have had to be insane (or out of love). But now it is easy. I must remember: there could be a sonnet:—

If I could doubt I loved, I should not love,
and that would be better—"

Suddenly he became altogether conscious of the tennis-game. Like a blinding sun it blotted out all his other thoughts, the past, himself, his love, into obscurity; and his whole mind became an act of pure contemplation. Up to now his thoughts had been, so to speak, corkscrewing in upon himself; now they leapt wholly into the environment, and were exteriorized. In a way equally abnormal, for there was still no relation between himself and the game, to enable him to act.

The sunlight inundated everything. The white field spread away before him as if it were on a globe that quickly vanished on all sides. The net, the markings of the field, were brighter lines, lit up, across the general whiteness. The duck-clad players leapt across the lines like naked angels. Back and forth sped the silvery ball. It sped from near him back across the field; and he was intrigued to see, flourishing and brandishing right before him, an angelic arm and a racquet with glittering strings (like the fiery swords of the cherubim before the gates of the garden of Eden). He could not perceive that this was his own arm and that he had just stroked a ball (there was a momentary twang, as of a guitar).

He was altogether dissociated. He saw, or rather contemplated, the game from far-off—the while he unconsciously made faultless strokes. Then, as he watched, everything became evident to him; all the rules and stylism of the game of tennis were standing about, invisible, but like so many real presences controlling the play. And they even began to be a little visible. He understood the Unity of the Form, of the ball bounding from side to side, of the leaping players, of the twanging of the guitar, of the muffled voices everywhere. Of the ball shooting towards him and away, and of the mysterious racquet that propelled it. Then, before his very eyes, this Unity floated into being and became almost a spirit, no longer made of matter and movement, but full of life and ghost, and the most beautiful thing that he had ever comprehended.

"I don't want to play any more, I want to look on!" he cried, hurling down the racquet he did not know he was holding. "Let someone else take my place."

"What's the matter with you, are you ill?" asked his partner anxiously, running over to him. The voice came from so far off.

"No, I want to talk to the game."

He walked over to where Cleveland and the children were, and sat down on the clay.

The Tennis-Game

After a brief pause, the tennis-game at once began again, with a substitute player, for it was only practice; but try now as Johnson would to concentrate on it, the silvery splendor was gone. The field had reverted to its more usual color of dirty buff, the lines of dirty white, the net grey; and the players garbed in loose-hung linen, the shirt-tail of one hanging outside his trousers. The ball dug up a puff of buff dust as it bounded skyward, not spinning, and scored with a visible stain like the cheek of dead, dragged Hector. The play was good; the drives low, fast, and angled. The players stood, or gained momentum across the field, with grace and ease. One volley of shots ended with so hard and angled a smash at the net that everybody applauded. But Johnson, whose perception had for a moment been wholly lost outside himself into that silvery work of art, and was now returning thru the normal experience of looking at a match of doubles from the side-lines, soon found himself again burrowing inward. He did not find the game interesting in itself, as a thing, but all manner of irrelevant thoughts distracted him, about the score, about the players, their tournament-ratings, for instance; about the spectators, about the boys in grey next whom· he was seated. It was all beginning again. By an effort of memory he recaptured the lines:

> If I could doubt I loved, I should not love,
> and that would be better.—

"Are you sure you are feeling well?" asked Cleveland, over his shoulder.

"Oh yes; I was a little tired."

"I should say you ought!" exclaimed Cleveland. "I have never seen such serving in my life."

"Gee, it was good," said one of the boys next whom he was seated.

Johnson put an arm around his shoulders. "Are you two brothers?" he asked. . . .

"But I cannot doubt I was in love!" he cried to himself, "that for two years I was always oscillating between self-

81

sacrifice and rage. I cannot doubt that there were in that person such qualities as compelled me to love, when once I had perceived them: such beauty, such fine-ness of grain, such erratic grace, such love of children. It would be easy now to maintain that I was deceived all that time and that the qualities I thought I saw did not exist; that it was only an ordinary person; that I was so eager to love anybody, that I found it easy to attribute any virtue at all to the first one to come along, just as I might now, for no reason, prefer one of these kids to another.

"But how could I deny that truth, it was so plainly so! Such mildness of manners, such precise uncertainty, such dignity in trouble! It was my *duty* to seek it out, to try to be near and contemplate it in an especial way; it was so plainly so. I confess I made no effort not to love, or to check my mind when it was not too late. But this is the duty of all who are naïve: when they see an undoubted value, to love it unhesitatingly, without regard to future pain or people's talk. . . .

"But what is this change for, then? Why am I not still in love?"

He smiled at the little boy distractedly.

"I cannot see it any more!" he thought. "If there is a change, it is in myself, not in what I saw. I used to be able to perceive a meaning in a certain body and soul; a splendor of form illuminated all its actions; but it is all gone; its walking, now, is only walking, and its moral beauty abstract, for I do not take fire altogether when I see, or shake inside like a tree full of wind (if I may say so), so as to understand it as this THING! For there is a special kind of perception in understanding a thing. . . . But the whole form, the moving form of my mind has changed, or I should still see it the same as ever. In respect to this at least, its sensitivity—its whole form, then, for it is a meaning and not a mere fact that is here to be perceived—has descended completely from one level to another, where it cannot see. There is as much difference as between the top of a mountain and the bottom. And this is why I have been so nervous, so hyperæsthetic these past days, for a revolution has been taking place inside me. This feverish movie-film of ideas in me, of the Receptacle, and how we think, and the boys who are twins, and the tennis-game, and how we fall out of love, so random and undisciplined—is really only my tumbling head over heels down the side of a mountain. Until I hit the bottom with a bang. And then there succeeds a time of apathy longer and more terrible than this delirium, until I become reacclimated.

"It is the meaning of death. The part of me that has perceived a value cannot any more, and there has been a real annihilation of an activity of the soul. There was an interior model of the one I loved, but it has died, and that one is a stranger.—"

Now Johnson began to cry, still seated on the ground. Tears streamed down his face and taking his arm from around the little boy's shoulders, he hid his face in his sleeve.

"I knew it!" said Cleveland, bouncing up, "he is really ill."

[New York City]
1932

Out of Love

Johnson became split into 2 personalities inhabiting the same body at the same time. On Friday morning, one of them awoke from a dreamless sleep, refreshed, ready for the day. Looking in the mirror on the wall, he saw himself—sleepy and happy.

The other awoke from horrible nightmares. Thruout the night he had kept breaking into consciousness. He was strangled in the bedclothes, saw brick houses tumbling on him, and underwent many others of the usual nightmares. Several times he got out of bed to throw open the window, open wide already.

(Meanwhile his other self slept soundly on.)

But it was only toward morning that these confused night-thoughts began to assume any definiteness or symbolic meaning. Then little by little, they—and he—became identified with one picture, one painting, by di Chirico: a cloister with a pool, bathed in a vivid midnight sun—far off, a puff of locomotive smoke. A scene infinitely desolate! he felt himself into the isolation of it—a summer sun without heat—arcades a thousand years old, yet intact but for a little crack in the plaster—drama frozen (which is a contradiction)—a thin long shadow of one person fixed forever on the pavement. With this one scene his mind was totally occupied. But outside the frame, from the peripheries of consciousness, he could hear the muffled shouts—the puff of the locomotive—of all the other dreams. It was only in this cloister that the walls were not tumbling in, but hung in the balance; and

85

that he was not being strangled by the bedclothes, but was breathless. Amidst the bedlam, was this vacant zone.

But as he awoke and opened his eyes, he realized with horror that the dead zone in the middle of his mind was persisting. The ceiling seemed a hundred miles away, as far off as the moon. True, the sharp outline of his dreams faded, it was no longer a picture by di Chirico; but everywhere he looked, he saw quite the same picture. The clock on his night-table receded a millenium; the bedclothes were like sand-dunes. The void, inside him, got up, traveled with him about the room, and at the same time the far-off shouts. When he looked into the mirror, he saw abstraction multiplied by abstraction.

"How hungry I am!" cried the other. "To rise, like a child, hungry from sleep—for years I have not had such appetite. Johnson, Johnson, you are surely cured! I am going to eat even before I wash." He stuffed a roll into his mouth and began to look around the kitchen for more food. On the shelf was a blue and white box: at once he knew that what he wanted was rice and milk. "Rice and milk with sugar and cinnamon. I've not eaten that since I was a little boy, almost a child; I used to eat it all the time then. It is at the tail-end of memories of the kids on 151st Street, when I used to sit on a little step-ladder in my aunt's kitchen. I recall a hundred bowls of steaming rice and milk.—All are from a different age." . . . He watched the water boil in busy bubbles. He poured in the shower of white kernels. But he did not at once *abstract* the hundred embodiments of form here, forms of motion, counting, patches of color; he enjoyed only the sensuous substance itself. At the same moment, the sun glanced from a faucet, a drop of water fell, and a fly zipped past, yet he failed to notice this at all.

(The other, however, saw it all.)

"Surely I am cured," he thought, "rid of something, of a void—as if some other person had taken it all away into himself, just as certain saints, they say, can absorb our diseases and our sins." He placed three greengage plums on the white cloth. His mouth watered with the foretaste

of their sour bite before the rice, milk, and sugar, and the
flat savor of cinnamon and coffee. The grains of rice began
to absorb water, grow plump. The coffee started to perco-
late and give off an odor. "For the first time in fifteen
years," he cried, "I am out of love!"

He sat down to his breakfast. He had everything at once,
a bite, a spoonful, a sip at a time. He added a Spanish
marmalade, very bitter. He thought: "Hitherto, if I fell out
of love with one, I was already in somewhere else; having
gone from hope, to rage, to despair with one person, I was
already well on that cycle with another; my heart always
restless; and this happened many times. But now, at last,
after a dying out that was unperceived and a calm that has
crept up on me day by day, I find that I am free! self
sufficient! instead of a half-moon, a full moon. And the
symptoms of it are these: dreamless sleep, a mind without
a corner void, and this ravenous appetite for rice and
milk."

The other thought: "I cannot fill up on gluttony. I am
trying to distract myself by the taste of foods, but there is
no satisfaction; I swallow everything as in a dream. Cinnamon, coffee, and sour plums—" As he recognized the
pattern in these tastes, he smiled, by a long habit; then this
smile, corresponding to no pleasure, froze bleakly on his
lips. "I didn't think," he said to himself, "that love and art
would go together, but now one has carried off the other.
Which was first to go?—perhaps they are the same thing.
There has been a clean sweep! . . . Everything I look at
today is athrong with forms—the rice showering into the
bubbles abstracted before me into a hundred forms—none
gives any pleasure. I do not seem to be feverish, but calm,
tho far off somewhere are the shouts of life, as if in another
world. . . . Likewise with the remembered faces that used
to play about each thing, in a golden glow, instilling such
light and terror in me, 'fear and trembling and clarity of
sight'—they are now like the negatives of photographs.
See, the face of Helen is in the glancing light on the
coffee—but it might as well be Helen of Troy."

"Free! free!" thought happy Johnson; "each person I
now pass on the street does not make my heart leap into

my throat; as if, perhaps it is she! Goodbye to all the Margarets and Helens!"—

"Negatives of photographs . . . there is no flow between photograph and photograph, but they pass from one to another in an instantaneous leap."—

"Now I am independent and can converse without dismay. Perhaps at last I shall be able to make useful friends."—

"Peace! peace! . . ."—

"Why, now I am at peace."

"Void! . . . I know that I have lost a part of myself," he thought, "and I hear its happy shouting in the distance. *I* am lost, not he. He was before me; out of him I grew, in some sense. Oh, I feel I am dying—*he* is returning to childhood, the time before I came. I have lost my connection with the world."—

"The Chinese, after a meal of delicacies, eat bowls of rice, just to fill up. But oh," thought Johnson, "that would obviously be the best part!"—

"How unlucky is di Chirico! He has always been driven to paint the ruins of Doric temples and a rearing horse of phosphorescent green."—

" *'If I want iron,' "* remembered Johnson, " *'if I want iron,'* I told my aunt, *'I can suck on the end of a knife; why do I need spinach?'* "

"I am sinking back into nothing. It is that he has ceased to be in love; I understand it clearly. Indeed, it was love that produced me, abstract as I am, as a concrete personality—but now love has flown off, I am void and already beginning to decay. What a loss for him! If I could only break thru, to rejoin him, recover my body, attract his attention!" He rapped loudly on the table.

"Who knocked?" said Johnson. He went to open the door, but no one was there.

He went into the shower-closet to take a shower.

Thousands on thousands of drops descended from the ceiling. Across them, the circular chromium fixtures gleamed. Runnels of water spread round his ears and under his chin, in the cleft of his throat, and between his breasts, in the channels between his shoulders and his breasts, under his armpits—and so down across his belly and between his legs. He moved, and the warm roaring water swashed and splashed.

"Perhaps I won't die soon," thought the other, far off, "but linger on in this torment for weeks and months."

From a square window near the ceiling, a sunbeam slanted across the shower, and the closet was filled with rainbows. The fine spray and mist created one system of rainbows, delicate and shifting and vivid; the heavy drops another, steadier, paler. They crossed each other in arcades, like arches of an Arabian Nights mosque.

"It's not with impunity we fall in love. There is a moral risk—"

Vanishing and shining vividly, here and there. The chromium circles, the golden drops, glimmered thru the iridescence. Johnson turned his eyes from side to side; he put his hands into the arcs, and at once, as the drops bounced from them, dozens of little irises leaped into being, like dancing elves. He realized that, from other points of view, he too, his gleaming yellow body, must be circled and swathed in rainbows. The water ran out at the bottom, with a gurgling sound, thru a round grate in the floor.

"It is not with impunity that a person falls in love; he is not the same after as before. Another self is generated and, when the nourishing love is flown away, how void and hungry this one is!"

The water became colder and colder. The drops glittered like diamonds. The frigid water spread among the roots of his hair and his scalp burned; it ran down his back in streams of cold. His dark hair, which was like a jungle wet and black in the rain, soon formed 4 channels hidden in the long weeds, to let the water stream into the corners of his eyes and in his ears. The roar became deafening, like shooting the rapids, or as when you hit the water after a high dive.

"How lucky for him," he thought amidst this clamor, "that I am split off and cannot torment him! I am better dead.—"

Suddenly the shower was over. He stepped out into a rough towel, which was warm and golden from lying on the tile floor in the sun. He stepped into some fresh linen and decided, before dressing further, to take a shave.

He had a razor-blade of Sheffield steel, more than ordinarily long. After a moment's stropping, it was sharp as the devil. Suddenly he became childishly proud of owning it; he felt a great affection for his razor-blade; he thought that with it one could chop a hair in midair, like Saladin in *The Talisman*. He began to have a number of such childish fancies. "Free! free!" he thought happily. "There is a lot of work to do, and today I feel capable of doing all of it! If only there were enough hours in the day. 2 calls on parents, a letter to *The Times*, then to school—" He was assistant-principal of a high-school. "—Today I shall call the faculty-meeting. They won't know me! They'll be surprised at the speed things are going to move at! I'll no longer spend too much time with people just because I'm afraid of being alone."

His cheeks and jowls were white with lather. In his round magnifying mirror, he looked like a department-store Santa Claus. He felt that there was nothing else in the world so pleasant as to shave with a razor sharp as his. The mirror presented his face twice as large; there were enormous tracts over which to pass the blade. Near his chin he cut a wide swathe, then began to piece out little chevrons and circlets above this. He behaved as if shaving were a kind of pantomime and he had all morning in which to pose. He could hear each hair of stubble thundering down as it was cut, like a tree in a silent forest.

His hand jumped a foot. He cut his throat, a bloody gash, on the left side.

"Now I have done it!" cried the other in a piercing voice, and died.

"What an unearthly shriek! who is there?" said Johnson, turning white. He was so bewildered that it was a moment—while the lather became red with gore—before he could apply the caustic tang of a styptic pencil, to try to stanch the flow.

Out of Love

He began to tremble. "I must be going mad," he said to himself. "First I hear no one knocking at the door; and then this uncanny shriek."

[New York City]
1933

Appendix*

Martin, or The Work of Art

I.

In the course of conversation with Larissa, Johnson learned that she had a brother named Martin; for the rest of the evening he moved the talk about him and nothing

*Note: Originally there were nine *Johnson* stories. One of them, "Martin, or The Work of Art," has a curious history. Like the others it began with a series of actual events, which Goodman transformed into fiction. He read the finished story, as was his habit, not only to the principals who had served as his models, but also to his literary friends, some of whom happened to be privy to the circumstances. One of his fellow-authors objected that his treatment was inadequate, and a sort of contest ensued in which a competing story was written from the same primary material. I have been told that there was even a third entry in the contest, but no one seems to know who the author was. The second still exists, never published. Whether or not this friendly competition had anything to do with it, Goodman made a rather special case of this story: he revised it in 1951, for what purpose I do not know; and again in 1968, for inclusion as a "new story" in *Adam and His Works*. The original manuscript has vanished, probably cannibalized in 1951, so that it is now impossible to know what the 1933 version was like, except by inference from later versions and from the competing story by his friend. It is not even clear where in the series it was to appear; perhaps at the end, if the references to Leonard as a past love are not later additions. Certainly its tone, and probably some of its incidents, were altered drastically. Johnson's question to Larissa about her brother's penis, is not likely to have appeared in the 1933 manuscript. Nor the television set in the bar. I print here the 1951 version, as the closest to the original, but as an appendix to avoid the clash of styles.

T.S.

93

else. He felt that this topic must be interesting to her, at the same time intimate and yet not so personal as to be embarrassing, since they had just met. It was a quiet tavern without television, and their voices became warm, earnest, and soft. With gray eyes glowing, she described how tall and black was Martin, unlike her ashen blonde to which she called attention. He was so slim as to be almost skinny, again unlike herself. He was three years younger than she. He was interested in astrophysics and baseball. He had a certain way of saying "Wow!" "So boyish!" cried Larissa, "just like you, Johnson." Before the night was over, because of the very animation of her recital, Johnson came to feel another, more essential, interest in Martin.

He thought that it would be a wonderful thing, an experiment fraught with doubt, to love both the brother and the sister at the same time. Without jealousy in the very lair of jealousy. This idea struck him just as he looked up at the clock and saw that it was 2:32 in the morning, a time when the resistance is low. Larissa was at this moment describing Martin's best friend, an Italian boy with violet eyes named Andrea, and how inseparable the two were, at which Johnson became so perturbed that he tipped over his glass of wine on the tablecloth.

In love, Johnson was disinterested and creative, and this allowed him to have sexual pleasure. By withdrawing and, like a sculptor, arranging the male and female figures in a beautiful group, he could then return and take his place in the niche left for himself. Sometimes, to be sure, the group worked harmoniously without him and he no longer found his place. Then he had the fancy that he was a Renaissance despot trying (according to the mighty Burckhardt) to carve a beautiful polity out of a troubled people. Also, he was reconciled beforehand to the disappointment and self-sacrifice that come from trying to make something worthwhile with recalcitrant material.

"When am I to see this paragon?" he said briefly to Larissa.

"Oh—I mean, if you and I are going to see each other again—"

"Of course I am going to see you again, soon. I must see

94

him too. Tomorrow. Now don't you miss. It's more important than you think."

She looked up at him with timid gray eyes as he arose. She was already in love with him.

"Look here," he said, "what's this name Larissa? Where did you ever dig up a name like that?"

"Oh—I mean—" she said. She explained that her mother had wanted to call her Laura, but her deceased grandfather's name was Isidore, so they called her Larissa. "We're Jewish," she explained; it was evident to her that "gift of Isis" was a Jewish name.

Sexually, Johnson was a Judeo-phile. "I'm going to call you Sarah," he said approvingly.

"Oh no!" she cried. "I mean—"

2.

But when Larissa came to the appointed place the next day, she came without her brother Martin. (And this was the first time.) She was late, too.

Johnson, for his part, was in the habit of being on time, especially when he wanted to keep the appointment. Now, after waiting, walking up and down for twenty minutes and wondering how he could have so miscalculated the girl, he had the added disappointment of finally seeing her running through the hotel-lobby alone, without Martin. (She was always late and she always arrived running, taking off the edge.)

"I'm so sorry to be late," she said in a fluster. "I couldn't find my hat." She pressed his hand warmly in both of hers and clung to it. He had to shake her loose.

"Where is Martin?" he said.

"Oh—he couldn't come. He couldn't come because he had to finish eating supper."

Nevertheless, Johnson soon recovered his accustomed cheerfulness and devoted himself entirely to Larissa. He did not so much as mention Martin, for now he felt that he knew her well enough to talk about herself, and he knew that it might seem unflattering to the girl to be talking

95

always about her brother. So he just kept starting her off ("wound her up," as we say) and let her prattle on about herself. Mainly she talked about her former lovers, how she had loved one person 75% and another person almost 90%.

"She really is stupid," thought Johnson wonderingly. "After all."

"You remind me of some one I used to know," he said suddenly. "You remind me of some one that *I* was in love with. He was a man, named Leonard. When you smile that way, and stick your tongue half out."

It was true that she reminded him of Leonard. At this time almost everything still did, any lisping speech, any off-color hair, any mention of vacation-spots that had either lakes or rivers. For just the opposite of his esthetical withdrawing mode of approach, once he had gotten engaged he could never cut loose from anybody. He would see in the fleeting expressions of a new face the ghosts of ancient loves. They revived before him, playing one after another on the face before him; or sometimes several traits at a time, the pout and lowered lids at once. Then he could not help but love the girl, he did not even see her.

When he left her that evening, he kissed her very warmly. They were very sympathetic with each other.

"You won't forget that I want to see your brother Martin," he said.

"Oh no, no," she assured him. But she said this smiling complicitly, for she understood.

For all of a sudden she began to entertain a singular notion about Johnson and Martin: that Johnson, far from wanting to meet Martin, wanted the very opposite. He spoke of "seeing Martin" only in order to have a pretext to see *her.* That is to say, the expression "I want to see Martin" meant "when shall I see *you* again, I am ashamed to want to ask straight out"—just as for Swann the expression *faire cattleya* meant "let's screw."

Larissa was so happy at the success she was having with Johnson. He was slim and had soft hair. When he kissed her she caught her fingers in his hair. His hair was varicolored. He was a man of the world. He was the most sympathetic person she had yet met, the only one to whom she could say certain things that were immediately caught up, as a spark shoots across an electric gap (and there is restored quiet). For instance, when she explained hesitantly that she was in love with somebody not altogether but about 90%, he said, "Yes, yes." He understood, he really understood. And he showed the same finesse in his ruse about "seeing Martin," avoiding embarrassment for them both. But since it was evident that he wanted to be *alone* with her, there was certainly no advantage in putting a fifth-wheel on the carriage—and especially a younger brother.

It did not occur to Larissa that Johnson might be interested in young boys.

3.

"I must make up a really clever excuse to explain him away this time," she thought as she ran down Fortieth Street, "in order to show that I can play games." But she couldn't think of anything.

When he saw her coming across the opera-lobby late and alone, Johnson was visibly agitated. He turned pale and red. "Where's Martin?" he asked sharply.

"Oh, he couldn't come. He couldn't come because he was making a telescope," she said, betrayed into the truth.

"Well for Christ's sake! what am I supposed to do with these three tickets I bought?"

"Oh, you bought three tickets?"

"*Here*—" He gave the extra seat to one of the City College students who wait in the lobby for such emergencies. The young man had ferocious brows and dark-rimmed spectacles and was quite ugly.

Johnson could scarcely contain his displeasure. Ordinarily he could not act rudely for anything, even with strong provocation. But now, sandwiched between the stupid girl and the owlish young man, he bit his lips and did not enjoy the music. He toyed with the idea of asking the young man to change seats with him—

"You know, it won't do," he said to her during the

97

entr'acte. "When I say bring Martin, I mean bring Martin. You mustn't trifle with me. This is the second time."

"But why?" she asked, bewildered, and near tears. "Why on earth? What interest can you have?"

"What difference does that make to you?" he said. "For heaven's sake, girl, wouldn't you want to see somebody if you thought he was beautiful and intelligent?"

She tried to change the subject.

Nothing doing. Tonight Johnson wanted to talk about Martin again; he did not want to talk about anything else but him.

"Are you fond of your brother Martin?" he asked her.

"Oh yes, I am very fond of him," she said.

"Good, good," thought Johnson; "they are fond of each other and I guess I am fond of them both"; and falling under the spell of the divine music he began to be quite in love with brother Martin. Excluding from his awareness the actual presence of the girl and the beetling brows on either side of him, he wandered into scraps of revery about the nature of abstract triangles, Euclidean triangles. "When you draw lines on a paper to form a triangle, this triangle is only accidentally contingent from the lines, for they could be drawn in some other direction and then there would not be a triangle." He was vaguely dissatisfied with this; he wanted the properties of the triangularity somehow to be working in the lines, moving in them to make the form of which they were the properties. These reveries were warm, clear, and buzzing, as well as irksome; the music was in the background—

"Will you please try not to mutter, sir: it's very distracting," said the young man on his left. With a start Johnson came to himself and found that his right hand was clasped warmly and damply in Larissa's.

The act ended and there was loud applause.

"Now tell me some more about Martin," said Johnson.

She told him an anecdote. Martin was standing at the window with his telescope and a man in the apartment across the court—they lived in Sunnyside, Borough of Queens—came out on the fire-escape in his bathrobe and shouted, "If you don't stop peeping I'm going to call the police."

They both laughed and the strained relation between them was relaxed.

Dimly Johnson registered that it would be extremely difficult for him to accompany to her door a girl who lived in Sunnyside, Borough of Queens.

"I thought you said he was just making a telescope," he said suspiciously. For the first time it occurred to him that the apparently simple girl was lying to him, just as he was trying not to lie to her.

"Oh, he's making a bigger one—" she faltered.

Naturally! thought Johnson triumphantly, Jews were interested in mathematics, chess, and music. They were intellectually combative, but also winningly docile; they stimulated one's best efforts to form them. He realized that he had to alleviate his guiltiness of his boy-loves by serving as a useful guide and mentor, even though this role soon stood in the way of his sexual ease and superseded pleasure, and then in turn lost its urgency for lack of animal fuel.

He knew little about mathematics and nothing about chess, but he did know a good deal about music. Perhaps—it was likely—the boy from Sunnyside, Borough of Queens, had little music. What Johnson wanted was somehow to re-live first hearing the E-Flat Minor Prelude and Fugue. Because now, inevitably, he heard it without *surprise*, and therefore without expectation surprisingly *fulfilled*. Even though he knew from experience that it was with disappointment and irritation that one breathlessly watched the boy's face and did not listen to the music oneself.

"Is Martin really intelligent?" he asked anxiously.

"Oh yes, he is very intelligent," she said. She was not sure what any of it meant, but she felt that this was what he wanted to hear and she had to make up for the frightening misunderstanding between them.

"Is he very very good-looking?" asked Johnson, rubbing his hands.

"Oh yes."

He wanted to ask a further question but did not know

how to put it. He took a breath. "Does he have a big penis?" he asked, reddening, as though he were not a man of the world.

"I—I don't know," she said, frightened.

Women! Their knowledge was always intuitive, when it was not merely illusory. They never knew the material facts.

4.

When for the third time Larissa came to the appointment without Martin, Johnson cried, "That settles it, the boy does not exist!"

"Look here, Sarah," he said quietly, "why are you lying to me? What's the matter with him this time?"

He looked at her sharply, almost for the first time. "After all!" he thought. "She has known how to play me. Perhaps the girl is more intelligent than I suspected. She is an artist."

Larissa was breathless and on the verge of tears. This time she had come late because she dreaded the ordeal and then had had to run in order not to be late. "Oh I'm so sorry—" she faltered. "I mean—yesterday Martin went away for two weeks to Lake Placid."

"Ah, ah," said Johnson, gasping like a landed fish.

He could foretell the entire future. He would end up marrying her. For she knew how to entice him in the preliminaries, and then, when she suddenly relieved his guilty anxiety—for there would be no Martin—he would be left confronting her, and nothing to do but fall.

5.

Now the real reason, this time, for the non-appearance of Martin was that his sister was ashamed to bring him. She began to feel that Johnson expected to meet some wonderful paragon, and that, in her eyes, was not Martin. Once he met Martin, he might be so angry that he would not see *her* any more. She was afraid. The more she faced it, the less possible it seemed ever to bring Martin. She scrutinized her brother; it was not encouraging. Yet since she had to produce him *some* time, she wished only that he could be improved a little, coached a little. She gave herself two weeks.

"Who was Aristotle?" she asked Martin, since from time to time Johnson mentioned Aristotle.

"Aristotle was a Greek."

"Good!" she said, surprised. "Who was Heine?"

"He was a Jew."

She was astonished. "Who was Marlowe?" she asked.

"What the hell do you want?" said Martin.

"How can you be so ignorant!" she cried passionately. "Aren't you ashamed?" Up to that moment it had been going so well.

"What am I supposed to be, a cross-word puzzle?" said the gangling dark boy indignantly.

Johnson could not make out why, when he talked to her, she kept jotting down little items on ends of paper, the backs of envelopes, and cramming them into her hand-bag. She was very sloppy (but she did not smell). "What can she have to write so much?" he wondered. "Can she really be taking notes on what I say?" This idea mildly flattered him.

He contrived to get hold of her hand-bag. It was in a tea-room. "I have to 'phone," he said, and as he rose he picked up his book and her bag underneath. In the 'phone-booth he explored the multifarious recesses: the lip-sticks, keys, key-rings, handkerchiefs, compacts, address-books, coins, combs, thread, innumerable papers. A mirror fell out on the floor and broke.

"Bother! She ought to keep such a thing on a string."

A gentleman opened the door of the booth and saw him on his hands and knees covered with powder.

"Damn!" cried Johnson and crammed everything back into the bag.

"How tall is Martin?" he asked Larissa vindictively.

"Five foot ten inches."

"Is he dark or fair?"

"Why, dark or course. I've told you a hundred times."

"Yes, I thought you might have forgotten what you said. What color eyes did you say he had?"

"Hazel."

"Is he sensitive? I mean, is he delicate, nervous, easily jarred, afraid of crowds?"

"Oh yes—oh no—I mean—He is naïve."

"Was he a quiet baby?"

"Definitely."

"So," thought Johnson, "she is beginning to contradict herself. The other day she said that he was noisy."

"Why are you asking me all these questions?" said Martin to his sister. "What difference does it make whether I know who Hannibal was? Anyway I did know that, I meant just what you said. What do I care if I'm supposed to meet this fellow Johnson? Who's he? Does he know anything about baseball? What difference does it make to *him* if I know who Hannibal was?"

"You ass! I don't want you to make a total ass of yourself. It's for your own good. Here, I've got some new bibliography."

"What's that mean?" he said in a toneless voice.

"That's books for you to read."

Frederick the Great. Sappho. *The Dialogue on the Two Systems.* Clement of Alexandria. Boswell's *Life of Johnson. War and Peace.* Schmutsky.

(Schmutsky was the painter who made his reputation by the ingenious retrospective exhibition: "Post-impressionism from Cézanne to Schmutsky." So Meyer Schapiro tells it.)

6.

It was all over. Johnson had to confess it to himself, sadly, for he really wanted to be happy, just like anybody else. He looked at the girl—she was a beautiful color—without interest; she had a sympathetic manner—he was not even hostile. His work of art had died in his hands; he didn't care whether Martin existed or didn't exist; or whether or not triangles could generate themselves. Instead he compared himself to another kind of heroes, for it was necessary for him to have some model or other. He was like Marcel who could never get started because the weather changed from day to day and one had to acclimate oneself. Or he was like Des Esseintes, who never did get to England.

With a mighty kick he kicked the tin waste-basket into the next room, where it fell with a tin clatter. Larissa looked at him more in stupefaction than fear, for to her he was considerate and polite, though a little distant. The life streamed into his legs, first the right, then, flooding stronger, into the left; and he felt that it was Leonard he wanted to kick—or whoever it was, long ago, who had cast a blight on everything beforehand, that he tried to hide with foolish projects. He went inside and carefully brought back the dented waste-basket to its place. He looked at Larissa but found that he could not stand the sight of her, she looked like a parody of Leonard—or whoever it was.

"Just go away," he said aloud to her and gave her a push. "I don't want to *see* you; don't you understand? The sight of you makes me sick. Good bye."

He crammed his hat on and went out, leaving her alone in his apartment.

"Don't you want to meet *Martin?*" she wailed. "He's coming back tomorrow."

7.

"But I *want* to see him!" cried Martin hotly. "You said I was to see him, now you're trying to back out of it."

The boy had worked himself into a passion and was panting. His sister was more cool and vindictive.

"Be a reasonable boy, Martin," said Larissa. "What do you want to see him for? You know what a man looks like, don't you? A postman, a door-man. A man. A man like any other," she added sententiously.

"Then why can't *I* see *him?* Why? That's what I want to

103

know."

"You can't see him because. Just because."

"For Christ's sake!" he roared. "Then why did you TELL me I'd see him? WHAT DID YOU TELL ME FOR?"

"Don't shout at me, Martin. What difference does it make to you why I told you? Supposing you knew, how would you be better off? Now there's a question. You answer me that question and I'll answer the other question."

Martin said nothing.

"The trouble with you, Martin," she pressed her advantage, "is that you think everything people do has a reason. Sometimes people do things *without* a reason."

"Ah," said the boy quickly, "did he give you a stand-up?"

"The reason I said you were to see him," she said coldly, "was that he *asked* to see you."

"Why can't I see him?" His voice was flat and inexorable.

"*Why* do you *want* to see him?"

"I can answer *that!*" said Martin. "I want to see him because he takes an interest in me. Not like those other dodoes you bring around who wish I'd fall through the floor so they can get you on the couch and maul you."

She tried to slap his face, but he cracked her forearm away with his hard forearm.

"You hurt me," she said, tears in her eyes.

"You said he'd teach me something!" cried Martin passionately. "Do you think I like to sit here in Sunnyside with nothing to occupy my mind?"

"You can't see him because I don't want you to see him," said Larissa.

"Ah! So. So. You don't want me to see him, that's what I thought. Why? Out with it."

"Why? Because."

"Come, come—don't be a fool, girl. I said out with it."

"Don't you dare call me a fool."

"I didn't call you a fool. I said don't be a fool. That's not *calling* you a fool, is it?"

"Well, don't you call me a fool."

104

Martin, or The Work of Art

"Did Johnson call you a fool? Come on, out with it."

"Do you think I'd tell you that, even if he did? No, Johnson didn't call me a fool."

"Why don't you want me to see him?"

She said nothing.

"Out with it."

"Why do you think?" she said. "I'm looking out for your own interests, that's why. He's no good, that's why. I don't want you to meet him because he's dangerous for you."

"Oh! So you don't want me to meet Mr. Johnson because he's dangerous for me. *Why is he dangerous?*"

"Will you stop repeating everything I say after me? What do you think you are, a tape-recorder?"

"Why is he dangerous?" said Martin.

"Why? Why? Out with it!" she mimicked him. "I try to do something for his own good, and then he asks me why."

"Why is he dangerous?"

"MUST YOU KNOW EVERYTHING?"

"Why is he dangerous?"

"All right. He's dangerous because he's a pæderast."

"What's that mean?" asked Martin sharply.

"That means he makes love to boys."

"Gee?"

[*New York City*]
1933-1951

105

ELEVEN STORIES
(1933-1935)

The Wandering Boys

From extreme points of the compass wandered 6 boys: 1 from the North, 1 from the South, 2 from the Southwest, 1 from the East, 1 from the Northwest. They were isolated and disorganized, without goal, home, prospects, food, or occupation. Wherever they went, they went some place else; till all came together in Ohio. Between being apart and being together: what a difference! and this story is all about that. They were Luke, Harry, Henry, Herman, Roger, and Robert.

The Search for Food

1. In the hot sunlight they set about robbing a truck-garden.

Harry and Henry, who were kids, 14 years old, stood guard outside the hedge, while the others sneaked under like 4 suspicions.

Last week, before they met, the kid Henry cried without cessation. Altho he got out of breath and tears, he continued with the same hollow in his chest and burning eyes; he could hardly swallow; when he ate he tasted snivelling in his food. Really, he was ill with a kind of colic or dysentery. When his health improved and he had wept out all his misery, he got over it; but the brutalizing effect of such a cure, by just "forgetting about it," was worse than anything, for it made the kid more like a man. Too late, a farm woman took him in for a couple of days and he robbed her of 40 cents. But he hadn't really gotten over his fit of crying, for he was again about to begin.

Suddenly he and Harry found that both came from the Southwest.

"Arizona is yellow on the maps because it is full of sand," said he.

"New Mexico is green because it has a few trees," said Harry.

Inside the hedge, 3 boys were among the vegetable-rows on their knees; Luke, the oldest boy, 17, stood, and told them hastily what to do, for he knew more about it than they. They pulled some turnips from the ground, but he told them not to, "because you have to cook them in a pot, but we want only potatoes that you can roast. We don't want nothing that is a nuisance."

They plucked, a few at a time, of the parsley-like green heads of limp yellow carrots, coming from the ground in bunches of 5, like an artist's fingers. Luke took off his shirt and collected a shirtful of half-ripe pink tomatoes, streaked with deep green stars. Hot in the sun and dust, these tasted to the lips like flesh when you lick it, in love, on an excursion; but when bitten, they proved hard and tart. "This red tomato," said Luke, naked to the waist, "is for the kid who has the bellyache."

Herman, a heavy boy on his knees, said sullenly, "He thinks he's wise and can boss us; but he can't. Look at 'im, he's lightweight."

Like 4 posts they stood up in the field; their hands were full of orange spikes and green foliage. Luke had a pendent white bag like an inverted balloon.

Outside, the kid Henry began to cry again. The tears streamed out of his eyes and he kept wiping them away with his hands.

"Are you crying?" asked Harry, coming closer to look.

"Yes," said Henry. His 10 fingers kept forming a lattice before his eyes and his muddy face was streaked with parallels.

"What's there to cry about?"

"I'm crying 'cause I can't help it," said Henry. His 10

fingers kept forming a lattice before his eyes and his muddy face was streaked with parallels.

The other kid began to be unnerved by this unreal exhibition of crying for no cause; just as people at all unbalanced are, by its unreality, by the weird scherzo of Beethoven's C-sharp minor quartet. It is something that files away at the very base of the spinal column. Tears brimmed in Harry's own eyes and he bit his lower lip. Finally they were both sobbing bitterly without a sound.

Then, accidentally, they touched each other, and as soon as they did, they fell down on the ground in each other's arms. And they lay clasped so. And their minds together, particularly since their half-open sight was wet and dim, were shut in a crystal globe; they were within a warm soap-bubble blown from soapy water. The iridescent sphere lay poised on the grass.

At this moment the 2 kids were more deeply in love than anybody in Ohio. I want to make this clearer by recalling the good lines of Keats:

> I wandered in a forest thoughtlessly,
> and, on a sudden, fainting with surprise,
> saw 2 fair creatures couched side by side
> in deepest grass . . .
> they lay calm-breathing on the bedded grass.

Now the farmer came by, against whom they were supposed to be on watch. He was extremely tall. Being nearsighted, he also saw everything in this bright day in a haze; in a sense, he also was within the warm soap-bubble. He saw the 2 brown-overalled kids clasped to each other with their 4 legs scattered, like a tan glove flung anyhow on a billiard-green.

He knew that the others were on the other side of the hedge for he could hear them talking. Their conversation came and went on the warm air. With the 2 kids (clasped together) at his feet, the farmer peered thru the hedge; and had they in the field looked, they could have seen his grey-blue eyes peering thru the long wild stems.

The hedge was an ordinary privet-hedge allowed to shoot tall and wild. The tops of the stems flew out in all directions. It was more like a bush than a hedge, except that it was long and formed a boundary.

The farmer cried: "Hey, come out here with those vegetables!"

2.[1] In a chromatic blaze, one after another, the 4 crawled thru the hole in the hedge.

Like classic boys with offerings, all 6 stood about the farmer, who was a foot taller than any of them.

"It's all raw vegetables," thought Henry fearfully, eying them, his eyes full of tears. *I want cooked food.*"

"He's 1 against 6," thought Luke; "if he bothers us, we could knock him down."

"We could leave him dead under the hedge," thought Herman.

"What do you boys want to steal for? Is that right?" asked the farmer.

"O mama, I'm sick of raw carrots," thought Henry. "My gums bleed pink on the yellow edges."

"If I tackle him by the legs, I'll be kicked in the head," thought Herman.

. . . "What possibly can we say?" thought Luke finally. "We stole it to eat it."

"Couldn't you come ask me if you were hungry?" said the farmer. "There's lots of food in the United States. I'd have given it if you were hungry."

"Everything is going to wrack and ruin—everything is going to wrack and ruin," he thought.

"See, I come closer to my friend Henry," thought Harry.

"O Harry," thought Henry, "let's stand close to each other. I'm scared of this man. I wish I wasn't here."

"If we'd 've asked, maybe you wouldn't 've given it," said Luke. "Then you'd 've been on the watchout and we couldn't 've taken it."

[1]In the manner of this part I have tried to borrow from Virginia Woolf's *The Waves.*

"What's he *blabbing* for!" thought Herman. "I could sock that guy."

The boy Robert stood with heads of lettuce in his arms, and the boy Roger with carrots and cucumbers. Henry and Harry, the kids, had wisps of straw on their overalls, from lying in the grass.

"Why, you boys are BUMS!" cried the farmer. "You! you haven't a shirt on your back" (this was Luke); "none of you has shoes on your feet. Where do you come from? Why didn't you *stay* there? Aren't you ashamed?"

"Not our fault," said Luke obstinately.

All the boys were ashamed because of their shoes. Luke, Herman, Henry, Harry, Roger, and Robert looked at their squads of toes.

All 6 stood like classic boys with offerings, about the farmer.

"Unlucky kids!" thought the farmer. "I tremble because of them. I don't know what I am supposed to say. I cry for my country's economic suicide."

"See, we are like an organization!" thought Luke exultantly, "we are alone no longer. Here we stand together and talk with him, like diplomacy. Jumping on him we could knock him down. I am proud to be the spokesman. I am like an ambassador from Canada to America. We are alone no longer. Because I am the oldest, I am the chief. Of the 2 kids particularly I am fond. In just this way we could organize a Republic; and perhaps have cooked food."

"Everything begins to decay," thought the farmer. "The arch has a broken back. But the Law is worth more than bread. Not to starve, they have taken to wandering in packs like hungry beasts. Yet men die every day: it is better to be in order than to eat."

"Now I want to be with Henry all the time," thought Harry, "because he is my friend. I should rather be just as tall as Henry than an inch taller than he. I do not feel cheap alongside him because my shoes are worse. On the other hand, tho he is always crying, I have no desire to make fun of him. It has not even occurred to me to wonder whether

113

or not I could lick him. . . . See, he is going to cry again. O Henry, Henry, don't cry no more."

"Why are we standing round?" thought Herman. "Why don't we step in and knock him down? I'm gonna beat hell outta those kids for not laying chickie like we told them! What's the good of traveling in a gang if some don't obey orders? We'd a'been a mile away."

"What's your name?" whispered Henry to Harry; and his face, like a burst of sun among thundershowers, lit up 100 candlepower brighter.

"You! you with the lettuces," said the farmer, pushing Robert in the chest. "Where do you come from? why don't you go back?"

"I ran away from thah," said Robert dully.

"Why don't you stay home? Don't you love your parents? Don't you want to be educated?"

"Warn't nuthin thah," said Robert.

"Why don't you work on the farms or cities there? Why do you roam about? That's not right. Everything becomes disorganized this way."

"Warn't nuthin thah," said Robert.

"The whole United States will be lousy with bums!" cried the farmer, "with 15-year-old kids traveling in gangs, in packs, like beasts. Unresponsible to anybody. Not recognized even by the Law. No rights, no duties."

"Can't you see, perhaps he didn't have any home to stay in," said Luke.

"You! you! you!—" cried the farmer, pushing them all, on the shoulder, in the chest, "why don't you go *home?* You don't want America to break in pieces, do you?"

"Don't shove," said Herman, "You know what your father got for shovin'."

"What's in that bag?" said the farmer. He took the inverted balloon from Luke's hands; the tomatoes rolled out over the grass. They were pink. "Look at those tomatoes," he cried, "they're *green*. You'll die if you eat poison like that!"

114

"Here," said Luke, stooping for a red, squashed one, "this ripe one's for the kid. He's sick."

"*Aaannnhh*," whinnied the farmer, and spat, and ran away, plucking at his collar.

"What's the matter with him, is he nuts?" said Herman.

"My shirt is wet with squashed tomato," thought Luke. "It is drenched and pink-streaked and full of little seeds. I must put it on. My white soft flesh is burning in the sun. I put my forefinger on my breast and already it leaves a white print. Furthermore, it is indecent not to wear a shirt."

"The tomatoes are hard and they are dry," said Harry and Henry, low and timidly.

"They are not!" said Luke. "There is more water in a tomato than in a glass of milk."

"How I hate that guy!" thought Herman. "Why does he have to *blab* so?"

Search for Love

3. In the evening, Herman became amorous and he went forth alone. He left the others, saying that he would be back, for all were going to leave in a box-car at 10:20. He walked along the road, so sleepy he could not hold up his head, nor keep his eyes open. He was quite alone. Somnolence tore at the top of his eyelids as you might tear meat with your teeth. Fatigue set up as a crick in his neck, torturing him. Yet he couldn't drop off to sleep because a hot, amorous, dry, salty longing kept him awake; it had localized itself not in his pubic parts, but an inch or two above, at the pit of his belly. The poor sleepy boy was really in agony, like Io tormented by the gadfly. There were 3 pits of fiery infection and longing for rest: above his eyes, and at the nape of his neck, and at the pit of his belly. Unaccountably jarred into his mind as he half-stumbled on the road, was the song:

> My muvver told me
> if I was goody
> that she 'ud buy me
> a wubber dolly—

He had an elder sister who used to sing and whistle this ditty.

> But some one to'd her
> I kissed a sailor,
> now she won't buy me
> a wubber dolly.

He was alone on the road. In his body, the 3 pits of fiery infection at first formed a triangle, like intense torches in the dark; but then (as 3 points determine a circle) the pain spread in a round round ring, like a branding iron, round his head.

The night was calm and moonlit; it was shadowy and white. By the trees on the left, long black shadows were cast across the road. Now among the shadows came this wheel of red fire, poised about 10 feet above the road (for his aching feet seemed far below). It moved, in the black night, like a halo on the head of an exceptionally tall saint, say John the Baptist. Herman felt himself being eaten away in all the pulpy parts of his body: his eyeballs, the forebrain behind his brow, the medulla oblongata at the cap of his spine, the scrotum. He was ready to drop.

"Love and sleep are sweet and good," he thought, "especially when they come together. But I can't ever have them together because I'm not home. Only at home is comfort. If I had a place to live I could bring a girl to, then I could sleep. Sometimes you could just remember and say a girl's name over and over. Now I feel like hell. I am also going to lie down in the road and . . ."

Suddenly on the moonlit road before him, running away, he saw a girl. It was the click of her fleeing heels on the asphalt that called his attention. Without noticing her, he would have overtaken and passed her; but she looked

116

back, and ran, and her heels clicked in the quiet. If she hadn't been afraid, he wouldn't have noticed her, and surely would not have pursued. In the 16 years he had lived, Herman had never raped a girl; and he would not have now, except that he was four-fifths asleep. But when he saw her running away—naturally, automatically, he pursued.

When she saw him break into a run, she shrieked; but they were in the midst of fields and thickets where none could hear. Swiftly he overtook her. By this time all fatigue and somnolence had left him; or rather, the burning ring of pain had suddenly contracted, shrunk away into an infinitesimal point of blinding intensity. His whole mind was afire with it. It was like a narcotic needle, goading his brain and anæsthetizing it at once. Down the road its brightness sped like a shooting-star.

And when he came on her, with a blow of his right hand he knocked her over onto the embankment on the dark left side of the road. (She was very slight and perhaps only 14 years old.) Falling among Queen-Ann's-lace and berry-bushes, her head was brought up, with a crack, on a stump. The intense point of inward fire brought him on. But then this point began to widen out, to swell, once more into a circle, or better, 3-dimensionally, into a globe, eventually filling his whole skull, full of moonlight. For the red heat of the old circle (that had been like a branding-iron) gave way to cool gray light, a globe, a skullful, like a bushful of fireflies at night, throbbing and brightening, like the waves we picture round a radio-transmission ærial. The globe of pure light lay in the dark bushes of the embankment at the side of the road. At the same time, from its crack on the stump, the poor girl's head was ringing like 6 or 7 brass bells in the quiet.

At the same time, up the road came an auto with its streaming milky lights and the hum of its motor and hiss of its tires; and disappeared in the darkness.

"What is your name?" said Herman to the girl in the darkness.

"Frederica Heritch Allen," she said.

(He asked her her name as the kid Henry had asked it of Harry; and the globe of pure light lay in the dark bushes, as, in the daytime, the iridescent soap-bubble had poised on the grass.)

A quarter of an hour later, Herman awoke and found himself alone. He was literally groggy with the poisons of sleepiness and fatigue. He could not stand on his feet. Finally he did. Fatigue and the need for sleep were like a solid iron bar from the nape of his neck to his brow, right thru the middle of his brain. But he remembered that he was to rejoin the other 5, waiting for him in a box-car; for he did not want to be left completely alone.

He sped back down the road, having the shadows on his right hand. He came to the siding where were the empty freight-cars that were going to be hauled to Cincinnati. The proper one, in the pale moonlight, was yellow; he climbed up into it, thru a crack left open in the sliding door. Inside, the others were talking in low voices. Their conversation came and went on the air. Herman, without a word, threw himself on some hay he had provided in a corner; and dropped off. Luke, who had a flashlight, let the round beam play on him for a second.

4. Without previous warning, the car started to move. All 6 were safe in it.

"We are 6," thought Luke, "all together now for the second day."

After a few hundred feet on one siding, the car stopped, grinding, and began a slow progress in the opposite direction for 20 minutes. Then again it stopped, and there was a long delay for coupling and uncoupling, activity in the night, an inspector coming by with a lantern; but all the cars were empty. Finally, suddenly, the car started to move with a jerk, picked up speed, began to tune to the beat of the rails.

At one end of the dark box, Herman lay on his straw in the corner. Across from him were sitting Luke, Roger, and Robert. Between the 2 corners, under a tan frayed quilt they had found, the 2 kids were sleeping; they lay clasped

118

in each other's arms. The other end of the box spread away
in an all-generative obscurity that even the flashlight
could not penetrate. Thru the crack in the door filtered a
moonbeam.

"Together, together," thought Luke, in a rising exaltation. "I come to know them! and everybody, then, is not
entirely unknown. We 6 at least are readily located: Herman, dark and heavy, having returned dog-tired, has flung
himself in the corner. The 2 kids are here between—"

"Why don't you make them stop it!" said Roger angrily,
"the kids. It's not right for them to be kissing each other all
the time, and to sleep together, keeping each other warm.
When I look at them, I'm ashamed and disgusted."

"Innocent! it's all innocent!" cried Luke, who was in
such a state of portentous excitement that he repeated
everything twice. "The kids are friends; that is why they
lie down together. Can't you see they are in love with each
other? Henry isn't going to cry any more."

"That Herman ain't very sociable, and that's a fact,"
thought Robert, "the way he came in without Hello."

"3, 2, 1—" thought Luke, "that's how we are arranged.
That makes 6 altogether. 1, 2, 3 equals 6. We have the
whole box-car to ourselves. Enormous; it is like a hall, or
like a bowling-alley; but there is no one in the darkness at
the other end."

Going uphill, the box-car rolled and tilted, and lost
speed; lumberingly delicate it rounded a turn, swinging far
out. But in every way it acted like a stationary world, a box
of still space, and as if the world outside were rising and
falling, and deaccelerating.

Because of the rising and falling pressure of the rails far
beneath, against his back, Herman began to have various
dreams.

"How curious and interesting it is!" thought Luke, who
all this time became more and more excited, for, in fact, he
had begun to run a fever more than a degree above normal,
"all the persons of the world are not just scattered about,
but they come in friendships and families. The 6 in the car!
the 6 in the car!" Everything he thought of, he repeated, as

if he were drunk and seeing double. "6 we are necessarily; for if one kid were missing, who would there be for the other; and if not Herman, against whom would I have to fight; and if not I, who would be the leader? We are not only 6, but 1. Roger and Robert—"

"How still the car is!" he said aloud to them. "Have we stopped?"

Suddenly Herman started awake, with a terrible nightmare at his throat. He felt that he was being pursued; but if he remained here in the car with the others, he thought, surely he would be caught, for it is easier to hunt 6 than 1. Beating the air with his fist, he drove the nightmare away. Then he rose, groggy, and thru the crack that admitted a moonbeam, he leapt from the train.

The 3 boys who were awake, ran to the door to look out, but could not see him, behind in the darkness. They saw that he had fallen into an embankment of soft shale. The moon dipped out of a cloud and shone on the gray meadows going slowly past. He had dropped out of one space-time into another.

"Now we are 5!" thought Luke, exalted and dreamy, as if he were drunk on gin. "With the loss of this one, we are stronger, we are less divided. He is a wild boy. He among us all was contrary. He is a wild boy. Of the 3, 2, and 1, he was the 1. His life is to leap off during the night. Perhaps he hates all those things which are at home. I am sure that he holds home in aversion. I myself have had no home, because I was an orphan in an institution from which I ran away because there were too many there and I had no friends. This was in Canada. Now we are 5. Perhaps this is what a home is, and no more."

In the car, Roger, who had taken Luke's flashlight, let the beam play on the 2 kids. One of them, Harry, was awake. With the tips of his fingers he was touching Henry's cheeks and lips, lightly, experimentally, putting his fingers in his mouth—half-blinded in the light, but not noticing it.

"Why don't you make them stop it!" cried Roger angrily

to Luke. "You know it won't end here. When I look I am ashamed and disgusted."

"Innocent! Innocent!" Luke cried exultantly. "Switch off the light, Roger. You will hurt their eyes, and waste the battery."

The words flew high above the heads of the 2 kids, like a distant wind, not distinguishable below.

"He and I are going asleep," said Robert briefly, designating Roger.

They divided Herman's straw between them and lay down, back to back. In a moment, because of the rocking of the train, they were asleep.

A dream entered the sleep of the child Henry. He dreamt that his cheeks, his face, were being rubbed by a damp washcloth, in the hand of his mother. He was dressed in a white sailor-suit with a blue collar. All the schoolboys were piling into a bus that was to take them to Tucson. It was early morning and it was a still day; indeed, it was May 30, or Decoration Day. There were many pennants. One dangled, blue and white, tickling, before Henry's face, and he caught the tip of it in his mouth and it had an acid taste. Rocking from side to side, the bus lumbered on its way. Henry, with many other boys, cried *Hurrah!*

A little formless grunt came from the sleeping child's lips, over the everlasting monody and healthy beat of the wheels; and all these, as has often been pointed out, only accentuated the quiet by giving it a form.

"Now," thought Luke, "I am alone."

His exaltation began to reach its climax, of ecstasy—as an aeroplane rises above the clouds—and to hang for several seconds in a nervous balance.

"All are asleep but me. I have sat up watching till 1 by 1 my friends have dropped off; and this is one way to become alone. Another way is to have no one there. But if I were by myself, I could not be so alone, only more lonely. So, in the car, the random noises make it more quiet. I know where all these 4 are located. Now I am alone in the car.

"Their dreams are wandering everywhere about, like the flocks of birds that migrate all the way from Louisiana to Hudson's Bay. But all, if I called them, if I said in their ear 'Harry, Harry!' or 'Henry, Henry!'—all must come flocking back to this car, as to a nest, or home."

New York City
1933

Pictures of Things Moving Toward Their Goals

The Philosophy Class

Sometimes in the philosophy-class, there was commotion; sometimes "breathless quiet" reigned.

The commotion was not vocal, but silent; it was in the turbulent minds of all the disputants, students, wrestling. Silently, silently, as on Long Island Sound the waves, wind-swept, slap the sides of sailboats or climb up on the piles of docks. At most it was betrayed by drumming fingers and darting eyes.

Imperturbably the blue-eyed professor sat in the middle.

After a while, quiet supervened, and then, often, there were voices. A young man talked in sober tones and everybody approved. Like the waves and floats of the Sound appeased into a hundred parallel ripples, less than an inch high, progressing swiftly across. Or as

The Dewdrop slips into the shining Sea.

This is a first approximation, of things in sight of their goal.

Analysis of a Petting-Party

Now indeed, they draw closer and closer.

On the bear-rug in my bedroom, a boy and a girl fondled each other "in fond embraces." I intend to analyze this in a little detail.

123

The quantity of common boundary of their bodies will be called *Intercorporeality*. There is a difference, as they discovered, between the continuousness of Area, and a number of discrete Points of contact, 5 or 6 that they could distinguish. And there is also the question of Motion.

The glow of warmth belongs rather to continuous Areas; heat (and pain?), a more epicritical sensum, to points distinct. Another way of analysis is by the senses involved. Is it only the sense of feeling? No, for taste and smell become increasingly important. Sight is rather a propædeutic to this kind of fondling than an element in it. As they came closer, the importance of sight dwindled. "$I_S = f(D)$ . . . the importance of Sight is a direct function of the Distance!" cried the mathematical boy. The girl closed her eyes altogether, as they kissed.

Of feeling, there is pressure and thermic, moisture and movement (light and heavy, hot and cold, wet and dry, at rest, in motion). What of dynamism? can it be analyzed without remainder into a kind of motion? I think not, for there is a muscular sense, a sense of "true time" or process or cumulative Power; and this we might conveniently summarize as the "principle of the tendency of Intercorporealization." . . . There are salty tastes and dusty tastes. There is the odor of hair.

Still another methodology is to isolate (or define) separate acts. For instance Biting, earlobes or lips: the lips swell and are assuaged by a kiss. Another thing is protruding the tongue, during kisses, so as to stick it, stiff and pointed, in the beloved's mouth. (I suppose this is a transparent symbol.) Kisses are also sucked in, as Plato says,

> my soul on the lips of Agathon, my lover,
> I held, for she came impatient to pass over.

What a Platonic conception it is! to suck in another spirit, or let loose one's own.

Still another way is to investigate Intentions. As: when on the bear-rug in my bedroom, Henry and Harriet (for so they were called) fondled each other and embraced and kissed, their intentions and their joys were altogether childish. From time to time they stopped kissing and laughed, and they set each other off giggling as one fuse ignites another. Thus, all these acts may likewise be considered according to Intentions, and may in this way be categorized and analyzed. And this kind of childish intimacies, untroubled by the intoxication, or "poisoning," of passionate sexuality, has often been called Petting, sometimes Necking. Henry and Harriet were *Petting*. As a sign of childishness, the 2 now began to bump their noses together, as is done, it is said, by the Esquimaux of North America. They became lost in a flurry of movements, and wisps of hair, and incipient dynamisms, and breaths, and laughter. Then they embraced very close indeed.

A Sharp Sword

Let me describe the thinness of a certain sword.

It is like a needle.

The hilt is heavy and firm, but the blade is like a glittering wire. It is a cavalry-sabre, but made rather for thrusting than for cutting.

It is like a frozen line; no scabbard is snug enough to sheathe it.

It is sharp, what?

The hilt itself is solid gold and carved, carved in a deep scroll with etching and filigree on each of the whorls, like pubic hair, "stiff auburn curls like Palmer Penmanship." From this Renaissance and gaudy handle, the blade came so rudely and nudely forth.

The only scabbard snug enough for such a blade is the human body between the ribs.

In the warm flush of torn flesh, the flush of blood I mean, flooding into the crevice about the steel, dark and wet—so tight enclosed, a sword can at last rest, fulfilled. This is in the heart.

For the end, or peace, of a sword is the icy egress of death. It is the end and the end.

The frozen line rests at last in a frozen solid.

(The hackneyed metaphor whereby love is compared to

125

the blow of an Arrow, has lost all power to picture and move: Revive it a moment! Consider the soft flesh underneath the violet penny of the breast *pierced* by a twisting barb; and the searing stab inside; and then the warm and loose flooding of heart's blood at the *shock*. Consider it, for instance, as an incident in primitive Amerindian warfare.)

Return to the Philosophy Class at Sunset

Now I returned to the philosophy-class and took my seat there amid the silent tumult and the quiet given form to by a talking voice.

The philosophy-room was a cube with a square table, and a great window in the rear wall. About the table sat 5 or 6, and the minds of all were open, sunny, dreamlike champains, with horses and telegraph-poles, a tractor and a plowman struggling across the sod. The problem was the greatest one of all, that of Being, and all the boys wrestled with it, like Jacob with the angel, coming closer and closer.

Each one pursued it his own way. In the cube, in all the meadows, the air was rather a summer-like buzz than a conflict; it was alive with insects and spiders. Imperturbably the blue-eyed professor sat on one side of the square table.

"If it *is* not in *every* way, I have not understood it!" exclaimed Rafael, a dark boy, whom I admired and as best I could tried to imitate. He spoke to himself, not to me.

One youth was always trying to think of his thoughts, to think of himself thinking them, and to think of himself thinking about thinking. In a systematic augmentation of self-consciousness, he hoped to find a clue to Being, tho he was likely only to hypnotize himself. Coming back on himself again and again, he met himself coming. I have heard this process compared with a dog's chasing his tail, round and round, in the middle of a field. Yet one can at least learn, in this way, the nature of a circle.

Another way, is to examine the forms of the *contents* of thought, not the thinking of it; this is the esthetic mode of

126

discovery—proper to painters and to all whose minds discover forms in things.

Somewhat ruddy on the tan linen shade drawn down over the window in the rear of the cube, the sunlight streamed. In a dark parabola the shade-cord hung across the shade, and underneath there was a hatchwork of shadow, shadow of a wire screen. To me and to one other, the contemplation of this design became a matter of the utmost moment: why was it *together*? what was Form? Suddenly the professor, who had his back to the window, facing us, and could not see what he was destroying, rose to pull up the shade and let in the fading light. "O don't do that!" cried the other boy to him, to himself.

"You had better not do that!" I said to him under my breath, almost threateningly.

He snapped up the shade and behold, on the orange sky, the clouds crossed each other in long flattened brown X's, with the wire net underneath.

A similar thing can be done with words, as we say: to be, being, to have been, I am. I am, I was, they will be. If you were to have been. Oh they were! they were! Be: *bhavati* (√bhu), φύομαι, *fuisse*. Let there be. Let be. Is. This is just an example.

"It must be *acted* as well as thought," thought Rafael. "It is not only a form, but a power." As soon as he thought this, joyous at the discovery—I felt immediately that it was so; I tried to pattern my thinking along the lines suggested. I concentrated on my rapid pulse, and for a while tried to increase its rate of beating by holding my breath.

The cube began to be full of a queer light, evening, and thick black shadows underneath the chairs; but our thoughts buzzed on in the quiet meadows. Oh what a negative existence has quiet, except as a vehicle for the forms of sound!

Imperturbably the professor loaded a pipe (we doing likewise). I reached-across a flaring match to light his bowl. The twisting stick of carbon blackened almost to the tip between my thumb and finger. Clouds of smoke began to hover above the table.

I glared at him, so imperturbable. "If he *knows*," I cried, almost aloud, "why doesn't he tell us? Why does he merely sit there, when it is getting late, since it is getting late! And sometimes he looks at us and sometimes not."

But altho I said this (always to myself) I did not mean it. For suddenly I began to know that all were finding some answer, even myself, who did not understand metaphysics very well. It was that by now the illumination coming thru the window was edged with violet; the air above the table was full of smoke. But the darker the cube, the lighter it became, with a queer light. Our thoughts and senses had become extraordinarily acute. The room was becoming exceedingly quiet—just how this was the answer to the problem, I find it very difficult to explain.

My friend Rafael kept darting quick glances about the cube. At last he was still. Then everybody was still.

He leaned towards me and whispered: "Look how the professor sits in the darkness! He is the pre-established harmony."

"Do you love *him*, then?" I thought. "Oh." I put my hand over my mouth. "It is only in mathematical demonstrations that things do really touch their goals."

Theorems about Circles

I conclude by appending, without proofs, a few theorems about Circles from Euclid and the Calculus:

Pictures of Things Moving

A. *Thru three points not in a straight line, one circle and only one, can be drawn.*

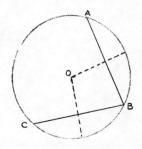

Given A, B, C, three points not in a straight line,

it can be shown that one circle and only one can be drawn thru A, B, and C.

(for the locus of all points equidistant from A, B, and C must lie on the perpendicular bisectors of both AB and BC. But since AB and BC are neither parallel nor in a straight line, these bisectors must intersect in one, and in only one, point.)

B. If a circle be drawn thru three neighboring points P_0, P_1, and P_2, on a curve, and if P_1 and P_2 be made to approach P_0 along the curve as a limiting position, then this circle will in general approach in magnitude and position a limiting circle called the Osculating Circle of the curve at the point P_0. And, *Theorem: The Osculating Circle is identical with the Circle of Curvature.*

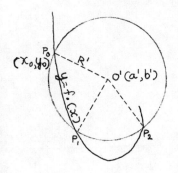

Given $y = f(x)$ and letting P_1, P_2 approach P_0 along it as a limiting position,

it can be shown that $O'(a', b')$ falls on the Center of Curvature of $y = f(x)$ at the point P_0, and that R' equals the radius of Curvature at that point.

THE BREAK-UP OF OUR CAMP

(This can be done by means of Rolle's Theorem, which will give equations to solve for a', b', and R' in terms of x, f(x), f'(x), and f"(x).)

New York City
1933

The Propriety of St. Francis

Coming to the top of a hill, St. Francis hitched up his habit and threw back his hood; he smiled sweetly to whatever was on the right and left, such as boulders, shrub-trees, and the tarry road. "Dear Highway," said he, quoting from Sir Philip Sidney, *be you still fair, honored by public heed.*" There were likewise in the air, everywhere, thousands of little diamond sparkles, such as on any sunny day you can see in pavement mixed with ground glass. And toward these, Francis did not know how to act, for he could not greet so many, all insistently sparkling and blinking; so he snubbed them by closing his eyes to say Paternoster. "Their joy is already sufficient for the day," thought he.

"The magnificent group of factories!" he cried, as he surveyed the valley, "so multiplex and fanciful. In some are made bicycles, and in some window-glass, and in some, last of all, typewriters are made. How bright and hard the plate-glass is rolled, so that you would not think it could have been soft, and before that, rough sand on the seashore! And the iron typewriter is a formidable device. If it could print letters and not move from space to space, that would have been sufficient. If it could move from space to space and not print capitals, it would have been sufficient. If it could print capitals and not advance the ribbon on its roller, it would have been sufficient. If it could advance the ribbon on its roller and not ring the bell, it would have been sufficient. But there are letters and

131

capitals, and rolling, and the ringing of a bell; and the basket of type is almost as beautiful as the miracle of the loaves and fishes. Each separate die, too, is delicately executed.

"Praise be to Thee, my Lord, for Brother Fire—" hummed the Saint, "who illuminates the night. Fair and merry is he, robust and strong." He sang this strophe because at this moment on 8 tall chimneys below, flames began to glow, like noisy hot flowers at the ends of stalks.

"And praise be to my Lord for the Child, Machinery; for willing and well set-up is he; he gives us a duplication of blessings, and preserves us all from arduous labor in old age."

("All this enthusiasm," thought the Saint distraitly, "is suited to the fine day.")

Now when he had expressed himself in this canticle, the saint beheld walking towards him up the tarry road, a laborer in brown overalls with a blue monkey-wrench on his left shoulder. "Lamb of God, how stoutly built!" thought Francis, "like a shepherd-collie. His eyes are brown and moist; how large his red hands are. Obviously at this hour he ought to be at work in the factory below, not loitering; yet I am glad to see him also enjoying the Lord's weather. But why is he so dour?"

"Young man," he said, "observe how among the 8 chimneys the darting of a white bird glitters like a wire."

"Bah," said the laborer, "I was just fired."

"Why that's too bad," said Francis.

"The lousy cock-suckin' sons a bastards," said the laborer animatedly, "threw 300 a us out on our—"

"What, 300! with an army!"

"Naw, the fucks told us t' go, 'cause they gotta shut up shop . . . God damn it!" he added.

"Child, don't take the Lord's name in vain."

"Yes, father."

"*Oh, oh!*" cried Francis, for at this moment, his breakfast having well digested, he felt invaded by the Holy Spirit, and he decided to make a speech. "Wonderful are

132

The Propriety of St. Francis

the proprieties of Nature.

"The great Sun, for instance, forecasts his coming with colored signals, and he dies, as we might say, in a blaze of glory. Or electric storms, before their cannonading, emphasize the stillness by minute noises, by rustling the leaves, by cracking shutters shut. I mean that many things are *proper* (or formal) in their places and now I am praising Propriety.

"There are those who think that the whole glory of the creation was in the visible things that God made, the sun and stars and trees and fire (as I myself have written about them). But there are other glories invisible. The rising and setting of the planets is fairer than the planets themselves, and the invisible Law than either the rising or the setting; that which is seen not, than that which is seen. And the proper time for things—decorum, formality—is of this sort; and it was created with everything else, in the mind of God before the beginning of time, as it is said:

> To everything there is a season, and a time to every purpose
> under the heaven:
> A time to be born, and a time to die;
> A time to plant, and a time to pluck up what is planted;
> A time to kill, and a time to heal;
> A time to destroy—

"And likewise in language, there is this propriety," continued the Saint. "I hate to see a man use Billingsgate every day, for then, when he is really in a rage, how can he make himself emphatic? Young man," said he, turning to the laborer; for most of his words, as was his wont, had been directed to the clouds and the birds. "—By the way, what's your name?"

"George," said the other.

"*Your* speech I approve of. There is a time to be courteous, and a time to curse. On the other hand, there is never a time to take the name of the Lord thy God in vain."

"Yes, father, of course you are perfectly right there," said the other.

"But there is also a propriety of deeds. I hate to see a man violent every day; stable institutions are a great thing. Yet violence also is one method of moving things; as Aristotle used to say (if a Franciscan may quote him), there is natural motion, which moves a thing from inside, according to its own nature; and there is violent motion, that pushes it.

"But is it really true," asked Francis, relapsing into a more conversational tone, "that they fired 300 of you without an army?"

"They told us."

"What, 300?"

" 'Cause they was gonna shut up the fuckin' shop."

"What a great number of lambs of God!"

"The paper they sent round had a yellow seal—."

"A yellow seal?"

"There was also a police with a gat."

"How thick his wrists are!" thought Francis. "They are as thick as Jess Willard's. Child," he said, "let me measure your wrists."

From the fold of his habit, he drew out a yellow oilskin wallet (though the fraticelli are not supposed to have possessions—but after all, he was the founder). From the wallet, tangled with a top-cord with a wooden button at the end, he drew out a yellow tape measure. Cord and tape were knotted round an ebony crucifix with a broken arm. Dangling at the end of the cord was a green top. In the wallet were still a sky-blue copy of the *Song of Songs*, and the bowl of a corn-cob pipe.

"These are all the things I own," said the Saint naively, "a tape-measure and a toy top, a broken crucifix and a copy of the *Song of Songs*. But especially a tape-measure."

Patiently the laborer submitted to the measurement, shifting his monkey-wrench from hand to hand.

"8 inches!" cried the little grey friar, his fingers tangled in the knot and in the red hand.

"Come, George, we shall put all the men back to work. What is done by words can be undone by words. What is maintained with force, can be taken by force."

134

The Propriety of St. Francis

"Yes, father," said the young man, walking, a foot taller, by his side.

A monstrous Packard sped past them in a swirl of dust. "Think," said the saint, in increasing wonder at his own idea, "there is one law proper to pedestrians and one for equestrians, and one for cyclists, and one for motorists!"

They descended into the valley and came, in a flood of sunlight, amid those elegant boxes of white concrete and glass, the factories. Circulating among the oblongs the hundreds of men, all in brown overalls and blue shirts— the out-of-work, the fired. Some were playing baseball with ash bats; others stood about in angry groups.

Among so many, such a great number of lambs of God, the little saint in grey habit moved joyously, supremely inquisitive—amongst such a variety of human beings.

("Perhaps I ought not to become so ecstatic," he thought, eyeing himself sharply; "after all, I have seen crowds of people before." But he became more and more so.)

"Show me around," he said to George. "Who is the white-haired man sitting on the soap-box? He seems more broken up than the rest."

"He was the foreman. He is fired like all the rest, though he is smarter than any of us. He invented the idea of having a bell ring when the carriage comes to the end of the line—" (for all these men had been engaged in the manufacture of typewriters) "—yet he is fired like all the rest. He is also a fine speaker, though he is not so big and broad when he gets up as he seems when seated."

"Introduce me to him, introduce me to him," breathed Francis, excited at the prospect of meeting so fine a man, and saying everything double as if he were drunk on gin.

"My name's St. Francis," he said to the foreman.

"Mine's Kerrigan."

They spoke for a moment on the respective merits of portable typewriters and regular heavy-service typewriters. It was evident that portables were handier, but the others gave better wear and were more solid for rough work. "In the end," said Kerrigan, "it is the difference between a racing-bike and a road-bike."

"Yes—yes—" said Francis. "Tell me, who is the pitcher on the ball team? His drop breaks too soon. How blond he is! Does he too work in the factory, so young?"

"His name is Haskell," said Kerrigan. "His father and brother are dead, and he too works in the factory."

The boy came walking back across the diamond, carrying his glove. Kerrigan in a loud voice called him over. Francis at once remarked that his eyes were olive-green with flecks of amber.

"Haskell, this is St. Francis," said Kerrigan.

"Oh, are you he?" said the boy.

"How peaceful all is," thought the Saint; "you would not think it was a factory-town."

Suddenly he felt quite at home in this valley (as indeed it was proper for a saint to be anywhere). "I have known each man 100 years," he thought. He felt, with a thrill, that strange sentiment of having lived thru it all before— whereby each successive moment becomes inevitable beforehand, perfectly *formal*. The men in brown and blue walked among the glass buildings as if it were a dance.

"I have not heard the arguments of the owners," he thought exaltedly, "but on every count I can prophesy that they are wrong!"

The sun kept passing behind a transparent cloud, thru which it could be seen as a small white disk; and it was this sight especially that cast him into the dream-state of having lived thru it all before. Full of the "sentiment of prophesy and inevitability," he glided into the factory building itself, past 2 private-police with shotguns at the door.

But inside the cool building, he returned to his normal self with a little bang; and entered the Director's room.

"You see," he said peremptorily, "there is entirely too much silence round here. When you walk along the corridor, your sandals ring."

"Silence is good," they answered (in chorus); "we have been trying for years to perfect a noiseless typewriter."

"Let us not argue the relative merits of noiseless

machines and ordinary ones," cried Francis. "It is evident that one defect of the noiseless is that it muffles the merry clicking of the keys."

To this they had no answer.

"Obviously there is no propriety in this ghostly stillness enshrouding a factory," he said. "Is this a holiday? The object of a factory, evidently, is to keep going, to give the people useful machines, I mean typewriters and bicycles, and canned goods, as well as baseball bats of ash-wood."

"No, no. Have to shut down," said they.

"What? What? do all the people in America who need 'em have typewriters? You overcharge. Cut the profits down. You gentleman have made all the money you're ever going to make."

"No! no!" cried they. "Make him go away. Suppress him! Throw him out on his ear! Is there no policeman?"

"Children—" said Francis, holding up his head, "you cannot injure saints and philosophers—."

"Lynch him! Electrocute him like Sacco and Vanzetti!" they shouted, working themselves into a real frenzy.

"—and what we say, will come to pass despite you."

To this they had no answer.

"And another thing!" said the grey-friar, "what do you mean by firing a man like Kerrigan? It's quite absurd, you know—a fellow like that, who invented the idea of ringing a bell at the end of the line—.

"You have no notion of *propriety*. (It's a pity for me to have to preach a sermon to grown men like you, as if you were birds.) As Confucius says:"

"What does he say?"

"The important thing, he says, is for the Prince to be Prince, the minister to be minister, for the father to be father, and the son son. It is for the people to be fed, and the rulers to be servants."

"Oh! oh!" 5 of them said, as if they were remembering an ancient admonition.

"But that is only half the truth."

"Only half?"

"Only half, obviously," said Francis. "For the counsel of perfection would be to be even as am I; that is, nought. I mean, to have no rank, neither man nor beast," he cried, "but to seek in every creature's way the Lord our God! . . . This is accomplished by love and abstraction, as I could explain if I had the time."

At this, 5 of the 15 that were there, decided to give up their profits and become followers of Francis. On the spot they took off the blue worsted suits with a pin-stripe, which all were wearing, and they donned grey cassocks which Francis doled out to them.

(I mean to show by this that one can never tell, from a man's station in society, what his innermost thoughts are.)

But the other 10 sullenly and grimly shook their heads. "No!" said they, and again, "NO!" implying by the repeated negative that they agreed to absolutely nothing that was said.

At this moment Francis beheld, on the plaster wall, a porcelain push-button bell. "Look!" he pointed it out enthusiastically to his 5, "a bell!"

> Praise be to my Lord for Signals,
> for shouts and warnings and premonitions.
> By these we are less unprepared: everything becomes more
> proper.

"Look where the double-wire extends along the molding above the door, and then into the wall! who knows how far or where it runs, in the walls, the ceilings, the floors—so that the whole building is netted; with a strong potential waiting to leap the gap and make itself heard. (Not altogether unlike the Holy Ghost, I fancy!) I push the button.—"

He did so again and again, and from far off, at the other end of the long, long corridor, came the faint, repeated jangling of a bell . . .

Now when he emerged into the sunlight—after all these long corridors, mystical utterances, and this highly questionable ringing of bells—Francis nodded amiably to right and left; he was greeted with a loud noise of shots. The men had decided to reopen the factory by force; the private-police had opposed them; and now they were firing hotpoint at each other round the corners of the buildings. Seated on a boulder in the middle of the field, old Kerrigan looked on stupefied. Francis nodded to each bullet as it sped by, each death-dealing little daughter of God that flew perilously past his head.

"I told them that they wouldn't make any more money out of this factory," he said.

In a ring, the men kept closing in, 20 of them; half a dozen policemen stood firm at the doorway. Somewhere the dispossessed workers had gathered a few rifles. *Furor arma ministrat,* Fury lends arms (quoted Francis)—

> *. . . cum saepe coorta est*
> *seditio, saevitque animas ignobile vulgus.*
> *jamque faces et saxa volant: Furor arma ministrat.*

"when suddenly an insurrection breaks out, and the ignoble mob rages in spirit; already rocks and torches fly; Fury lends arms—."

In the hot noon, the interchange of rifle shots crackled like the thunderous static of a midnight storm in radio headphones. The blond boy, Haskell shot thru the head, lay in the buff dust with green eyes staring.

In the middle of the field, Francis knelt apart from everything. He did not notice the shot boy nearby, nor the bullets whining over his head, nor Kerrigan sitting stupefied not far off. For, in a flash, he had been rapt away, altogether, into a vision of his Beloved (where unfortunately we cannot follow him). For everything there is a season, except for this free gift, that comes at any time.

The laborer George grasped his shoulder and shouted to him, above the loud reports, to go away to a spot less exposed. The dead pitcher, his glove still on his hand, stared up at him. But Francis was not to be distracted from this contemplation by any person or thing; and not to embarrass or bewilder us all, he had buried his face in his sleeve.

[New York City]
1933

139

Dresses, Architecture
and Church Services

1. Recently I was offered the occasion to compose a critical article on the work of Elsa Schiaparelli, the dressmaker. I wrote it, comparing her admirable technique with that of the "constructivists" in architecture, who also plan from inside out and concentrate on the structural (rather than the merely visual) form; I tried to illustrate this in some detail from her creations. Almost at once, a kind of hue and cry arose (among the few who know me), accusing me of a certain frivolity in using such a method on such a subject, in writing more or less formal criticism about women's clothes, and in treating a dressmaker as if she were an "artist." There would have been some justice in such strictures, I felt, if Mme. Schiaparelli were a follower of seasonal fashions, rather than the possessor of so striking and definite a style of her own, with its inner development; or if she strove merely to be practical, rather than tried in every way to modify utility in the interests of abstract form. But in any case, the motives that led, and lead, to such an accusation of frivolity (when any one tries to write seriously about dressmaking) were in themselves interesting, worth noticing; and I think it is clear that they sprung from the fact that such things as clothes are perishable, commonplace, and practical.

2. Architecture, of all the major modern arts—literature, music, painting—is that which has been most neglected by critics. I suppose that nobody would deny this. Perhaps the cinema is equally disregarded, but this is

because this art, though major, is still too new for academic criticism to have gotten to it, and at the same time there is a good deal of a kind of cinema criticism in the daily papers. But architecture is both ancient and disregarded, at once. Yet there are buildings all about us. . . . Now perhaps it is just because there are so many buildings and that they are always about, that criticism of them is lacking; for the objects become commonplace, and thus fail to be looked at (until they become ancient and strange). Another factor is this: that buildings have a practical use and thus we are not constrained to inquire further about them; using them, we do not have to judge them. In brief, it is possible that the same commonplaceness and practicality, 2 of the factors that prevent criticism of women's clothes, likewise prevent criticism of architecture; except that in the one case such criticism is considered frivolous, whereas in architecture, if actual practice is a criterion, it is considered irrelevant. Again, dresses are not worth criticism because they are perishable; but it is useless to criticize buildings because they are so long-lived! It is useful to condemn a play or poem, for then it is no longer played or read; but once a building is built, you have to put up with it.*

3.   Now it is not evident that such properties as commonplaceness or necessity should exempt an object from the requirements of formal beauty (or from the province of criticism). Indeed it would seem clear that the reverse is true: that it is just the things that are always present to

---

*In the ancient history of architecture and in the foundation of the Beaux-Arts system, as is well known, architecture was a craft, building, pure and simple. Being so, it was subject to formal criticism only secondarily. But then, when it began to be considered as an "art," and so subject to criticism, it was in the most ominous fashion, for architecture at that time began to be considered mere decoration and completely divorced from building or structure. Thus, it became an object of criticism by ceasing to be architecture, and so architecture never became an object of criticism! But what criticism of architecture would mean, would be criticism of the formal arrangement of the very functions and structures themselves. The "practical," not the ornamental, is too formalized.

142

everybody that ought to be most carefully judged in this, as in every other, respect. Ruskin and Morris, of course, were great champions against the public indifference in this regard: the former (as part of a general socialistic scheme) designed æsthetic containers for tea, and the latter devoted himself to what he considered graceful patterns for cretonnes. . . . Thus, it is cutlery, crockery, foodstuffs, and furniture, door-bells, street-cars, and precisely architecture and dressmaking, that should merit the most, not the least, critical attention. The point here is not that these are the materials for the best arts, since obviously a complicated piece of music or cinema can achieve effects far more subtle—too subtle often for the common ear or eye to discern—than a dress by Mme. Schiaparelli. But the point is that the dress, in so far as it is formal, should not be neglected by critics.

4. Everything is formal; abstractly viewed, anything *could* be arranged. The utilities of one level are made the values of the next higher level—just as in former times, it is said (sometimes with more poetry than truth), economic life used to be illuminated by the social relations, pleasant and dignified, that it itself produced. And thus architecture may be regarded as the harmonious arrangement of a number of functions. . . . In actual practice, however, I think it will be found that in the case of practical and commonplace objects, it is so difficult to *isolate* them, that it is almost impossible to judge them formally. Let me explain what I mean. The possibility of a formal judgment, it seems, all depends on the ability to choose a proper frame. The frame is very important. With a painting, play, or piece of music, the selection of a frame is quite automatic (it is the result of training in what to look for). We come to a theatre, for instance, and the lights go out: then we know it is time to begin paying attention. By disciplining, too, we learn what kinds of observations are irrelevant, so that it is only children or women who say, "I saw *Andromache* last night, but the first act was spoilt because I forgot whether or not I had closed the door"; or "The *Italian Concerto* does not come off when you have a toothache." But in judging a coat or a street-car, made for

ordinary use, all such commonplaces seem to become mysteriously relevant, and the "object"—that is, the frame—seems to slip away into the surrounding environment. It is harder to judge an interior than a painting because there is no one place to stand. When we say of a house that it is "full of wonderful surprises," we mean that for the life of us we cannot comprehend it as a whole. So, to sum up, a house, clothes, being ordinary and necessary, ought therefore to be most carefully formalized and judged—but just because they are ordinary and practical, demanding action on our part, they become involved in all the details of living, and when we come to judge them, we are faced with a complicated choreography.*

5.   Now if this much is evident, I should like to make one more observation, and it is this: that æsthetically, it is a calamity that people today are ceasing to attend church-services, school-graduations, and such other ceremonial public gatherings—which the radio, a certain cosmopolitan sophistication, and a growing indifference in both state and church, are making things of the past. And yet, for many, particularly for the common people who read no literature or hear no music except of a low order, such occasions (unctuous as they are) have been, altho ethical in inception, the deepest æsthetic experiences afforded by their lives.

A few months ago I attended the wedding of my friend K.; the ceremony was a simple one, in a Lutheran Church. This building, in the interior, was a plain hall painted white and gray; it was devoid of architectural features (except that, just over my head, in the rear, was a little organ loft, with a choir of 4 voices there); but on this particular afternoon sunlight came streaming thru the windows, which were frosted but not colored, save for a small leaded medallion in the center of each. The people in

* So complicated, in the opinion of some (my brother among them), that in the case of practical things, that must be used by all types on any and every occasion, it is better to make the thing as nearly *invisible* as possible, reduce it to its lowest utilitarian level, so that it may thus give the minimum of offense. The theory here is that the only formal quality common to a great variety of environments is nothingness.

the place—it was moderately filled—were Germans, mostly relatives of K. and the bride. After a while, they were all there and the organ launched on the Processional. There was a clock set high high on the white-washed wall, that kept moving—20 past 3, half past, 20 to 4. Every one stared at the backs of the 2 up at the altar; and meanwhile, suddenly a solo soprano voice began to sing, neither very tuneful nor very pure (for it was not a concert), a long hymn, 8 slow stanzas, each one like the one before. At this moment I knew that there had been created a pause, or frame; and the first thing I saw in it was a kid, of 6, who threw a spit-ball at a girl 2 pews behind, and when she stared at him, he made a gargoyle face by making a pug-nose with the index of one hand, and pulling down the lower lids of his eyes with 2 fingers of the other, and protruding his tongue. In a flat, matter-of-fact voice, the minister kept on charging the couple, expatiating with almost no inspiration, on Luke xiv, 34: "O Jerusalem, Jerusalem, which killest the prophets and stonest them that are sent unto thee; how often would I have gathered thy children together, as a hen doth gather her brood under her wings." Afterwards many objected to his flat tone, but others—and I think they had the right—said: "This shows that he has an ordinary and practical place in the community; for on certain occasions, generally critical ones, like birth, marriage, or death, it is necessary to call in some one, and he is the one." The Church was St. Eustace's, after Eustace, that chevalier who, riding in the woods one day, beheld an elk with a crucifix grown between the antlers. Overhead the clock registered 4:20, but of course no time had passed. Till suddenly, in the silence, the organ could almost have been said to thunder, *Ein feste Burg*, which the choir and many of the congregation gradually took up. In a hubbub, almost, it seemed to me, they started to file out, to Mendelssohn's rather rapid march. K. was grinning, moderately amused, half pleased. For a moment, in a sea of faces, I caught a framed glimpse of the bride, whom I hardly knew; she was very young, and I was struck right between the eyes by the almost archaic cut of her dress, obviously imitated from a mother's dress, and that from a mother's before, and that from a mother's before that. A whole landscape of time and custom seemed crammed in a brief moment, on the steps of the church. (I recall that she wore a short necklace of seed-pearls.) A thick composite of choreography, dress, and architecture!

6.   Such ceremonials are another kind which ought not to be, but have been, neglected by formal criticism. There are, of course, numerous manuals on church music, the order of services, and so forth, many of which, indeed, show a taste, decorum, and sense of the whole, far superior to what is found in more pretentious works. But it is rarely that we discover anything on the subject with a broad comparative view—such an essay as that of Matthew Arnold's called "A Persian Passion Play."

[New York City]
1933

146

Iddings Clark

Lo! on every visage a Black Veil!
—*Hawthorne*

1.

In the assembly-room of the Northport High School they were celebrating the day before Christmas. All the children were present in the seats and a crowd of parents in the rear, and many graduates—some of whom were parents and some collegians home on vacation. The greatest hilarity and yet decorum prevailed, as always (so that many held that "the best part of the holiday season is the High School celebration"). This year was given a pageant of the Nativity, but only half-reverent, for at intervals a great burlesque Santa Claus rolled in, did tumble-saults, and so forth, while two end-men bandied jokes. All this was invented and directed by Mr. Iddings Clark, M. A., a teacher of English, a mind so spirited and original, with modern notions of Art (considering the community); and these masques have since been collected and printed. He was also in charge of the singing. To see him high on the platform, waving his arms, lifted everybody to enthusiasm; ordinarily a shy, almost reserved man, on such occasions he was red with pleasure and crowned with joy. Recent students of his, home from college, crowded beneath him to the platform. The song rang through the hall:

> Jingle bells! jingle bells!
> Jingle all the way!

—when suddenly, in the midst of a note, the conductor fainted away, and fell from the platform on his face. A cry

147

of horror rang through the hall. The young men who had been at his feet now bore him up; they laid him on the platform and loosened his collar—he was pale—and dashed a glass of water in his face. His eyes fluttered open and he came to. "It's nothing," he said. "I see you all clearly. I am so happy having around me my friends so bright and close. Everything is exactly as it was."

The fact is that at the moment he was about to faint—perhaps because the blood rushed from his head, or that the electric light faltered, or for some other reason—at that moment he beheld over everything a cast of darkness. He saw on each face a veil. It was the Black Veil in the harrowing story of Hawthorne (from which I have taken the motto for this story). At one instant all faces were lit up—the lights overhead ablaze and the falling snow outside—and all printed with an indulgent smile at the well-known song; the next instant, though their mouths were open wide, the sinister shadow was everywhere apparent! A teacher of literature, Iddings Clark was only too well acquainted with Hawthorne's unnatural romance; twice a year for eight years he had read through with his classes the tale of the Minister's Black Veil. But although each time he came to that awful outburst "Why do you tremble at me alone? tremble also at each other!" he was so moved that the sweat appeared on his brow, he hardly thought that it would come to this. As if we experience works of art with impunity! The next instant he fainted away.

He sank in the dead faint and the light came and went. Then there was no more light and his soul was profoundly torn—accompanied by violent trembling and shaking in all his limbs, so that the students among whom he had fallen felt the body quiver in their hands. Thus quietened, he began to rise again through the zones of light, and he had a dream: that he was walking on Hooker Street in the snow and he saw, with a sense of appalling loneliness, that all the passers-by wore half-masks like highwaymen; then he entered the school and stark naked stood before his class. With a cry, he awoke.

2.

That night, Christmas Eve, Iddings Clark went to the home of Otto, an instructor in chemistry, to trim the tree for his five-year-old daughter. To spend the night thus had become almost a custom. "Yet soon," said Otto, "she will be beyond the age for Christmas-trees."

"I am all right," said the English teacher in a strained voice. "Anyway there is a compensation for everything! How well Emerson put it!"

He was famous as a decorator of trees! For here also—as in the clever masques he composed—sparkled such fancy and originality, in the dramatic contrast of white lights and the deep boughs, not without a touch of wild wit, such as a jack-in-the-box in the heart of it. People dropped in at the house where he had decorated the tree.

"How strange your tree is tonight, Iddings!" cried the chemist. "It looks almost sinister; you can't mean to leave it so. All the tinsel, the silver globes, the dolls, candy-canes, and lights are crowded down in one corner, pell-mell, without beauty or order. The rest of the tree is black. Why have you cut out a little recess in the dark boughs, and there put, so lonely, the silver star that is supposed to ride so brightly at the top? And around it four upright candles, one above, one below, on the left, and on the right, so rigidly?"

"We must snatch at least this much order from the riot."

"But the star itself is not balanced; it leans to one side . . . . Why did you arrange the candles in a cross? It doesn't fit Christmas."

"They are four soldiers."

Frau Otto looked attentively at the young man and said, "You are feverish—I can see by your eyes."

"Remember this afternoon—" said Otto.

"I've been neglecting a cold; it's nothing. Perhaps you could give me an aspirin tablet."

She dosed him with two, and a cup of hot milk to wash them down. "You can't go out now in a sweat," she said. "We must put you up overnight."

149

"Oh!"

"We'll sit up just a few minutes."

At the opportunity to stay and talk the English teacher was overjoyed. He smiled and at once started to talk about himself, saying, "I remember when I was a boy, I lived in Boston, and at night I used to walk on Washington Avenue, among the bright lights, and look in the faces of all the people! Dr. Otto, did *you* ever do anything like that? I mean, not necessarily in Boston . . ." He sped on in the same vein. After a few moments, Frau Otto rose and excused herself—though indeed there was nothing scandalous that he had to say; for what could a person so young and sober have to confess?

"You're strange, Iddings!" said Otto, thinking of the uncanny tree, which, he felt, would frighten his child. "Maybe I ought to call the doctor."

"A different person exactly!" said Clark. "I don't apologize for talking about myself because nothing is more important than that we understand one another."

"I understand you less and less."

Soon it was past midnight. The chemist began to foresee that the Christmas in his house was ruined; in the morning he would not be up to greet his daughter; and what a rude fright was in store for her when she saw the Christmas tree. He speculated on the possibility of putting his guest to bed and then stealing down to redecorate it. He could not foresee that this tree would be the merriest his daughter ever had; for throughout the morning, her newly-gotten toys—dolls, a house and furniture, a mechanical fire-engine—all lying neglected, she kept climbing a chair to right the lopsided star and then, dancing for joy, knocked it away again with paper balls aimed from across the room.

In the afternoon, several visitors, teachers, dropped in at Dr. Otto's—Messrs. Bell and Flint; Dr. Croydon, the dean; and Miss Cohalan, the registrar. Iddings Clark continued, in the same nervously intimate strain; his sleep had been only moderately feverish, enough to generate almost pleasant dreams—and these he now proceeded to expound in minute detail.

150

Otto took Dean Croydon aside. "He's not well. I tried to keep him in bed but he won't stay."

"What is his temperature?"

"Normal."

"You see," cried Clark, "there is nothing we're not capable of!"

"Nothing is more false!" said the Dean sharply. "Nothing is falser than when we think ourselves creatures of any chance fancy, not as we really are—just as, brutally frank with rage, we tell our friends what we think of them in a rage, not what we really think."

The situation rapidly became strained; the social atmosphere spoilt. Each of the friends cast his eyes upon the ground to avoid looking at the others; only Iddings himself eagerly sought them out with his eyes.

"When all know too much, all are ashamed," thought Otto.

"It's lucky he's taken ill during the holidays; he'll be better by the start of school," thought Dean Croydon.

3.

On New Year's Day, which fell on a Tuesday, Iddings Clark was scheduled to deliver the annual Hooker Lecture on Literature, in the auditorium of the High School. And this year an extraordinary audience had gathered, for not only was Clark always a treat as a lecturer, but every one remembered the dramatic incident that had befallen him the week before, his dead faint in the midst of the singing. Many children, as well as the grown-ups, came to stare at him in curiosity; the ushers were given orders to shunt those boys not with their parents up into the balcony—and there they sat, staring down, their lips pressed against the shiny rail.

Dean Croydon introduced the speaker as their "beloved friend who occasioned so much anxiety on the day before Christmas, but who has since quite recovered." The subject of the lecture was "The Incentives of Poetry."

When the English teacher stepped to the front, however,

he seemed the opposite of quite recovered—thin, white, with somber eyes. Everywhere there was a leaning forward to see him better. He said in a strained voice, "I had intended to speak of poetry as objects and forms, and of the excitement of *inventing* something: for there is a pleasure in creating a new structure, or in elaborating a living plot, as if a man were Prometheus. But instead I shall speak of it as communication, and why it is that one person talks to another.

"But talking to you, as Meyer Liben said," he cried suddenly, "is like talking to a wall!"

As he spoke the pink color mounted in his face, and his dark eyes burned. He made no gestures, but with white-knuckled fingers gripped the edges of the lectern, and his voice came forth over his hands. *"Come alive Galatea!* cried that famous sculptor, *that I may talk to you!* and he kissed a statue not yet free of the formless rock. What a sad pity that the centuries of evolution could not create a human friend for him!"

People looked at each other.

"Very lonely," said the lecturer. "Such exact symbols—but only poets pay close attention, and they adopt this language for their very own. The poets speak only to the poets. To talk to you is like talking to a wall!"

"Our friend Iddings," whispered Miss Cohalan, seated behind the speaker, leaning across to Dean Croydon, "he seems beyond the bounds of order. His sentences come in gusts."

"I have not heard more moving eloquence," said the Dean sharply. (One would not have expected him to say this.)

"The French poet, Charles Baudelaire, wrote:

Le bourdon se lamente, et la bûche enfumée
accompagne en fausset la pendule enrhumée,
cependant qu'en un jeu plein de sales parfums,
heritage fatale d'une vieille hydropique,
le beau valet de coeur et la dame de pique
causent sinistrement de leurs amours défunts—

'in a game full of dirty perfumes, the handsome knave of hearts and the queen of spades, gossip sinisterly of their dead loves.' Why did he say *this?*

"And he wrote:

> *Et le printemps et la verdure*
> *ont tant humilié mon coeur*
> *que j'ai puni sur une fleur*
> *l'insolence de la nature—*

'the springtime and foliage humiliated me so, I took punishment on a flower for the insolence of nature.' Why this?

"*J'ai plus de souvenirs que si j'avais mille ans—*'I have more memories than if I were a thousand years old!'"

At this sentence many in the audience started.

In the balcony the children began a whispered debate.

"He says he is a thousand years old!"

"No. He says it was as if he was a thousand years old."

"Mr. Clark is a *thousand years old!*"

"Quiet! quiet!" said the usher.

The afternoon growing late, the snow outside falling thicker—the hall became dim. Yet all, straining their eyes in the dusk, thought that they saw the speaker clearly.

"This is a common experience," he said, "young people in love are unable, no matter how hard they try, to keep from talking about the person.

"But when they are *out of love;* still wounded, not yet healed, hopelessly hunting around in every direction for sympathy—then they *still* talk (making all ashamed)."

Suddenly—just as he had begun, and as he continued—he stopped. His voice no longer came in separate gusts across his white-knuckled hands. But the faint light that seemed to play on him on the platform persisted.

They began to clap and abruptly found themselves in pitch darkness. The applause grew loud. There was a hub-bub of people trying to put on their coats and galoshes in the dark. At last the lights came ablaze. Blinded, the people took this opportunity to add to the infectious applause, but the speaker had slipped away during the darkness.

"Would the young man have us go around confessing each other?"

"No. It is only that we read poetry more sympathetically."

"Come alive, Galatea! cried that famous sculptor."

"How pale he looked at the beginning; then how flushed he became."

"I thought that he was going to keel over again."

"How was he at the end?"

"You couldn't tell, it was so dark."

4.

The next day, it was a Wednesday, school reconvened. The snow lay deep on the ground, but the sun shone brightly; it reflected from the snow and sky, and poured into the large-windowed classrooms. At nine o'clock, flushed and damp from a snowfight, the boys and girls came trooping in.

Out of his little cubicle off the English lecture-room, Mr. Clark stepped to face his class: he was stark naked except for his spectacles and a Whittier in his right hand.

With cries of fright the young people fled up the aisle and through the doors they had just entered; before the period-gong had finished sounding, the classroom was emptied—except of one small girl who sat spellbound in the front row, and a boy who stopped near the door on his way out.

"I'll tell Dean Croydon," he said, and left.

Now Rea, the small girl, and the teacher of English were left alone, facing each other, she seated behind a desk, he standing naked beside his table.

"Why don't you run off with the others, child?" said Iddings.

"I'm hot and tired with playing; I'd rather stay here for the class."

"They have an unexpected holiday out of me."

154

"Won't there be a class, Mr. Clark?"

"The assignment was *Snowbound*, by Whittier."

"I read it all!" cried the girl.

"It's not a great poem. What the devil prompted him to write it?"

She stared at him closely, from head to foot, and said, "Is it true, what they say, Mr. Clark, that you are a thousand years old?"

"A thousand years! Heavens no."

"They say that you said you was a thousand years old, and I see that in some places you're grown all over with hair."

"I am 31," he said smiling.

"I'm 13, just the opposite," said Rea. She kept looking up into his face.

"What's your name, girl?" he said sharply, "my glasses are sweated over and I can't see you clearly."

"Rea."

"Rea! that's a strange name. It means the guilty one. Rea. Is there any of the boys you love?"

"Donald Worcester."

"Come here, child," he said in a tight voice. "Have you told him that you love him?"

"I wrote on the school-wall with chalk," she cried, "REA LOVES DONALD W. Just as if somebody else wrote it."

She rose from her bench and came beside the teacher.

"That's *right!*" he said "Now he must tell you."

At this—as if for no reason—she burst into sobs. At the same time the door in the rear opened, and in came the Dean with a posse of instructors summoned from their classes for this extraordinary occasion. With a cry of fright the girl fled across the bars of sunlight out of the room.

"She's crying. What did you do to her?" asked the Dean.

"I did not!"

"Iddings! what's the meaning of this?"

"It's the story of Hawthorne's, *The Minister's Black Veil.*"

"I don't remember. It's many years since most of us read Hawthorne," said the Dean.

"I at least shan't wear a black veil!" exclaimed Iddings

155

Clark exaltedly, and a wave of color swept over him, from his feet to his forehead.

The Dean took off his coat and flung it round the shoulders of his trembling friend.

"This is serious; this is awful, Iddings Clark," he said. "We won't hear the end of it. Where are your clothes? Get dressed. It's *my* fault; I knew it was coming. At least we'll try to hush the matter up. It won't come before the School Board. But how can I answer for the consequences?"

New York City
1933

The Fight in the Museum

The Apollo Belvedere, in plaster, held out his thin arm, already motionless two thousand years, and, underneath, the 4A class scraped their torn shoes against the edges of the pedestals. All around, the tall, strong gods, brought in crates over the waves, were looking on.

Like a magnet, the unclothed figures drew the 4A eyes, and the little girls turned in confusion from one statue to another. Miss Flynn tried to hurry them past this court, but they straggled, vanished in alcoves, were seen far off through the legs of horses and between the fine, bent limbs of athletes.

Now the entire class of P. S. 24 was brought to a halt until they found the little Jewish boy, A. Gold, twenty minutes behind, staring in dark-eyed awe at Pharaoh.

"Were all the statues made before George Washington, Miss Flynn?" asked Hilda.

"Yes," said the distracted teacher.

"Were they all made before Christopher Columbus?"

"Yes, yes!"

"Have you counted everybody?" she asked the monitor, but this girl, too, had disappeared. Her head began to swim, and, through her spectacles, amid dancing black spots, she saw the statuary tilt.

Obscure desires, like beans in the dark soil, began to germinate in the youngsters; and the whole court, ruddy under the skylight, began to glow like a hot field full of buzzing bees; and the pastoral gods stood, half coming

157

alive, in the grass that stretched to their knees.

"Who was Artemis?" asked Luke, fascinated by the full quiver and bent bow of the moon goddess.

"She let no man touch her!" cried Miss Flynn in a high voice.

Some of the boys began to feel martial, making experimental thrusts with imaginary short-swords. Two by two, they slowly danced, wielding invisible round shields on their left arms, and shaking invisible helmets crowned with horse-hair plumes. . . . The amber court was filled with the resounding noise of waves.

Brushing past Betty in her middy blouse, Luke pushed her against the sharp point of the pedestal of a huge equestrian and bruised her arm. He wished that the upraised hooves would stamp down on her head.

Then they all passed into the Room of Ancient Musical Instruments. Miss Flynn said, "Mark time: *March!*"

Tramp, tramp, *tramp*, tramp, *tramp*, tramp. . . .

"Please, ma'am," a guard at the door said, "not to have them march in step, it's too noisy."

"*Halt!*" She did not know what command to give to have them break ranks not in step, so she drifted uncertainly off by herself. With the echo of command, a few clavichord strings stirred under the dust, and a huge gong hummed.

Venus of Cnidos said, in a voice as far off as a high bird, "We stand apart from each other—Mars, Neptune, and my husband, Vulcan—ancient statues, each perfect in himself, when you look at them from *afterwards.*" The Poseidon was made in 370 B.C.; the Hercules in 512 B.C.; the Pharaoh in 1350; the Apollo in 711.

In the Hall of Musical Instruments, a single note—middle A-flat—from a cembalo, lay on the dusty air.

"Who did it?" snapped Miss Flynn. "Who did it? You are absolutely *forbidden* to touch anything, or we go right back to school for a written examination in arithmetic!"

A sad note, not quite C-sharp, quivered from a hunting horn.

"Jack!" she cried. The boy's mouth was full of ancient dust.

The Fight in the Museum

"I didn't hear what you were saying," he said.

Then with all his strength, Luke punched Gregory in the nose. At once a fountain of blood gushed from the nostrils of the black-haired boy. Silently they pounded at each other, rolling under the legs of the first pianoforte built in America.

Like snow melting, the children fled silently from the room. The boys raced up the stairs and down a long corridor of Dutch chiaroscuro masterpieces on either wall, two guards in pursuit. Giggling shrilly, the girls ran round in circles, clapping their hands, while from the wall, a clear print of Gluck with a stave from *Iphigénie* listened to the din.

One small boy, who had gone back to the statues, now white with fear, eluded an old man's hands by climbing the vast equestrian Galeazzo. He boosted himself up by the stirrup and spur and stood in the lap of the monstrous rider twenty feet above the paved floor. The guard silently gesticulated from below. From the door of the Hall of Ancient Musical Instruments, Miss Flynn beheld the little boy in the lap of the iron rider, and she leaned against the lintel and wept.

With an appalling clang, a suit of armor fell, and the children froze, one with the left leg lifted, one with a hand about to grasp, a call half-uttered, and they seemed like statues. *"À casser les statues—on risque—d'en devenir une—Soi-même!"*

Luke and Gregory lay clutched in each other's arms under the pianoforte, and they could feel their hearts beating against each other. The dust from the old instrument had snowed down on them as they kicked and scratched, and it mixed with the blood on Gregory's face. Luke half attempted to lick some of it off.

"I did not punch you on the nose on purpose, Gregory," he whispered.

"What was that noise?" they hissed together.

At the thought that they must soon be discovered, they both began to weep, mixing their salt tears in the dust and blood.

159

A guard was talking to Miss Flynn, "It's no matter; don't cry; nothing is broke," he said kindly.

"Isn't the suit of armor broken?"

"Designed for harder use than that!" he answered.

"I am afraid," said the curator, "that the museum-privilege will have to be rescinded from your school. It's too bad, really."

Six girls in pinafores stood around the fallen knight with his huge iron muscles. Through the lowered visor, one seemed to be looking into a profound and empty mind.

Again the twenty-five children were lined up. Behind them, the Apollo Belvedere stood high on his pedestal, his right arm extended.

"Gregory! Wipe off your chin!" Miss Flynn said. The boy pulled out his handkerchief, and two marbles rolled out of his pocket and bounded away on the floor.

"Miss Flynn says we are all to be put back to 3B," Hilda said.

The guards stood waiting about expectantly, as if the chase were going to begin any minute. "We are really too old to catch them one by one," the guard explained to the curator. "We ought to hunt them in relays, each one taking up where another gets tired, as the Greeks did hunting wild asses. . . ."

So, in the foreground, was the 4A class, and behind them were the panting guards. In the far background were the statues of Zeus, Hera, Poseidon, like spectators in the amphitheater.

"How draughty it is!" thought the father of the gods and men. "The time seems to blow by faster now than it did."

A green bronze of Pan spent twenty-two years at Delphi; three hundred and seven years at the bottom of a pond; one thousand, two hundred and six years in a cellar ten feet underground.

The curator was looking in increasing wonder from one age to another.

"Even in my time, the ancient glory had vanished," thought Apollo, his right arm firm. "The Chariot of the

The Fight in the Museum ·

Sun that I drove was a pale cold thing, hardly bright enough to dazzle the eyes of men, much less my own."

[New York City]
[1934]

Phaëthon, Myth

Looking down at the earth, at the wooded plain and the silvery streams, the cities with towers and quadrangular streets, young Phaëthon burst into tears. Going before his father the great Sun (who was invisible to his eyes, but the spirit of the god electrified the room), he blushed and was confused.

Phaëthon said, "May I once drive the chariot of the Day?"

"Why?"

"Perhaps I had a mortal mother," said Phaëthon. .

With his great (invisible) eyes, the god swept the boy. "Why do you say that, boy?"

"When I think how pale and cold the light falls on the earth—"

"And how we—"

"And how we in these courts enjoy its blazing presence, the gold lamp and coal-black shadows—then such a grief—"

"I have heard this story more than once," thought Phœbus.

"—comes on me to bring down the sun among the men!"

"You mistake the nature of seeing," said the god. "Seeing is proportionate not only to the power of the external light but also to the light in the eye. Like causes like: we could not see the sun if it were not within us. (Let me tell you that the cause and the effect are the same thing.) Here forever on fire, we live in the hot focus; on the distant

163

earth the light falls cold and dim. But their eyes are not receptible of our light, nor can we bring them this temperature without catastrophe. Our cousin Prometheus was wiser; he took only a curling flame protected in a fennel-stalk against the wind. Even this was dubiously useful."

"Father, is it because I am half mortal that I think of this?"

"On the contrary, this is your divine part. It is an ancient error that the god descends thru defect; this is his proper act. As for men, they would not know us if we did not come. Have I myself been an unserviceable god? driving my car on schedule a hundred thousand years. If I do not drive closer—as you today will—it is because I, like all the older gods, have more regard for the most of those below, and less for the few who need more light. (They *have* this divine desire; why do they need satisfaction, too?) Only my sister Aphrodite, mother of calamities, goes down among them and spreads ruin and destruction on every side."

"Aphrodite!" said Phaëthon in a hushed voice.

"Perhaps hers is the best way—how do I know?" cried the god, more moved. "Each of us acts as he must. It is only the god of prophecy who am so frightened of catastrophes. The year 1000! the year 2000! There have been *many* accidents in the past—who is the worse? Phaëthon! when the sun nears the earth, the forests will catch fire, the rocks melt, and the ocean go up in smoke. Some of the men will be blinded by the dazzling light without and within. Then, start out at once, for it is time."

"The round Sun! dynamo of heart and head—" said the boy.

"You are the son of Clymene, a mortal woman," the god said. "This is how gods mingle with men—let no man contemn it: the mingling of gods with men is like the love of a man for an animal, a furry goat or sleek horse; whence are born fauns and centaurs, and other charming monsters. It is like the infatuation of the sculptor Pygmalion with the granite. The joy of a teacher in the soul of the youth. Or as I myself, often, seize on the soul of the prophetess at Pytho."

164

Phaëthon, Myth

At this, the 4 high-headed horses were brought in. The gates sprang open.

2. *scherzo*

Out sped the fiery-wheeled car toward its catastrophe, while the young master cracked the whip.

Rubens, Actæon, Lampus, and Philogeus were the names of the 4 horses.

"Now," thought Phaëthon, "I am on my downward way; how swift the space whistles thru my hair!"

So light and quick beat the hooves on the clouds, that sparks of lightning played about the 16 feet. Meanwhile the round sun poured forth its flat beams.

The chariot-wheels made 1400 revolutions a second. Far behind, deserted by its lamp, the Heaven was already growing gray.

"Ho, *Rubens!*" shouted the young driver exultantly to his lead-horse (for the 4, noticing the new course and feeling an unaccustomed hand at the reins, began to grow restive). "A different road: down, down. As yet we're only picking up speed, but wait. The closer we get, the faster we'll fall—till we hit with a bang in a blaze of glory!"

Fascinated, like a boy in the top-gallery leaning over the rail with his eyes on the stage, he stared over the edge of the car.

"*Rubens* is the ruddy one, the horse of Dawn. The horse my aunt Aurora mounts when she goes hunting. It is the horse of the Springtime, whom they say to be the son of Memory."

Now, on their precipitous course, they began to enter the signs of the Zodiac. All about stood the calm stars. Truly there was nothing to be seen in the heaven but the gray eyes of the boy and the many shining stars. As he came to the 3rd abode, the constellation of the immortal Twins, he reverently bowed to Castor and Pollux, the brothers of Helen.

In the great and starry stillness, he felt obliged to cry out. "*Actæon!* is the shining one, of high noon. Now we are in

165

full career. How calm and fast we go, as if this course could continue unchanged forever. One would hardly notice how we are accelerating; the miles glide by as if they had no being; there is nothing but this course of ours, unchangeable forever. Actæon is the horse of shining Summer, the time when everything is reaching its peak and there is no end in sight."

Much in this way, they sped between the claws of the Crab and past the Lion, rampant in one place.

But to those on the earth, the present progress of the Sun—far from seeming a state eternally the same—began to suggest the wildest alarms. They were used to the lordly ease of Phœbus' daily round; but now the sun fell in one streak across the zenith. Many hoped, many feared a coming catastrophe; some expected it, some doubted. Thousands of people who had never thought of the sun turned their attention to it and hurt their eyes. Trade was done in black glasses.

Phaëthon entered on the 3rd stage of his journey to the earth, and a sadness crept into his heart. At the same time he attained the height of skill in driving. Hitherto he had let the reins loose, letting the course create its own future, not knowing for sure what might occur from moment to moment. Now the whole was clear to him; he understood at what rate they had been accelerating, and how long they must so continue; he even saw, in a flash, at just what spot they would hit. "It is the afternoon, the hottest part of the day, yet already stricken with a chill. Tho I am driving his very chariot, I know I am no longer part of the sun's course. This is because I so clearly understand the finish of it, and I am outside of it all." At the same time he began to experience the keenest delights, no longer in driving (for each stage has its own delights), but in looking about at the scenery, estimating the speed, and thinking up figures of speech. Always accelerating, they skipped by Libra, proceeded thru Scorpio. "After the moment of the Balance," thought Phaëthon eagerly, "we get to know the sting of the Scorpion's tail."

"Lampus!" he called, with such youthful intensity that

the horse looked about, half-expecting to behold a mare gifted with speech. "This is the blazing one—the golden harvest moon, a coin, a pumpkin, or anything full and golden."

Meantime on earth, the excitement became intense, as the huge ball of fire grew larger and larger. Entire races began to migrate at once (not only men, but animals: the men going into the forests, the beasts running thru the streets), passing each other, going in opposite directions. It was at this time, some say, that charred by the approaching fire, the Africans became black-skinned. Others hold that, on the contrary, in the beginning all races were black—but the northerners shone so in the blazing light that the reflection stuck fast and they became blond and white. Some were stricken by the sun outside, in their bodies, others inside, in their souls.

"Now," thought Phaëthon despondently, "I long for the wreck. Let it come!"

The reins hung loose in his hands. No longer under their own momentum, powerless to stop, the horses dropped like a plummet, drawn downward by the earth.

"Let come what may," he thought, falling faster and faster. "Why did I ever risk my soul on this monotonous journey? At first I had the joy of starting out; then of the speedy course; now I ask only for the end. On all sides I am hemmed in, it seems, powerless to stop. I have lost control not only of my horses, but of my own thoughts. What is this uncontrollable lust in me for the crash?"

Passing thru the sign of Aquarius, the Water-Carrier, he began to weep.

He remembered the name of the 4th of his horses, Philogeus. "The Earth-lover! We two, Philogeus. The others are rearing, turning their heads wildly upward, trying in vain to escape; but we two have our heads outstretched to one love." The horse made no response to this, other than to keep his eyes fixed steadfastly on the looming earth. "Now for the first time I understand the sense of all this ride," said Phaëthon—"I am like the playwright whose play has come to life against his will and

167

destroys its own hero."

The whole earth was bathed in tongues of flame. Extensive tracts of forest set ablaze. With one sizzle, mountain-streams went up in smoke, the rocks melted and themselves started to flow in the stream-beds. Even the ocean began to shrink away. Such dense clouds of vapor enveloped everything that it is no wonder that only the most contradictory reports have come down concerning the events of that momentous day.

With a roar and a hiss—and dashing the rider out on his face—the chariot plunged into the Ocean. Coming to the surface, snorting and spitting out the hot foam, the 4 horses turned their faces to the West and swam off, leaving a bright wake behind them, all the way to the horizon.

3.

A certain individual, a philosopher of the Hebrides named Rogerus Insulareus—Roger of the Islands, was stuck blind by the sun falling down like a shot bird; and he buried his dazzled eyes in his sleeve.

"I cannot recall," he thought, "whether I am some victim of the sun, struck blind, or whether I myself am the great sun tumbling down. Everywhere I cast my eyes—" (for he did not realize that his eyes were buried in a dark sleeve) "—the trees, the rocks turn

> yellower than the plates of honey
> that pass among the bees as money.

Surely I am the great sun painting everything yellow."

In waves the blood rushed to his head and flowed in red channels about his golden eyes.

"How swiftly we are falling thru the sky!" he thought—quite beyond himself and holding out his hands as if he were grasping the reins. "We two, Philogeus! . . . I see where we must strike in the western sea. . . . But there below me is a madman in the Hebrides, named Roger. He has buried his eyes in his sleeve. 'How swiftly we are

168

falling!' thinks he and looks over the edge of his imagined car. 'We two, Philogeus! . . . But there below me in the Islands is this fellow . . .' "

Unable to restrain himself for excitement and inspired by the notion of falling faster and faster, he leaped off a high cliff and was dashed to death.

4.

But Phaëthon, coming to his senses in the water, shook out his golden locks, brighter than the wake of the retreating sun, while the droplets flew about in the air like amber beads—and with long strokes he swam to the shore. There, being tired, he lay down on the edge of the sand and fell asleep. Then arose Diana the moon, shining far and wide.

Now a young maiden, daughter of the king of the Anthropophagi—for it was off the coast of these man-eaters that the sun sank into the sea—came down to the shore to play ball.

Her name was Clymene, the same as that of the mother of Phaëthon (if indeed it was still he, on the shore, and not Apollo himself—for often, in these myths, we insensibly glide back into the past, and the many generations merge).

After she had thrown the ball up and caught it, Clymene spied the golden form on the sand a little way off and thought it might be a large fish cast up by the recent convulsion of the elements. (In the moonlight, you would hardly remember those golden flames.) Struck by memory, so deep, her strength failed her and for a moment she leaned against a tree, her hands over her breasts.

Phaëthon, meantime, dreamed a dream that seemed to have no form and yet was strong and full of portent. In fact, it was a dream of the ancient Chaos. In the midst of his troubled sleep, out of nowhere—rose a name, and he called it out: "Clymene! Clymene!"

Stunned already by memory—for Clymene was one of those who having seen the falling sun could not forget the sight—how profoundly stirred must she now have been to

169

hear her name called out in the lonely night!

"Here he is who called," she thought, looking at him. "If there were golden seaweed, his dank hair would be compared to it."

She sank to her knees beside him.

For the first time in her life, she observed a person sleeping. She heard his fitful breathing, saw his limbs twitch, his features grimace—with no cause for it all. He sang 4 clear notes of a song. Indeed, these events were taking place in a different world from hers—and one could not guess the meaning. Just as when there is a flurry on the surface of the sea, arising from nothing, you cannot tell whether sea-monsters are fighting below the surface or a volcano has erupted in the depths.

A doubt began to assail her. "Perhaps my name is not Clymene at all, and I have let myself be bewitched into thinking that the first name I heard called was *my* name. Perhaps no one ever called out."

Finally she lay down beside him, rested her face on his shoulder, and drew his arms about her. Yet Phaëthon did not awake, but received her also into his chaotic dream.

Thus always, *asleep*, the gods cohabit with mortals.

With a start, the boy awoke. His gray eyes, clear and cloudy (in which you might look right thru to his ancestor the beginning of the world), opened up on the bright moonlit beach, and his ears on the tinkling of the billions of drops of water in the breaking waves. Disengaging himself from the girl's arms, he stood up.

She was now lying asleep at his feet, just as he had been at hers. "What bad luck!" he thought, "to come into a country where the first person I meet is asleep." He saw, however, that her eyes were not shut, but were staring at him—great circles of golden fire. This did not make him think her any the less asleep.

"Her eyes," he thought, "are golden and a person not skilled in genealogy might think that she, and not I, grayeyed, was the child of Helios. But I, like all the gods, take after my great-grandfather Chaos."

All this time, the golden gaze of Clymene did not leave him. He felt ashamed to have her staring at him. "Rise up, girl," he said, touching her with his foot. "Tell me, what place is this?"

She rose. "I did not think that the Sun was so young—in the afternoon when I saw him come down," she said. She was asleep.

"How do *I* know?" cried Phaëthon. "How do I know whether or not I am he? My memory tells me that I left my father's court in heaven—"

"In the court of the Sun is a well with a windlass, and alongside it—"

"—yet maybe I never took the headlong ride, but am myself one of these miserable folk."

"—alongside it is a statue of Hermes with broken arms."

"How did you learn that detail, girl?" he said sharply.

"I am reading it from your face," she said.

He lifted his hand to his cheek, but found it smooth and downy.

"Did you ask me anything, my lord?" she said humbly.

"I asked you, What place is this?"

"Oh! it is the country of the Anthropophagi."

5.

As if summoned up from the ground by a name, 5 or 6 of the Anthropophagi stood about, "aged men, of venerable mien." With a start, Phaëthon saw the round golden eyes of each.

"*All* the people here are blind, it seems," he thought. Clymene had vanished.

"Wonderful!" he thought, beginning to feel the exaltation of one who, not yet seeing clearly where his work is moving, knows by sure signs that it is near the end. "See how the next is upon us! I mean the End. Surely this morning I was with my father in heaven; I drove thru the air and I fell into the sea. Who are these blind sages springing up on every side? there must be more than a thousand."

By now there were more than a thousand.

"2000 circlets of gold!" he cried, referring to their eyes.

"Wherever I turn—" they prompted.

"Wherever I turn my eyes, I look into the same profound and fiery soul."

"A strange acquaintance—"

"I seem to have a strange acquaintance with every one around. Where can I have met so many?"

"Mirrors—" they prompted.

"How easily suggestible I am!" the young man thought. "The moonlight seems to flash from one to another of them, standing on the shore, as if they were mirrors."

"Hold out your hand," he said to one of them, "and see if you can see yourself in it." He held out his own hand and saw that he could see his face in it as in a glass.

A loud shout rang out. The many thousands began to rest their weight first on one leg, then on the other, as if at the beginning of a dance.

A spokesman stepped forward and said to Phaëthon, "It is our custom—

"It is our custom," he said, shifting to the other leg, "to eat up every glorious stranger that comes to this land, in order that we may inherit his virtue. (But if any mean personage comes, we feed him our children, in order that he may inherit ours.) Do not be angry, but consider the matter from our point of view: when the wolf-god descends here, we become possessed of the lust and fierceness of wolves; when the lovely armless statue of Aphrodite is found on the shore, washed up by the waves, we are stricken with repose—then we grind up the marble and bake it in little cakes for all. All this is reflected in our eyes, where sometimes—as in a glass—you can see the prowling wolf, sometimes the immobile statue, or sometimes the golden Sun! How various are the sights of the eyes! Yet often we fear that there are invisible presences all about that we cannot see."

"Tell me, good man," said Phaëthon, "what are the genera of your race?"

"Lovers, musicians, dialecticians—"

"Then is it the fate of Phaëthon to be eaten up by these!" cried the young man. "I started out at dawn, drawn by an

172

intolerable longing, as I said. I travelled thru the air all day and fell into the sea. I slept and reproduced myself—"

"Do not be alarmed," said the spokesman, seeing that he looked this way and that for Clymene. "The girl will be well taken care of. It is not every day that we have a daughter the mother of a god."

"—and now die.

"Let me give you instructions," he said, "how to cut up this body of mine—this flesh," he said, laying his finger on one breast. "The head it is best to dismember by features, making 6 parts in all, counting the ears. The fingers take separately except for the thumbs, which ought to be bisected the long way—giving altogether 6 pairs, or 12—

"I give them these directions and magical numbers," he said to himself, "merely in order that they may have a complex formula, a ritual, by which to revive the memory of me again and again. Perhaps any other numbers would do as well—(who knows? these particular ones have come into my mind). It is well to give men something concrete to go by, so they may start off."

[New York City]
March-April 1934

Gamblers

Messieurs, faîtes vos jeux," said the croupier in a pleasant voice, at the next table. He turned to me and winked the left eye.

At the card table, my friend Jason clicked the yellow chips on that dark green baize. Standing behind him, pretending to look elsewhere, I closely watched him over my shoulder. Finally he lifted his eyes, shot a quick glance at Monsieur, and almost imperceptibly nodded. "Ah!"—I took a breath—"he is going to play again." The pasteboard cards flew through the air. I looked over his shoulder while he picked up the King of Clubs with the globe and the rosy Queen of Hearts.

"Rien ne va plus!" cried Jacques, the croupier. With a whirr, the roulette began to whirl and the pellet to hop and dart about the bowl.

There were several of us bystanders, not gambling, staring fixedly, not at the game, but at the gamblers.

"They fly to me on the wind like the oracles of the Cumaean Sybil written on leaves," said Jason. "Each card, as I raise it from the cloth and the bright face appears, is like a bolt of lightning, accompanied by the rumbling thunder of the pulse. So the Law was revealed to Israel from Mt. Sinai. Now this law—the law of these cards and *his* dealing"—he spoke with hatred of Monsieur, the dealer—"is imposed; my fate is dealt—no will of mine. How little manly of me to submit myself again and again to this passivity." He picked up the last card, its bright face from the baize like a bolt of lightning—and he blanched.

175

"Your friend Prescott," said Jacques in his pleasant French accent, "seems to have the same rotten luck as ever. Why do you come here, not to gamble, but to watch him? It must be very discouraging."

"Look, the Five Books of Moses!" said Jason with a bitter laugh, holding up the poker hand for me to see: King Queen Jack Ten Seven. "Big promises and look where the Jews are!"

With a little click, the roulette ball found its resting place. There was a flurry of excitement at that table. Jacques raked in the losings. One golden plaque fell from the table and lay on the carpet; and a rosy bell-hop, a kid of fourteen, darted after it among the legs of the gamblers. "You may keep it to bet with," said Mme. de Coudray. "Put it on number 22," said Pierre.

"Why do I come here and watch Jason?" I said to the croupier. "I come here and watch Jason in order to learn patience. He is an example to me. How many times I have sworn that I would not try again to be happy! There is a limit to how often one can be disappointed and still want to succeed, for even success, after a while, will leave a bad taste in the mouth. Yet what a nightmare, to think that any of us, as we are, are better off than no matter what desperate risk! Then I come and behold Jason, and, always losing, he plays again and again. See, he has again signalled to Monsieur!"

"*Messieurs, faîtes vos jeux!*" said Jacques.

Through his eyelashes the gambler observed the long fingers of Monsieur shuffling the cards. (I watched him in a mirror opposite and I could see the narrowing of his eyes.) The cards rustled and snapped, as Monsieur alternately employed two methods of shuffling, first by holding the deck in one hand and redistributing the cards with the other, then by cutting the deck in two and snapping the halves together. His hands moved in a sinuous way, and the fingers and cards seemed to flow into each other.

"These alien combinations, evolving in the quick hands of Monsieur," said Jason, "—if his little finger held one card a split-second longer! Yet what is he to me that I should hang on his little finger! I am a slave by nature;

176

Gamblers

they ought to mark me by boring a hole through the ear, like those slaves of old who refused their freedom on the seventh year. Yet he doesn't promise anything; all the royal flushes are in my imagination. I wait for the opening of the doors at two o'clock, in order to give up my world of freedom, where, ah! I could command this or that according to my whim, to submit myself to the arbitrary rules of this shuffling! Isn't it a disgrace to take a chair at this table again and again!"

With a dry little tap of the deck on the table, Monsieur adjusted his cuffs and dealt.

"Rien ne va plus!" said Jacques.

"I would not be so sure," I thought, "that this shuffling is arbitrary, and that Monsieur is not cheating."

The roulette began to whirr and whirl, and every one at that table leaned forward.

The cards flew out to right and left like fateful little telegrams from a war-zone.

"The fact is," I said bitterly to smiling Jacques, who had asked me why I came to watch the gambling, though I did not play, "one has to learn patience. Take the case of falling in love—" I was already near tears, as people often are when they are pressed as to why they do something and they try to answer honestly.

Jason turned pale as death. In a visible tide the redness left his face and neck, leaving his flesh a mottled blue. With a haggard look, he handed me his cards: Six of Hearts, Jack of Hearts, Eight of Hearts, Ace of Hearts, Ten of Spades. I flung them onto the table.

"43! rouge!" sang out Jacques, amid a flurry of excitement, as the wheel clicked to a stop.

Little Pierre began to sob bitterly.

"What's the matter, kid?" I said. I took off his little cheesebox hat, and one could see that he was a mere child, with red hair.

"I put it on 22," he said, deep down in his throat.

"Why, you didn't really expect to win on a single number, did you?" I cried. "Here's another chip; try again."

"It was the *first* time," he sobbed; "I thought I might be

177

one of those people who are lucky."

"*Messieurs, faîtes vos jeux!*" said Jacques.

"I see that I am like everybody else."

The child was disconsolate. He would not take the silver chip I offered him, but ran from the room. He sat down in the lobby and sobbed out his heart. In the lull of the conversation, during the turning of the roulette and the dealing of the cards, this sobbing could be clearly heard.

"Once I had the following dream," I said to Jacques. "I dreamt that I was playing solitaire in eternity—but in *this* game I had all eternity to get my game, and I understood that by strict mathematical laws in a billion deals or so I should almost *have* to get it, and come out. Yet this did not prevent my pulse from pounding, and I woke in a sweat."

"Ha!" said Jacques in pride and scorn, "if you would not masturbate, you would not be troubled with nightmares. . . ."

"*Messieurs, faîtes vos jeux!*"

"Now I have caught you in a lie!" I cried triumphantly. "For we are all in the same boat. Have you, a Frenchman, never read Pascal?"

At the mention of this name, he lost color. I seized the advantage:

"Pascal says, at the beginning of the Ninth Section of the *Pensées*, that the state of man is to be compared to one borne, asleep, to a fearsome and desert island—*déserte et effroyable*—and who awakes without knowing where he is or how he is to get away. And he sees others like himself nearby, and he asks them if they know any more about it, but they are in the same plight. . . ."

As I progressed in this narrative, he grew more and more pale. His hands trembled and his voice faltered.

"*Rien—rien—rien ne va plus!*" he faltered in an uncertain voice, as though he were no longer sure of himself.

When he spun the roulette, his hand shook. The result was disastrous for the House (for his manipulation of the machine, just like the dealing of Monsieur, was dishonest). If Pierre had now wagered his first chip, he might have won, he might have won. Was I not right to feel the glow of triumph at that which I had accomplished?

"All, all are in the same plight!" I cried in joy.

The blood froze in my veins. Monsieur was about to deal but Jason was slowly shaking his head from side to side. Monsieur kept looking inquisitively toward Jason for the accustomed signal, but Jason, with head bent, was stacking his few remaining chips, preparatory to leaving the table.

"Play on! play on, gambler!" I cried in a loud voice, so that people everywhere in the room turned to look at me 'neath arched eyebrows. "Shhh," they said. "Silence!" "I have a wonderful premonition!" I cried. "Who knows? perhaps next deal!"

"I have so few chips," said Jason. "Look how beautiful!"

"They have no value except in this game," I said. "Once up from this table, they are worthless. It's no good saving them."

"My friend," said Jason to me in a deep voice, "to tell you the truth, I have gotten to a point where I don't care whether I win or—"

"Hush!" I said, cutting him off, lest he prove a bad example to me. "What a thing it would be, Jason, if we became disgusted to such a point as to be satisfied to go on as we are!"

I reached over his shoulder and tossed a chip from his pile into the center.

Blazing with fury Monsieur glared at me. He dealt the cards.

In the mirror opposite, Jason was looking at me with moist eyes, glinting with hate.

But I, my heart beating hard with mounting joy, thought: "O Alfred de Musset, fear not, old boy! Fear not! we still play the old game:

> *Après avoir souffert, il faut souffrir encore,*
> *il faut aimer sans cesse après avoir aimé.—*

to fall in love again, having fallen out of love!—

"Play on, Jason, play on!"

Monsieur restrained himself no longer. Eyes ablaze, he

rose to his feet and said: "Young man, in this establishment it is customary for the players to play their own hands. After all, it is their chips they are risking."

"You!" I said—in so loud a voice that all the polite people left off their gambling to turn toward us throughout the room (and from time to time a voice was raised in support of mine)—"It is your cheating that is on trial here, not our luck. I, who do not play and am therefore not bewitched by the fascination of *this* game, have been observing your shuffling very curiously. I could point to many irregularities if I wanted to cause a scandal."

"Yes, yes!" cried a voice from the other end of the room, "we who can watch the players as well as the cards see many strange things."

"A good many of the gamblers," cried the voice of another observer, "are not in a condition to defend themselves."

"The worst of all," said another voice, "is that these chips they are playing for are absolutely worthless in themselves. Go out on the street and you will find that you cannot pass them. Even if they won, they would not have anything."

"My friend Jason—" I said, "my friend Jason does not expect to win, but he will gamble on and always lose; and believe me, it will look worse and worse for you in front of all these people!"

My voice broke into a sob. There was a deep silence in the room.

"*Messieurs, faîtes vos jeux,*" said Jacques appealingly.

Slowly the people turned back to their tables, at first with some hesitancy, but soon they were throwing down their chips with as much clatter as before. Monsieur broke into a warm and friendly smile. He called an attendant and spoke a few words to him behind his hand, looking all the while in my direction. Both burst out laughing. I became more and more uneasy.

Monsieur sat down, adjusted his cuffs, and resumed dealing where he had left off.

Jason turned round in his chair to say a word to me. "The fact is, Ben," he said, and smiled wanly, "I play because I like the game. It must be a kind of vice with me, I suppose."

Humiliated, I felt a perfect fool standing there, not playing at anything. I strode across the room into the lobby, where Pierre was drying his tears and putting on his little hat before a glass.

New York City
1934

The Detective Story

Long ago when I had fallen out of love, I decided to write a detective story, and this was to be the plot of it:

> A famous detective is assigned to the solution of a number of crimes which bear the mark of one criminal. As he pursues his investigations he feels that more and more closely he can understand, and sympathize with, the mind of this criminal; this gives him an increasing insight into the crimes. "No one can solve a crime," he declares, "unless first he puts himself in the criminal's place." And at last, at the last crime, he discovers himself committing it; he, the criminal, has been pursuing himself all along!

Fired by this interesting idea I set to work and soon had written many pages. I called the detective Mr. Fort George after the neighborhood in which I happened to live. "Soon at this rate I shall be at the end!" I thought happily. But this very self-gratulation—which was perhaps the last I would enjoy in this work—constrained me to pause a moment, to reread what I had written. Here began my troubles.

What I had written was very nice, but it was not worthy of my fine plot. For all at once I came to see my idea not as a simple detective story but as a detective epic, a narrative of crime detection in its most general form, as the philosophy, indeed, of detective stories. But who was I, and how was I fitted, to undertake such an enterprise? I had as yet committed no crimes, I had no experience of the

183

police and no knowledge of criminology.

Like many other novelists, I began to engage in research. Even while I was hard at work on a little crime, I struck up an acquaintance with the corner policeman. He lent me his nightstick and blackjack and playfully imprisoned my wrists in handcuffs. I loitered in the station house and played poker with the gang. I planned and executed a complicated robbery of the Great Bear Butcher Shop and got thirty-two dollars, most of which I later returned through the Post Office. I also read Ferri and Lombroso and the celebrated Essay of Beccaria.

All this was not done in a day. To execute the robbery alone, as I planned it, I had to seduce and then train an idiot-boy to knock down a blind old hag at the one moment when, every morning, she passed in front of the butcher shop, so that in the confusion I could rifle the cash register. Altogether, seven or eight weeks passed by; but always I had the burning confidence that finally I would be able at least to return to my story. While I was doing everything else I have described, the idea of my story shone bright above it all, like a lamp that lighted the other things but was itself constantly before my eyes.

To my dismay I found myself farther afield than ever: I could no longer unify my material. I now found myself in the perplexity of a problem of style. Where previously my plan had been adequate but only my experience limited, now the result of my researches, my material—the Irish humor of the police station, the fear and trembling of the crime, the remarkable statistics that I had learned from the anthropometric school—all these refused to be collapsed into a story. I took the matter this way and that way, by a hundred different handles, and again and again I wrote a first sentence but could not write the second sentence. As soon as I put down a word, a world of experience was excluded forever; and, of course, the harder I tried, the more thronging memories came into my mind unwilling to be omitted. This could be expressed by saying that that lamp of mine had illumined so much that I could hardly raise my eyes from the ground and had but a distant and hazy image of it itself.

The Detective Story

I turned to the experts in this kind of unity, to the creators of Sherlock Holmes and Arsène Lupin, and to Gaboriau and Poe and Wilkie Collins, and even to dozens of the modern small fry. I read two hundred episodes of Nick Carter, gathering the only complete collection in New York—which I have since sold at a small profit. Altogether, in two years I read 1,712 detective stories. In the end a positive physical loathing overcame me; I could not conceive of myself adding to the detective literature of the Western world. In despair I wrote the following two verses of an epic poem:

> Of those who look with sidelong sight
> at the blue police with gloves of white—

and this effort killed the idea forever in my heart. What! was I never to write a detective story?

2.

In this crisis, suddenly—for every transformation in this curious history caught me by surprise, though I can only too well account for each one—my problem presented to me an entirely different face, because I was desperate and, what is equally true, because the foreknowledge of this very change made me turn away from what I had been doing up to now. "The trouble is," I now thought, "that up to now I have not conceived of my plot in a manner profound enough. Up to now the conception has been superficial, on the level of a detective story or a realistic sociological description; but obviously the true, the profound story here is the case of a Dual Personality rediscovering his ego."

I immediately saw that my story of the detective who pursues himself from crime to crime was nothing but the self-analysis of a split personality disturbed by the irruption into his life of a number of alien symbols and compulsive acts (those are the "crimes"); spurred on by a need that becomes ever more acute and passionate, he achieves reintegration by discovering the truth about himself! That is, a simple clinical case, but what ancient literature! for it was half Dr. Jekyll and Mr. Hyde but also half Œdipus the King who with growing horror hastens on at an accelerating pace to discover that he is the man who slew his father at the three-forked road. A dual personality by ignorance, the bedfellow of Jocasta was two persons, her husband and her son, but one of them came to confront the other: the cunning Œdipus who solved the mystery of the Sphinx, engaged on his second piece of detective work.

My new plot. But what was to be the cause of the hero's initial loss of half of himself? Sophocles, to be sure, did not find it necessary to explain why a finite desirer should be in ignorance and come to grief; but I, fired with enthusiasm by my new and remarkable plot, was determined to explain this too. Once more I began my studies, more soberly perhaps than before, but with undiminished energy, just as if I had gained a second wind. I no longer hoped to dash off my work in a month, once I could get started, but the idea of at least starting burned before me like a lamp.

I read about the multiple personalities of Miss Sally Beauchamp, as described by Dr. Prince; and Dr. Rivers on shell-shock; and here and there in Freud. The phenomena of hypnosis and somnambulism occupied my attention, and the twin sister of somnambulism, the act of falling in love.

Ah! "Why do I want to write a novel at all, and why have I invented this particular plot?" I asked myself; for where previously, writing a detective story, I had been obliged to leave my desk to fraternize with policemen and execute a robbery on a butcher shop, I now naturally turned in the opposite direction, inwardly, and began on every occasion to question my own motives.

"It was when I had just fallen out of love that I began to write this novel. Was it because I was afraid that I should have nothing to fill my time that I turned to the writing of a detective story, an exciting and fantastic occupation, not realizing how deeply I should soon become involved, but inwardly knowing it very well?—for it is not by chance that this business has come to fill all my time day and night. Or on the contrary, was it the very prospect of undertaking a novel—but not that novel which I was then thinking of!—a prospect not yet born in me but operative all the same, that made me fall out of love, so that my love was dead before I knew it, and before ever I invented the reasons, such as they were, which allowed me consciously to fall out of love? If indeed I ever did fall out of love? and all this novel is not just a screen, a strategem to distract my attention.—But look! what is the plot of my novel!" I cried. "It is nothing but the story of a man who thinks that he has fallen out of love; but he is troubled by the irruption into his present of experiences which he no longer recognizes, for they were organized under the forgotten signs of his ancient love. Disturbed, anxious, soon panicky, he hastens on from clue to clue, until he finds that he is still in love. . . ."

At this I began to tremble violently, at the thought that perhaps, after so many years, a certain face would return in nightmares as she used. But my dreams were far less suggestible than my waking, and no face reappeared; for indeed I had fallen out of love. Instead, I proceeded with the greater assiduity to study for my novel; for it kept seeming to me that very shortly I should start to write again, although now, looking back, I see that every step was taking me farther afield.

You cannot understand the criminal, Fort George had declared, unless you put yourself in his place. This was the first guiding principle of the whole work. But now I added to it a second: The first step in detective work is a self-analysis, an inquiry into the mind of the detective himself. What is his mind? what are his motives? For if this is not known, how can he put himself in the place of the criminal?

Thus the new self-analytical frame of mind that I brought to my novel became reflected in the plot itself; and my detective story became a novel of the psychology of the empirical ego. I changed the name of my hero and called him Paul, after my own empirical name.

It was during this period of my life that I married and, so

to speak, settled down. (I became a kind of anarchist and committed very many public crimes.) All this, as I then thought, was merely a means to an end: to satisfy myself, in order to hasten on to my novel—which all the while was really becoming a dim memory.

I purchased a home in Brooklyn and the years passed slowly by.

3.

Once again, despite my hard work and even humility, one morning I awoke to discover that my story had changed itself again. I could not recognize what I had been working on; and indeed, when I thought of it, that old story seemed a worthless and superficial object to waste so much time on; it seemed as if it were somebody else's work. What sort of fellow must I have been to be absorbed in such a thing. The only serious study, I now saw, worthy of engaging a man's attention, was the following problem in logic: how is it possible for any proposition to be adequate to its truth?

Not the case of a detective tracking a criminal in order to convict himself; nor of a split personality feverishly seeking out himself; but of how the minds of all of us try somehow to understand those objects given to us (these were the "crimes"), try to make themselves adequate to the thing.

But this effort of the mind seems futile, for the mind—I momentarily thought—is only rational, and all things are infected with irrationality, since they are given to us in an arbitrary way. The contradictions multiply and the investigation becomes more and more desperate.

When this transformation of my plot into a problem occurred, I was not in a state of disgust, as I had been previous to that prior transformation; nor did I now become joyful and enthusiastic. I realized that I was not the master of this transformation, but as if looking on, with fascination.

I imagined I saw by what process my psychological

188

novel must have turned into a problem of logic. For how was it possible for my detective, by looking into his own consciousness—on the maxim, to analyze himself—to find himself there? If he was there, how could he be looking from outside? Or to put this another way, how was he to know that what he found there, the strange memories and impulses, was really himself? How does a person know, in general, that when he has found something it is what he was looking for? Only by having a criterion (so I decided at that time!). Thus Paul's search for himself became the search for a criterion of the adequacy of subject and object in general; and there was no longer any use in calling him by my empirical name.

My detective was to have a third maxim. For first he saw that in order to understand the criminal it was necessary to put himself in his place. (What a strange thing for a detective to think of! obviously it was only he who had committed the crime who would ever have thought of it.) But secondly he discovered that even before that he must find himself out. (What a peculiar inference! obviously it was only he whose personality was split, etc.) Now he realized that the foremost thing of all is to have a criterion of adequacy, otherwise how is one ever to know that he has indeed found himself out. (What a curious dilemma!—)

I read the *Theaetetus* of Plato and Aristotle *On the Soul*; and what St. Thomas Aquinas had to say of the *Criterion*, and the *Discourse on Method*. I noticed anxiously, as I came to the later writers, that the search of the subject for its object was becoming more and more desperate; until, in the *Phenomenology* of Hegel, I was face to face with a detective novel like my own, a hundred years old. I read the *Appearance* of F. H. Bradley and was persuaded that it was impossible in principle, when once the subject and the object have been split asunder, ever to bring them together again.

For the first time I began to feel that my novel would never be written after all, for it was impossible in principle to think it through. Heretofore I had been buoyed up, if not always by enthusiasm, at least by the sober conviction that the longer and harder I worked, the more substance I would give to my novel, as an animal long gestated is most perfectly formed. Now, whichever way I turned I saw that there was no use in proceeding any further. For if the subject were different from the object, how could it know it? and if the subject were the same as the object, how could it know it?

Occupied with this conveniently endless perplexity, which I soon saw lurking under a thousand different disguises, so that everything, even the most simple thing, was seen to be a fatal paradox, I do not know how much time passed during which I did not sit down to work on my novel. (And these were the years, of course, during which I divorced my wife and did not bother to live anywhere and followed every kind of excess that suggested itself to my heart.)

Very thoughtful, I read over some of what I had written so long ago, and for the first time several passages became clear to me. I saw, for instance, why I had said that my great detective, Caspar Fort George, would never convict anyone except on circumstantial evidence; for how was his mind to come to grips with the actual crime?

> His methods—I had written at that time—were pure. He never experimented, tortured the facts; never laid traps for the criminal, nor an ambush to nab him in the act; never extorted a confession by the third degree. His attitude was entirely passive: let the facts come, do nothing to force the issue.
>
> This seemed unreasonable! Why should one not expedite matters by entering actively into those "facts" and making them talk? All of his activity was in the mind. He used to say, "I refuse to infect the object with myself . . . I have never gone to work on a hunch. Just because I should myself have committed such and such a crime (this is the hunch), shall I convict somebody else on my manufactured evidence?" Again, "My mind is nothing but a schematism, a framework of thousands of classes into which fall the clues—till they form a legible pattern."
>
> "What sort of classes?" asked Hepzibah.

190

"M. is a such and such, of such and such a physical and emotional type, in such and such a stress of circumstances. This pistol is a such and such; this bullet-wound is a such and such—

"In this way I will contrive an enormous fabrication and never come to the individual criminal!"

"Is not such evidence merely circumstantial evidence?" she objected. "The conclusion based on it is only probable."

"Right! if I were a judge I should never convict on this evidence."

So long ago! How far I had drifted from this original story. These fragments surviving, coming to light after many years and changed by the weathering (for in the beginning I could never have understood what I then wrote so lightly: "My mind is a framework" and "never come to the individual")—these surviving fragments made the original ruin far more ancient than if there were absolutely no trace left, just as the broken drums of marble columns, transformed by the weathering of years, perhaps sprouting weeds from the dirt in a crack,

> à chaque printemps, vainement éloquente,
> au chapiteau brisé verdit une autre acanthe,

says Hérédia—vegetation from the newest season of the world!—make Greece and Rome more distant than Atlantis, except that Atlantis survives in fragments even more antique, the fragments of legends. And I no longer thought, as once I had, "What a pity I did not hasten on when I was able and finish my story in one flourish!" for I understood that if I stopped at that time at the end of Chapter Two it was that something was already amiss, and that all my efforts subsequently were predestined by a contradiction from the first. Either in the plot or in myself—at first it appeared only as a difficulty of style— and I vainly tried to remedy it by new researches, introspections, points of view. Until finally the root of my error is laid bare: that I could not come to grips with things and I was brought to a stop once for all.

4.

Now indeed I have come to understand this novel!—if indeed I have. This is the plot of it:

There is a man who, still young, determines to convince himself of his freedom and power by making something, for instance, a story. After years of trying he finds that, being as he is, he is powerless to accomplish anything at all. He cannot give existence to any whole thing, for where is the existence to come from? The work dies in his hands. And indeed, far from being able to give existence to something outside himself, he learns that he cannot maintain even his own life. On every side he is beset by critical questions that he cannot answer, and he finally cries out at the very edge of despair, "Where, where, where shall I put my next step?" But in this crisis by the grace of God he is no longer cut off from his Creator, and is assigned to his proper place. (This is easily assigned by God.) At the same time he is not cut off from his story; it is easily completed, such as it is. For he imparts to it not the partiality and deceit with which he used to be so well acquainted (these are the crimes), but he regards it as a simple description of certain facts, known to him as one of the actual beings, that God who, being unlimited, can make anything, has made.

Was this, then, the story that had kept appearing to me in so many variations, like Proteus, god of the ocean, but perhaps now I have caught him in a net? In the guise of a detective who is able to solve the series of crimes only when he is himself the criminal; of the split personality who finds (let us say) that one of his symptoms is what he really wants; and so forth. But it is not by his own efforts that the split personality is made whole, or that mind and object are one with each other, for this act of unifying would be precisely impossible to such a divided substance as that split personality; but help comes—if of course it does—from elsewhere.

192

The Detective Story

It is not to write a novel, I think, that I have been brought on this long journey, this lifelong tour, as it were, among so many provinces and kingdoms; but to be made aware, again and again, of the true condition that I am in. For each time, faced with a question that cannot be answered and cannot be ignored, unable to cope, for instance, with a simple problem of style—I imagined that by retreating to a new vantage ground I would then have firm footing and could return to resolve every difficulty. So I retreated from my desk to the company of the corner policeman, and from there to myself, and from there to the theory of error. But I soon found the vantage ground itself give way beneath me; and indeed, if it was solid ground that I wanted, I would better have lingered on with the corner policeman! But the realization of my true condition, so salutary and necessary to me, could only, it seems, be effected by a painful retreat, struggling at every step. Without the sentiment of fighting a losing fight, I could not, it seems, come to the realization of the true perplexity of my condition, as it is said: Seek and ye shall find. (That is, in my case, precisely that "you shan't find.") And let me add this: that if I had not in the first place fallen out of love I should never have entered on this way at all.

I read the Book of Job and the Epistles of St. Paul. And it seemed to me that apart from the critical writings of Kant and Maimonides the books of philosophy were love stories. That insistent book that keeps posing a question, the *Commentary on the Epistle to the Romans* by Karl Barth; and *The Castle*, by Franz Kafka, a Jew like myself. I saw how so many men by the many different highroads stumbled into a dead end; but a certain foolish hope seemed to illumine them all.

Some get to the point, I am told, by brilliant successes, as it says in *Paradise Lost:*

> —greedily they plucked
> the fruitage fair to sight . . .
> instead of fruit
> chew'd bitter ashes which the offended taste
> with spattering noise rejected.

193

Others by a string of failures (for with some people nothing seems to succeed, even the most expected probabilities),

> Oft they assayed,
> hunger and thirst constraining; drugg'd as oft,
> with hatefullest disrelish writhed their jaws,
> with soot and cinders filled.

But after a while the meaning of the string of failures becomes clear enough. And still others, like myself, by continued efforts, more or less ambiguous, neither successful nor failing, but tempting one further.

Now, it seems, I could easily put myself to write any kind of incoherent paradox, for I am no longer troubled by a problem of logic. Or, on the other hand, this novel of mine could be a kind of *Odyssey*, the story of a sailor trying to return home; except that Ulysses knows there is an Ithaca, for he was born there, but we at the end of the story find that it is precisely this that we do not know!

Now it may be granted that I, too, shall one day be shown where and what I ought properly to work at, and what is to be the end of it. But I know, and this is a fourth maxim that I have discovered, that by myself I shall never be able to find this out. For first I learned that to understand the motives of the criminal one must first put oneself in his place; and then I saw that before that I had to learn the truth about myself, for who but myself was I to put in the place of that criminal; but thirdly I came to see that before anything one must have some criterion of the truth itself (and even if I had it how would I know that it was the true one?). But now I understand, or hope I do, that whereas from my side I cannot go on with this work, I need not despair but only wait, or I need only despair and wait.

New York City
1934-1935

The Joke

Crossing the 181st Street Bridge after a card game on the first floor of a house on University Avenue, Mr. Taylor was in high humor, for he and his wife had ended the evening with a small slam in hearts, redoubled.

"Do you want to hear a funny joke?" he said, unaccountably lapsing into a phrase, "funny joke," that he had not used for thirty-five years. (And this was his original mistake, for we must not revive memories of the time when we were seven and eight.)

Mrs. Taylor, who was in a temper, for good reasons that we need not go into, did not answer.

"Well, it seems," he said, hurrying on all by himself to destruction, "that in 1492 Columbus and his ships anchored off the island of San Domingo, and there were two Indians on the shore. So Columbus took out a megaphone and yelled: 'Hey there, are you the Indians?' And they yelled: 'Yes, we are, are you Columbus?' And when he yelled, 'Yes,' they turned and waved to the rest of the Indians who were hiding in the bushes: 'C'mon out boys—we're discovered!'... Ha! Ha! Ha! Ha! Ha!" Mr. Taylor laughed uproariously at his joke.

But since Mrs. Taylor, who was cross, did not join him, his laughter rang out alone among their footfalls on the deserted bridge. For it was half-past two of the silent night, when many things can be done with a common understanding that there will be no scandal.

"Now, what's funny about it?" she said. "I can't see any joke. He did discover America in 1492, didn't he?"

195

"Yes, but how did he know that they were the Indians? Ha! Ha! Ha!"

"He was *looking* for India. He set sail to find a Western route to India, didn't he?"

"Yes—but how did they know *they* were the Indians, I mean? How did they know that *his* name was Columbus? Ha!"

"I can't see the joke," said Mrs. Taylor.

"How did they know they were *discovered?* What a thing to say: 'C'mon out, boys, we're discovered!'"

But at this, laying such stress, such undue stress, on the word *discovered,* Mr. Taylor started, and paled somewhat, as if someone had called his name, or tapped him on the shoulder.

"Frankly, I can't see it," said Mrs. Taylor. "It was bound to happen, wasn't it? They couldn't expect to remain there in isolation forever, on the other side of the ocean; somebody was bound to find them out sooner or later. Why shouldn't they say, 'Well at last, comrades, we're found out,' or whatever they said: 'C'mon out, we're discovered'?"

" . . . to find them out—sooner or later . . ." murmured Mr. Taylor, as if in a trance, and stopped walking.

"Well?"

"Look at the launch all lit up with green and red lights coming up the river," faltered Mr. Taylor, to cover his confusion, and account for stopping short. He moved against the rail of the bridge, where the waters of the Harlem River could be seen swirling far below; and he took out his handkerchief and mopped his brow. A street lamp patiently glowed on the secluded pavement under High Bridge. On Ogden Avenue a little white dog trotted after them, looking for a home.

"It's not a launch, but a tugboat; it's not going up the river, but down," said Mrs. Taylor.

Once more they started on their way. "About that joke," he said. "Can't you see how stupid it is, for them to think of being discovered? Nobody ever thinks, himself, of being *discovered*. He's *there*, he's known; *he's* the one who does the discovering. Let me explain it."

196

The Joke

In this way, Mr. Taylor persisted in his self-destruction, or at least in the destruction of an elaborate framework of self-deception, which amounts to the same thing. At this time, had he dropped the whole matter of Columbus and the silly Indians, Mrs. Taylor would not have been the one to remind him. But to stop, once he had started, was, of course, what he could not do.

"Who ever said that those Indians were stupid?" cried Mrs. Taylor. "Why shouldn't they think of the possibility of being found out, some day. It could happen to us, too, couldn't it? Supposing some explorer today—"

"*Where*, where could he come from?" cried Mr. Taylor.

"Supposing he came from the planet Mars, and he saw us, right on this bridge, and called out, or tapped you on the shoulder."

With an awful shudder, and a haggard look on his face, Mr. Taylor turned sharply around, to the right, away from Mrs. Taylor, to see if there was any one behind.

"It's all right; there's no one there, beau. We haven't been found out yet," said Mrs. Taylor.

"Is that so!" said Mr. Taylor angrily. "A lot you know about it."

"What now? Another riddle? One of your jokes that nobody can understand?"

"It was a *simple* joke!" screamed Mr. Taylor. "The joke's on *you*, for being such a FOOL—that's who it's on!" he bellowed at his wife. "WHY DID I EVER MARRY SUCH A FOOL?" he roared at the top of his lungs, so that there was a remote echo from the wooded cliff in High Bridge Park.

"Murray!" said Mrs. Taylor, perplexed.

"Can't you really understand this simple joke?" he insisted petulantly. He was about to begin to whimper, and Mrs. Taylor might have noticed if they had not just passed a lamppost and entered a zone of darkness, that there were tears welling in his eyes. To bring these coursing down his cheeks required but the words he now spoke:

"Those Indians—standing on the shore—when suddenly the three sails, or the three ships, appeared above the horizon: how could they possibly have foretold that the captain's name was Columbus, as if they had read it in

197

Merrill's 4A History Book, on page sixteen in boldface type, opposite a full page picture that I can no longer visualize?" (At this, the tears coursed down his cheeks.) "But maybe you're right," he faltered, "and if they had truly understood their situation, they ought to have seen that they were on the verge of being found out. And if they had analyzed it more deeply, they might even have seen that it would be a Genoese captain who would come—for the commerce of Genoa bred daring mariners—and why mightn't they even guess that his name was Columbus? People often have such intuitions."

"Murray, you're crying!" said Mrs. Taylor, thunderstruck, as they finally came into the illumination of the next lamp.

"What you said—that they couldn't remain there in isolation forever, on the other side of the ocean—makes me cry."

"No one is on the bridge; not even a streetcar."

"When you have to explain it, almost any joke is likely to make you cry."

"Well, it's not my fault, I hope," said Mrs. Taylor.

"If only I could recollect the picture on page seventeen, I'm sure I wouldn't cry. I think it was Columbus kneeling before Ferdinand and Isabella."

"Are you sure you aren't feeling ill?"

"I'll be able to stop in less than a minute," said Mr. Taylor in a woeful voice.

"Here, sit down on the bench," she said—for they had come to a stone bench built into the pier at the middle of the bridge; and he sat down heavily, defeated—but the fact was that he looked fifteen years younger than he had before. The lamp above him on the right, not far from his head, drew his profile in a sharp line on the pavement. At the end of the bridge sounded the distant rumble of a trolley car, causing a tremor to run through the entire structure, from end to end. The water tower of the High Bridge reservoir stood against the night sky. And in a doorway on Amsterdam Avenue, two adolescents who had spent the small hours in vicious practices, lit their cigarettes.

The Joke

Of a sudden, Mrs. Taylor saw the point of the joke about Columbus and the redskins; and although apprehensive, she burst into a fit of laughter. "Ha! Ha! Ha! Ha! Ha!" she gasped again and again.

"It's a good one," she said gaily: "'C'mon, comrades, we're discovered!'"

She could not contain her laughing; and there she stood laughing, and he sat there crying.

New York City
1935

A Prayer For Dew

" . . . *And the offering of Judah and Jerusalem shall be a delight unto the Lord, as in days of old, as in ancient years.*"

With this ending of the Amidah or "standing-prayer," the sparse congregation sat down. A springtime thunder shower was washing the windows, amid prolonged rumbling of thunder and many flashes of lightning. Inside the synagogue all the electric lights had been turned on by the negro janitor, according to the injunction: "*On the first day shall be a holy convocation, ye* [Jews] *shall do no servile work.*"

Rabbi Lipsky stood up in front of the closed curtain of the Ark, adjusted his sleeves, and said: "We now come to the most beautiful prayer of the day, *Tefilas Tal*, the Prayer for Dew. This prayer, said before the open Ark, is the quintessence of springtime longing. What could man do without the rain? The rain falls in order to fill the rivers, and the rivers flow into the sea in order to evaporate into clouds. Who will give me fifteen dollars for the honor of opening the Ark for *Tal, P'sichas Tal*, the opening of the Ark for *Tal?* What am I bid? Do I hear anybody bid fifteen dollars?"

"Four dollars for my son, in memory of husband Isaac Podolnik," called Mrs. Podolnik from the women's gallery upstairs.

"Six dollars!" said Mr. Brody with a quiet smile.

The Rabbi and the President, in his silk hat, looked up inquisitively at the widow Podolnik.

"What exactly," I turned around to ask my friend Leo, sitting behind me with his white-shawled father, "is the theological status of a bid made in honor of some one when it doesn't win the auction?"

"Seven dollars!" called a voice in the rear.

"Seven dollars is bid back here," said the beadle, hastening to the spot.

"What's the name, please?" asked the Rabbi, tending his ear, that was like a handle on the moon.

"Thumim," said the voice.

"Berman? Mr. Berman bids seven dollars."

"Seven-fifty," said Brody quietly.

"Seven-fifty is bid for the opening of the Holy Ark for the springtime prayer for Dew," said Rabbi Lipsky.

Meantime the rain, not yet prayed for, thudded hard against the windows and on the green-glass skylight. All about, the water could be heard flowing busily down the runnels and the drainpipes. There was a burst of lightning and the old men near the window, seated with their fringes over their heads, were sharply silhouetted against the window and brightly illuminated around their outline.

"Eight-fifty!" cried Mr. Thumim.

"Mr. Berman bids eight-fifty," said the Rabbi.

"Eight-seventy-five," said Brody.

"Nine!" cried Thumim excitedly.

"Nine and a half," said Brody.

There was a crack of thunder and one of the electric lights over the reading table went dim and dark.

"Nunny, go call the *schwarze* to bring a new bulb," said Mr. Mondschein, the President, to his little son.

Nunny ran down the aisle, bouncing a rubber ball on the red carpet.

Throughout the synagogue, conversation became general, a continually augmenting buzz; everybody began to comment on the weather; and, far in the rear, some one began to tell a new joke.

My friend Leo, the divinity student, finally enunciated an opinion on the theological status of the widow Podolnik's offer which had been outbid. "She fulfilled a commandment in starting the bidding off," he said in my ear.

"In Jewish life it is considered a *mitzvah* to start things off!"

Like wildfire the joke progressed from bench to bench, greeted at each retelling with a greater outburst of hilarity.

"Shh! shh! this is a synagogue!" admonished Mr. Mondschein disapprovingly, pounding the palm of his hand loudly against his open prayer-book. The buzzing fell an octave lower on the scale, as happens on a meadow in the month of August when the sun passes momentarily behind a cloud.

"Twelve dollars!" rang out the voice of Thumim, in a last desperate raise.

"Twelve-fifty," said Brody.

"For heaven's sake, Marcus—" said Brody's brother-in-law, tugging wildly at his sleeve.

"So?" said Brody, turning to him with a bland smile, "did I say I *want* the bid? I'm just—*raising* a little . . . . "

"Twelve-fifty is bid by Mr. Meyer Brody for the honor of opening the Ark for *Tal*."

"*Fifteen dollars!*" thundered a new voice, on the left.

"Sixteen," said Brody.

"*Seventeen!*" boomed the voice.

"Seventeen-seventy-five," said Brody.

Aaron, the grizzly-haired negro janitor, came down the aisle carrying a ladder and a frosted bulb, followed by six-year-old Nunny, now bouncing a different ball, a small red ball, at the end of an elastic string. The old negro climbed up on the ladder, stretching up his arm to unscrew the light, and the ladder began to wabble. The Reader seized hold of it, to hold it firm.

"The question is," I said to Leo, "whether you're even allowed to hold the ladder; isn't this just as bad as climbing up yourself to fix the light?"

"The answer is No," said Leo. "This comes under the rubric of helping to preserve a man from injury. This is allowed."

"*Twenty dollars!*" said the booming voice on the left.

"Twenty dollars is bid!" cried Rabbi Lipsky joyously. "What is the name, please?"

"Samuelson—Ely Samuelson."

203

"Ah, Mr. *Samuelson!*" exclaimed Rabbi Lipsky with the joyous and flattering quaver that he reserved most often for weddings. "Mr. Samuelson is not a member of our congregation," he exclaimed to everybody; "he is a visitor from Providence, Rhode Island. His uncle, however, is our dear President, Mr. Mondschein; and I am sure that you all join with me in telling Mr. Samuelson that he can regard himself just as much at home in this congregation as in Providence, Rhode Island."

"I'll give just one more raise," said Brody quietly to us, letting us in, so to speak, on his method. "After such a build-up by the Rabbi, how can he get out of taking the bid? . . ."

"Twenty-three dollars," he called out.

"Twenty-five!" said Mr. Samuelson, on the left.

"Good—take it!" said Brody, and turned around to us triumphantly.

"I bid them up all the way from four dollars to twenty-five!" he said boastfully. "After all, why shouldn't the money go to the synagogue?—it's a good cause. Have I been playing auction-pinochle for forty years for nothing?

"You see, you can always tell," he explained confidentially, "when you can bid them up and when there's nothing doing. A fine bid was seventeen-seventy-five—how could anyone refuse to go at least to eighteen? . . . But in pinochle, never say three-forty—always force them into it, and then drop your cards and say, '*Good, take it!*'

"Sometimes in a game," said Brody, "when I'm boosting them they have the idea that they're boosting me. That's where they're wrong."

The pinochle player of the Lord.

The Cantor and his choir of black-robed boys began to gather at the reading table under the light which had been repaired (but which now shone dimly in the brightening air). Several of the young sopranos were downstairs in the cellar, playing punchball, and their piercing cries could be heard in the distance from time to time.

At last, after its triumphant progress from the rear of the synagogue across the entire congregation to us in the

front, the joke arrived at our bench; but it proved to be a
hoary jest.

A sudden idea struck me. "Look here, Brody," I said to
the pinochle player, "supposing the Rabbi decided to
knock it down to *both* of you, having both of you up to
grasp the cord to open the curtain—then where'd you be?"

"It wouldn't happen," said Brody, turning pale.

The Cantor, who had a white hat with a pom-pom, now
stood up on a stool to tower, with his pom-pom, above the
boys; for unfortunately, though he was very broad-
shouldered and had a powerful black beard and a bass
voice, he was only five feet high. Like Ulysses, "when he
was seated he looked imposing, but when he rose to his
feet you saw that he was of small stature." From the top of
a stool he dominated the scene, and often, holding a long
note as if rapt, he would dart a sidewise and upward glance
at the women's gallery. He smote the table with his little
tuning-fork and held the sound to his ear, while the vibra-
tion welled out amongst us with the unpleasant ring of
pure, colorless music. The choir, catching the note, sang a
C-minor chord.

"Will the congregation please rise," said Rabbi Lipsky,
"for the repetition of the Amidah and the singing of *Tefilas
Tal*? Mr. Samuelson, will you please come up and stand
alongside me on the platform, so that everybody can see
you?"

"Blessed art Thou, O Lord, our God and God of our
fathers—" began the Cantor in a deep voice, accompanied
by a humming continuo of the boys.

The numerous and progressing chords of the choir and
the flowing line of the Cantor's baritone voice had pene-
trated every corner, like the sun.

While Brody looked on with an ecstatic and self-pleased
smile, Mr. Samuelson smartly pulled the cord of the curtain over the Ark and disclosed the ranks of a dozen scrolls
of the Law, dressed in white silk and wearing silver
crowns.

The congregation rose.

"Our God and God of our fathers, grant Dew!—" said
every one.

THE BREAK-UP OF OUR CAMP

"Grant dew, to quench the thirst of Thy land–" sang the Cantor, with no accompaniment.

> *"In holy joy, sprinkle Thy blessings*
> *on us–*
> *With a quantity of wine and corn*
> *Establish the city of Thy desire!"*

—"with dew!" shouted everyone, while the choir gave voice to a loud pæan.

The thunderstorm had moderated to a light, steady rain that could be heard tapping on the skylight and flowing down all the drains. Meanwhile the atmosphere had become progressively brighter, till the electric light shone dim and pale.

There were many stanzas to the poem, each comparing, in some trope or other, the state of the Jewish people in exile to that of a land thirsting and without water.

"With dew and contentment fill our barns—" sang the Singer of this agricultural people, accompanied by the continuo of the choir.

> *"Renew our days as of old–*
> *Beloved, according to Thy valuation uplift our name–*
> *make us like a garden well-watered–"*

"B'tal!" shouted all.
" . . . with Dew!"

New York City
1935

206

The Break-Up of
Our Camp
(1935)

*When the ice is soft enough to break thru and fall in,
the water isn't so cold as it might have been.*

I: The Canoeist

In mid-lake, Armand, in his canoe, woke to strains of singing. He had drowsed, the paddle loose in his hand; now his eyes opened wide. Darkness had settled on the water, and on the shore, whence came the gusts of music, was a row of starry fires. The young Canadian felt wide awake, but increasingly so continually, so that it was certain he was in no normal mood. Pointing his prow toward the camp fires, he paddled rapidly ashore.

Here I, patrolling the waterfront, stood waiting for him. "What are these fires and singing?" he asked in a strong French-Canadian accent. "This is Camp Katonah, a summer camp for Jewish boys," I answered in French; "who are you?"—flashing a light upon him—for we did not approve of strangers coming into our camp, especially after dark. At the same time, he was a traveller, to whom we owed hospitality. In the circular light he crouched thin and red, and somewhat intimidated. He explained that he was from St. Pierre, Province of Quebec, and was paddling to Burlington. "I dozed off," said he, "and I awoke and saw your fires on the shore."

"Any other night," I said, "all lights would have been out, but this is Wednesday camp-fire."

He opened his eyes wider still when twenty-five juniors rose to perform a swift dance among the fires.

"It must be dangerous on the lake at night," I thought. "This is like coming to a family-place," he thought.

There was a can of tea, and I offered him a dipperful.

"Roast us something to eat, Danny," I said to the tall boy who ran my switchboard backstage. (For I was the teacher of dramatics at this Jewish boys' camp on the shore of Lake Champlain.)

Singing began.

"In what language are they singing?" he asked with a frown.

"In Hebrew." It was the Zionist marching song, *V'im lo Achshav, Eimatai!*—"It means," I said,

> And if not now,
> When?

"That was what the old Rabbi said—" Then I saw how impossible it was, and even how absurd, to try to explain to this Canadian canoeist into what kind of world he had come. The song itself, a song of the East European Jews, was not in Hebrew alone, but in three languages, in Hebrew, Yiddish and Russian; how to explain it? What a curious, and even ridiculous thing for a hundred small boys to be singing, in northern Vermont, in Yiddish,

> Pioneers, quickly!
> pack up your packs,
> for the train is starting off—

"At the same time," I thought, ruffled (for no one likes to think that what he has grown used to is ridiculous), "any combination of circumstances would be equally improbable. What if they were singing in English—what if they were singing in Algonquin—beside the ancient lake." *Proschaiti psedruja!* the small boys now sang in Russian.

> Good-bye, comrades!—

Where were they all going to, sitting down?

The singing was rapid and smooth, had none of the wildness of the boys; they sang like a learned choir.

"What a peculiar place and what a peculiar crowd of people!" thought Armand, with a puzzled frown. He bit

into the steak sandwich; the meat was black and tender
with a sprinkle of salt on it. "I like it here" he thought.
"Everybody is singing and eating." The more he looked
about, the more mystified he became, and at the same
time the more he seemed to become wide awake under the
variety of novel impressions—becoming mystified and
seeming to become wide awake were to him the same.
"Your camp is a regular wonder box," he said.

"I'll show you around," I said, already a little annoyed,
for I absolutely did not approve of strangers appearing out
of the night to call our camp a wonder box. (His phrase
nevertheless, was not so very different from my own, that
"any combination would be equally improbable.")
"Danny," I directed "watch the shore so nobody falls in
and drowns."—"This waterfront is very dangerous; we
have to keep a strict guard."

"My boat?" said the Kanuck discreetly. "I shouldn't like
to be stranded here forever," he smiled broadly. ("Is that
so?" I thought.)

"Put Armand's boat with the rest of the canoes."

We went along Company Street, preceded by the circle
of my flashlight. On either side stood the ghostly tentalows with white canvas walls, and as we withdrew
further from the singing and the fires, the quiet of the
night and the sounds of insects spread round us. "Is this
where you all sleep?" asked Armand, but this innocent
question made me very cross. "Where do you think we
sleep, in the trees?" My crossness was apparently due to
his asking obvious questions, questions that seemed to me
obvious, as if he were a tourist and we were exotic, but the
deeper reason of my antipathy to him, to that stranger
asking questions not out of need but out of curiosity—it
was only in the course of time that I came to be aware of
this, my own disgust, and boredom, with our camp. *"Go
away, canoeist, before you spend one night here!"* I ought
to have warned him. "How many sleep in each bunk?" he
asked. "Five. Isn't that a good number?" said I aggres-
sively.

"What is your job here, you seem to give orders?"

"I put on the plays. Here is my theater."

211

I led the way inside and, leaving the canoeist in the darkness among the seats, I leaped on to the stage and threw on the green borders and foots.

Immersed in this pea-soup gloom and beholding me, a ghastly spook, on the stage, Armand faltered and lost color. At which, in momentary triumph, I flashed my most powerful spot full in his eyes; he recoiled and spoke a cry.

"Where am I?" he cried, like one just awakened.

Slowly I filtered the atmosphere away from the green until stage and theater were bathed in deep rose—wasting time while an idea that had struck me could become formed; then I left the stage white and bright. I was content. For several days I had been thinking what play to give as the last of the summer; and now, beholding the stranger in the white spot in the gloom, I decided on *Macbeth*, in a version for my boys. Like the ghost of Banquo come to the feast, he stood among the empty seats.

He climbed onto the stage and began to manipulate the switchboard, which I perfunctorily demonstrated. He was extremely childlike; he could not conceal his pleasure at the number of toys backstage. His lips revealed his gums in a wide grin as the wonder box proved more and more, extraordinarily, productive. Happening on the siren, he tirelessly sent lugubrious howls into the silent night.

"Make a storm of lightning and thunder," I said. He sent a howl of wind through the theater and up my spine, while the bluewhite tops of the cyclorama flickered on and off. In time to the lightning, I punched a metal sheet—*Double! double! toil and trouble!*

"I seem to have been here all summer!" thought Armand, because he was engaged in a creative manual activity.

From down the lane, at the girls' camp, as if in answer to our racket, came the strains of taps.

"Let's go up to the Lodge; they've put them to bed over in the girls' camp."

"Oh! are there girls, too?" said the Canadian ecstatically.

I looked sharply at him—he was wearing white duck

trousers over a bathing suit of Canadian red. "Don't you think you could put on a shirt or sweater—" I started to say crossly—"skip it," I said.

Now, just as we were mounting the hill to the Lodge, the full moon, whose light from behind the low hills had been more and more strongly irradiating the eastern sky, rose large and yellow; and, as if creating them from nothing, its light brought into vivid view both the boys' camp and the girls' camp across the covered bridge: the parallel rows of the boys' tentalows below, like an equal-sign, and across the face of the hill the arc of the girls' houses, where now everybody was asleep, and the dying fires along the shore, each circled by seated boys; and a quarter of a mile away, shining in the milky light (for each moment that we watched its effects the moonlight became whiter and brighter), were the mysterious markings of tennis courts and a baseball diamond, and farther on still, a stony meadow with the blots of animals.

"It would take a whole summer to get to know these large grounds," said Armand in a flat voice. (At this moment he decided not to paddle off on the following morning before breakfast.)

The moon rose high and bright. Out of the covered bridge, from the girls' camp, came three young women, my girl Maitabel, Louise, the dancing counsellor, and Naomi. These three came noisily laughing through the bridge. When they saw Armand they stopped short.

"This is Armand," I said; "he's paddling down to Burlington."

"Hello, Almonds," said Louise.

"Look," I said in Yiddish, "will you take away this mad dog before I shoot it?"

"O.K., let's go to town, *Almonds!*" cried Louise, thinking that she sized up the situation in her way. She clung to his arm. "Can you wrestle?" she said.

??"Why shouldn't I stay here for a few days?" thought Armand, bewildered and happy. "They all seem to like me, except that dramatics teacher, who obviously doesn't know what he likes (I've met that type before). I have never in my life fallen into such a curious place. They have no manners and talk over one's head in an incomprehensible language; at the same time I feel at home, as if I had been staying here all summer, though everything is strange and new; I seem to recognize everyone, rather than to be seeing them for the first time. I wonder if I am really so wide awake as I imagine, and not floating, drowsy, in the middle of the lake."

Inside the Lodge, a radio was playing

You're the tops, you're molasses candy,
You're the tops, you're Mahatma Gandhi—

and they dragged him off to dance.

"Good-bye, Armand," I said, holding out my hand, "I probably won't see you again; you'll be gone in the morning before we get up."

2.

When I came into the mess hall next morning for breakfast, there, at the main table, *in my place*, at the right hand of the head counsellor Dave Werner, and next to Dr. Kleinberg, sat Armand, grinning broadly with his brown face and eating spoonfuls of cornflakes. Seeing me enter, he did not stop eating but waved a greeting with his left hand.

"Look," said Danny, who came in with me, "there is Armand the canoeist."

"For Christ's sake, Werner," I said in Yiddish, "what is this *shaegitz* doing here in my seat? Don't you see that now we'll never be rid of him?"

At this main table we were at the heart of our camp. Behind, one could hear the conversation of the girls' dining room. Ahead, through the windows, spread the whispering lake. Out of the corner of my left eye I could see sullen Winkie, who did not yet know—but I knew—that he was going to be Macbeth.

"He claims that the water is too rough for sailing," said Dave, "and he won't leave till this afternoon."

"Too *rough!*"

214

The Canoeist

"I was just telling Matt," he explained to Armand in English, "that you were going to be with us till this afternoon." The Canadian smiled, and I gave him a hard look.

"*Attention, everybody!*" proclaimed Dave, getting to his feet and emitting a shriek of his whistle, so that the clamor of the mess hall fell an octave. "I want to introduce Almonds, the Kanuck. Almonds is on a canoe trip from St. Pierre to Burlington, down the St. Lawrence River and down Lake Champlain, a distance of two hundred and fifty miles. Almonds will stay with us all this morning and he will be glad to give any and all a lesson in sailing. *Give him a big hand, everybody!*"

Armand rose to his feet amid thunderous applause.

"Rabosai," said an authoritative voice: "Let us say Grace."

The noise hushed and Armand looked about while a voice began a prayer in a foreign language. . . .

The surface of the lake was blue and glassy, crossed once in a while by a fan of quarter-inch ripples glittering in the sunlight. Armand did not find enough breeze to put up his lateen-rig to give the instruction in sailing; instead he performed canoe tricks, of which he had a large repertory. He could make a canoe stand almost on end, or make it roll over without shipping water—while the excited Senior boys splashed round him and climbed on and off. He introduced to our camp the sport of canoe-jousting with brooms, which has since become a popular tournament amongst us with a bronze medal for the champion (so that in this particular, Armand played the role of the Culture Hero who came from afar and founded the institution). Finally, seeing our large pink war canoe, twenty feet long and meant for eight paddlers, he decided to perform also on this instrument and launched the boat singlehanded into the open; but it was too heavy for him—a gust of wind, the single gust of the morning, swung the nose around into the pier and broke the canoe's back.

"Very good!" I said to Dave.

"You were the one who brought him here, you with your lightning and your wind-machine," said Dave, reddening.

"Each one of us, at first, treats him hospitably; but there

are so many of us that he will keep getting the idea of a continued welcome. Mark my word, he'll be here tomorrow morning, too."

"What do you advise me to do?"

"The fact is," I said, "he likes it here, where, though everything is strange and new, he feels as though he has been all summer."

The eleven-year-old Intermediates were the next group to meet Armand and make him feel at home. (Thus he was welcomed by one after another of us, first by myself, then by Louise, then by the head counsellor, then by the camp as a whole, then by the senior boys, then by the inters. . . .) "Almonds, tell us how you shot the rapids!" the kids cried in their high voices, crowding round him—it was perhaps something he had promised earlier in the morning, and now for an instant, forgetting the sport to which they were bound, in their grey sweaters they came crowding round him in his flaming red and white, forming a flower. "Tonight after supper—" said Armand, laughing, trying to break loose. "O.K.!"—and they ran off to a new sport, forgetting all about him and his promise; but to Armand it now seemed that he was welcome in the evening, too, and would see the camp fires actually being lighted, not merely burning from afar. But he did not know that there were camp fires only on Wednesday nights.

Bernard, who was five, the smallest child in our camp, came running to the Canadian and said: "Uncle Almonds! piggy-back me to the wash-house!"

In the afternoon, Louise, the dancing counsellor, said to me grimly: "Please, you'll have to tell that nut you brought around not to follow me or I'm going to crack him. He wants to wrastle all the time."

I grinned at her uncertainly. By this time I was no longer cross at the coming of Armand, but ill at ease, as if I sensed, yet could not see, a bad ending in it for myself.

"He comes when I'm trying to teach a class and the girls aren't dressed."

"You oughtn't to have given him such a good time last night, and he wouldn't be looking for more."

"I ! You were the one who began it. He says that you

took him into your theater and flashed the lights in his eyes."

"Yes, I did—and he cried out."

"What did he cry out?" she said (I thought).

"I could not understand the word."

"You told me he was going away in the morning," said Louise, "or there were things I wouldn't have let him get away with. There's a special way of acting toward a person who is staying for only one night and we're never going to see him again."

"If our camp were not only for the summer, and we ever expected to see each other again," I faltered—and the tears began to flood my eyes—*"we, too, should behave more circumspectly. But there is no time."*

It seemed as if this canoeist, who had paddled in out of the night, seeing our fires from mid-lake and hearing strains of singing, had been around all summer. When he walked down Company Street between the rows of tent-alows, and could look through the wire-screen walls at the activity within each one, the naked boys with towels around their shoulders and the counsellor stealing chocolates from a trunk, he was a familiar figure, greeted by each one he passed, by the little boys and the big boys and the young men, with an off-hand nod or a strained smile, or by some such phrase as "Hey hey!" or "Nice going, Admiral!" or "whad'ye say?"—to all of which he replied with a flashing smile and a characteristic wave of the right arm bent at the elbow.

3.

Yet by the next morning he was frozen out; and when he walked down the windy street, for it proved to be a wretched day, every head turned slightly away, not more than a few degrees, but just so no one would be obliged to notice him. Twenty times, amid the gusts of wind, he half raised his arm and the smile decayed on his lips. The animosity against the stranger, which I, like a delicate barometer, had felt almost at once, had reached its full storm; and there were many ways in which it broke forth that I shall not set down because I want to hasten on to the end. The small boys, who were as sensitive to what their counsellors did not express as they were disobedient to what they did, peered with fright at Armand out of the corners of their eyes, so that the whites of their eyes showed like the under-sides of leaves before a rainstorm. Among all these, unable to find anyone to talk to, Armand walked across the empty athletic fields, and the more woebegone he looked the less willing was anyone to notice him. But I, who could rejoice in the general acceptance of my own dislike—and was this not what I desired?—instead found myself embarrassed; I could not bear to see him loitering on the baseball diamond (amid the first drops of rain) with no one to talk to—yet I could watch nothing else. "I wish he would finally go away; hasn't he had enough!" I thought—and I shadowed him at a distance from place to place, hiding behind a tree, so he would not see me.

Were it not for the troubled weather, he would have left already. The wind, slowly accelerating through the night and morning, had attained a formidable speed, tearing to shreds the canvas doors of the tentalows and whipping up foam of the lake into rapid bullets against our faces. The tossing sea of Champlain was white and black, yet despite the high wind the cloudy ceiling lowered so heavily that nothing seemed to move.

Late in the afternoon, far out on the pier's end, amid the whitecaps, Armand ate his luncheon, while I, from the porch of the theater, unable not to watch him, looked on.

Suddenly turning around, he caught my eye, and I was obliged to come down to him on the pier.

"I am afraid that I have overstayed my welcome," he said.

"You aren't going to go away!" I cried in anxiety.

"If you think it isn't lonely, paddling day and night down the St. Lawrence River and in this ocean!" he said, indicating with a brusque gesture the tossing lake. "I thought that by luck I had come amongst dozens of friends and pretty girls. Do you know that for a moment yesterday

218

The Canoeist

I was about to ask to remain here the rest of the summer as the boating counsellor? This is a good example of how different the situation can really be from how we momentarily happen to estimate it."

"We have a boating counsellor; my friend, Mike," I said.

"Up to a certain point—" said Armand, "up to a certain point from the time I awoke and heard the singing and saw the fires on the shore—up to a certain point from that time it kept seeming that I had come to a place that would take all summer to get used to and fully to enjoy. Then!— without any real reason for the change, mind you, for your camp is well enough in its way—all this was impossible, inconceivable. . . . The fact is," he said cheerily and broke into a quiet smile, "beyond a certain point your camp leaves me cold!"

"From the very beginning you didn't want to be stranded here," I said.

"After all, those friends and those girls—" he said with a grin.

"They're well enough in their way," I said angrily.

"Well, good-bye, Mathew, and thanks for everything," said Armand, holding out his hand. "Tell Dave thanks for me, and give my love to Louise."

A few large drops of rain now began to fall and I left him on the pier. Furthermore, it was time for Sabbath evening services, to be held in the theater, because of the weather, and not outdoors as usual.

I was in a black rage. It was very well for *him* to talk cheerily about the camp leaving him cold, but *I* had to stay on in it! I scowled at the ninety boys and the eighty girls, and at the counsellors of whom I had seen too much, collecting in the theater where I had staged too many plays, for a prayer service that I had said too often. Up to a certain point! Beyond a certain point!

"Look!" pointed Danny, standing at the window with his legs apart, "there goes your Canadian paddling away."

I peered through the square, dusty window pane, into the rain that was now coming down forcibly, the drops splashing on the unquiet surface of Champlain; and there, struggling in the teeth of the south wind, his double-

219

paddle rising and falling courageously on either side, rode Armand, forced back three-quarters of a length for every length of advance. A bolt of orange lightning split the sky, silhouetting the figure of the canoeist with a brilliant glow around his outline. (Three or four of the electric lamps in the theater went dim and dark.) "I pity him," I thought, "if he intends to be out all night on that sea." But the truth was that I did not pity him at all, but envied him, because he was going away.

Behind me, as I stood looking out of the window, the collected camp broke into that marching song, *V'im lo Achshav, Eimatai?* and this question,

> And if not now,
> *when?*
> And if not now,
> WHEN?—

this question broke in so hard in my depression that I had to lean with my hand against the window frame, not to fall.

> Pioneers quickly! pioneers surely!
> ... the train is starting off.

I felt ashamed, standing with my back to the others and my eyes flooded with tears that at the slightest shock would begin coursing down my cheeks; yet this extraordinary uneasiness meant, I knew from experience, that I was in the presence of what I should do well to disregard not lightly.

II: The Break-Up of Camp

The deeper sinks the sun, the longer grow the shadows.
—Nietzsche
The owl Minerva flies at dusk.
—Hegel

I.

Groggy with the lights and cues, I stumbled out the back door of my theater, gulping in the air. The sun setting, red and flat, called attention to itself. The shouting of the kids was retreating up the hill. The lake had begun to kick up.

Out on the pier, Mike was gesticulating to two kids to bring a canoe in. When they got close enough to clamber up, he beat them on the head. With a great heave, he lifted the boat onto the dock and drove his heel through the belly of it. This scene, this action of my mild friend, was so unbelievable that I observed it with simple curiosity. The feat of strength was such as persons perform when they become heroic in an emergency. The pink war-canoe was already lying with its back broken on the rocks, in the waning light, like another stage-property of the same fiction.

At supper the racket was extraordinary. The fourteen tables raged like games. I thought that it was always like this, that it was I myself—no longer occupied with the old show and not yet preoccupied with the next—who was suddenly attending to it for the first time: the cheering and snatches of song, punctuated once a meal by the terror of a falling tray of dishes. But there was an extra energy, in each bang on the table, and as if the tray had been not dropped but flung down; there were barbarous quarter-intervals in the tunes, as if all these booming boys, well-behaved Jews from Brooklyn and Montreal, had forgotten the thousands of years of civil culture.

The disorder became systematic. A counsellor began to call at the top of his lungs whatever popped into his empty head. It was of course Ostoric, the repulsive counsellor of arts-and-crafts.

Munching a roll, he approached my table. "Marvelous show, Matt!" he cried. "You done a wonderful job! The fire under the cauldron was—ah!" he kissed his fingertips.

I stared at him in absolute stupefaction. This was the character who had been hired (to be sure, he hadn't been paid) to *help* me backstage, with the properties; and never once had he driven a nail or laid a brushstroke—but my lads and I, we did it all. And I was resentful by disposition—

"*Keep* your hands off!" I warned; I was afraid that he would touch me.

"Three big cheers for Uncle Matt!" cried Huey Ostoric. "Rah! Rah! *Rah!*" And they cheered.

The color left my face. We were accustomed, in our close society, to cheer each other, to cheer each other on a little, to cheer each other up a little. These loud cheers would almost have repaid me for the whole season, if I did not hold back my answering gratitude.

The "whole" season? What had I recognized at last?

Beginning quietly in a corner, then taking fire and spreading everywhere in chorus, a well known song swept away everything else, all cheers and congratulations:

> Three more days of vacation!
> Off to the railway station!
> Back to civilization!

So.

As for me, it was my last little show and I no longer had any function at this place. For me too this stripped away a mask and put on everything a different face. "Mike! Harry!" I shouted across the dining-room to my friends.

The Break-Up of Camp

"*Wait* for me outside."

"Rah! Rah! *Rah!* Zuppy!"

"Let us say Grace," said an authoritative voice, and there was a pause of silence (not yet to be disturbed by the mere break-up of our camp).

> *Rabosai n'vorech,*
> *y'hi shem adonai m'vorach me-ato v'ad olam*

—"May the name of the Lord be blest from this time and forever."

But even while they were saying the prayer, there was a curious pantomime framed in the window. Mr. T., the owner, was nervously roping a trunk onto the back of his car. "Good bye, boys!" he shouted suddenly, and climbed in and drove off, and his lights were eclipsed in the dark.

"Where in hell does that mad dog think *he's* going?" cried Dave, the head-counsellor.

Ostoric laughed loudly.

Still we looked thru the window, at the untouchable reality in its frame. Two sheriffs in starred vests drove up, to attach the person of Ben Tumpowski for debt.

The prayer ended: "Blessed art Thou, Lord, who nourishest the world."

The sheriffs hung around, as if they expected him to come back. Ostoric said, "There's no use waiting, he's not going to come back."

I therefore went down to my theater, because it was the last summer. I turned the stage-lights on full, as if for rehearsal, but I sat, where I had never sat, on a wooden chair in the middle of the vacant stage. Amid the tag ends of the final scene of our childish version of the great melodrama—the branches and saplings, already drooping, of Birnam Forest, and the red tissue-paper uniforms of Malcolm's soldiers torn to bits. The broken end of string of the Dagger Scene dangled near my nose—loose, motionless, as if no one had walked on this stage for a hundred years, since the days of Edmund Kean. I fell to thinking, without thinking, of many performances, of many

223

wonderful and famous performances. One of the footlights brightened and went dark, and called me back.

All that summer I had wanted to get away from this boring place and these child-plays that no longer fitted me, and now I had what I most desired.

There was a sound behind me. I wheeled round, half out of the chair, and caught two kids fiddling with the door-latch. They froze fast, crouching, and I half out of the chair, looking across my shoulder—like a scene from a play rehearsed to its innermost reality, until it passed over into reality; like the reality, too precisely adapted to the sentimental circumstances, till it became merely a play. The two kids froze, an arm half-lifted,

a hand outstretched, about to grasp,

and I watched them out the corner of my eye, the broken string dangling, as if (but it was indeed the case!) this moment were the end result of the long process of time.

"Mad dogs! where in hell do you think *you're* going?"—They were Ottawa Red and Ba Ba of Manhasset, two of my best.

"We needed rope to tie up our trunks," said Ba Ba.

"Who said you could take it?"

"Uncle Matt said we could go backstage and take it," he lied mechanically to my face.

"You may take whatever you need tomorrow morning," I said in a voice that surprised me by its tiredness.

The two made no offer to drop the rope they were carrying, but they crossed and stood in front of me.

"Well, are you sorry the camp is over?" I asked.

"What I remember *best*," cried Ba Ba passionately, "is Almonds the canoe-man paddling off in the lightning!"

"They never fished up his drownded body!" said Red.

"Sonny saw his speerit over in the girl's camp."

"Every Friday at services he paddles it again and again."

"Ke-ram! he smashed the war-canoe."

"An' he's the one that breaks the other boats!"

They turned to go.

"*What* was that?"—I cried out with lively interest, and

224

this was my fatal mistake; for I betrayed myself into an interest that was out of season; and I clutched at the greatest thing, that I wanted most, the social legend, when the time for plays was past. *"Who* made it up? *Why* didn't he tell me?

"I am in charge of the stories," I shouted, and they left.

Bitterly I turned to taking out the electric lights.

The wind meantime, that had begun to rise earlier in the evening, was howling by at thirty miles. As I came outside I was knocked off the steps and my flashlight lay in grass. The canvas doors of the tentalows were torn to rags, and they flapped in the wind. It was near freezing.

Since no one else seemed to be on duty (it was in fact my night of duty), I made the rounds among the younger ones, from bunk to bunk, flashing a light on every bed, restoring the blankets that had been kicked off; and the kids lay there half-naked, shivering in their sleep, under the round beam.

2.

In the fresh sunlight there was a masquerade or carnival. On Company Street, some of the boys were parading city-clothes, other went quite naked. Some of the naked boys had on ornamental hats and were carrying tin swords from the treasury of the rifled theater.

The boy most disguised of all was our musical pitcher, Arky:

> Sacred Arky, angelically long,
> pitcher of a floater and a dark one,
> eerie flautist: Ophanim on high
> and the great Seraphim responsively
> emit cries: of thy Creator saying
> "Holy holy holy
> all the earth is full of glory!"

—this Arky appeared for the first time all summer in his college baseball-suit, as if he were a—college ball-player.

225

It blew *Fall-in-for-Inspection*, but no one paid any attention to this ludicrous command.

Now was evident the form of the confusion: Decadence, the accelerating dissolution of the parts of an organism when once the unifying soul has perished. Sports and varieties appeared. There were spontaneous powerful social combinations, enduring for two hours, of members loosed from their conventional associations, finding often more natural associations (but not yet the fatal natural associations of Brooklyn and Montreal). Some became celebrities, whom no one had ever seen. Last day friendships were sealed that have survived the years, for they sprang from instinct. And old half-forgotten practical jokes and nick-names from the ancient history, like Mr. T's *Huffski Puffski Ben Tumpowski*—these were turned up in the universal overturn, and they shone brilliantly for a moment, like first-water jewels.

But Mike and Harry and I, friends from before we ever came to this place, were not *in* it, in the general breakdown. We were standing on the sidelines.

"No," said Harry, "this is precisely *being* in it. There are always the three witches. Now is the day when we have nothing else to do. Our job is to see that nobody gets physically hurt."

"My conscience is clear," said Mike. "I kicked in the last of the boats."

But I said, "Listen, do you know the kids have a legend? Do you remember Almonds?—" For I was not reconciled to it, just as by disposition my childish heart would never be reconciled to anything. I would not admit the salient reality till the moment after, turning to each blow *after* it had struck. Yet at the same time (therefore) I kept repeating to myself my little motto: *If not now, when!*

Ostoric had on a red bandana and was carrying a bowie-knife unsheathed. He was contriving to look like a pirate. The idea of a grown-up being in it, at this level, aroused in us a deep disgust. Yet the truth was that he was not contriving anything; he looked just as he had always looked; he had always worn a red bandana and carried a bowie-knife unsheathed, and tried to look like a pirate.

The Break-Up of Camp

They began to march in step, up the hill to breakfast, a step satirically heavy, as soldiers use on furlough. *One* two *three* four; and to the rhythm of old slogans of the Color War: *White* will *Fight! Blues* can't *Lose! White! Fight! Blues! Lose!* . . . The last variant caught fire, and from now on could be heard, all day, in every distance, this lugubrious wailing: *Mad! Dogs! Blues!* let *Loose!* The first part they barked, the second they howled. So when our cities succumb at last (it seems soon) to their catastrophe, the wolves will come back and prowl, and howl.

I suspiciously did not touch the food. There were announcements about the trunks: how they were to be labeled, when they were to be ready for inspection. These announcements were official recognition, on the part of the head-counsellor himself, that the camp was *over*, virtually over. But the announcements should have been made by Mr. T., the colossus who bestrode the gap between the cities and our camp. Who was Dave Werner to make such announcements, as did not concern the shore, or the Teams, or the calls to my rehearsals? His voice lacked authority. They howled while he talked—*Blues! Loooooose!* He dissolved the camp, but he did not represent the Fathers: no one accepted this idea. The only existing world was the dissolving one, and *Blues! Loose!* and *Huffski Puffski* were the outcries of this dissolving world. "We want Huffski Puffski!" "Fuffski Huffski Puffski!"

"Why aren't you eating?" said Harry angrily.

"I'm not eating," I said.

"You don't have any *evidence* anything is spoilt, do you? Then shut up."

"Not eating," I said.

I took some eggs. They were not poison.

"This is the day to live *through*," said Mike, who used to be a boatman.

"Oh Christ, why should *I* be the goat!" cried Harry bitterly—for he was responsible for the smallest ones.

—Tomorrow! tomorrow when they would be waiting around, and watching the trunks piled into the truck, and the Montreallers already gone; regarding the grounds as no longer their own, hesitating to suggest a set of tennis—then the campers would become resigned to the fact that the summer was over, we'd never return to this place; then they'd feel bad and burst into tears. But today was part of the life of our camp, yes! (this is what our camp was worth) the best part of all!

There is a famous saying: When rape is inevitable, relax and enjoy it.

"Mad! Dogs!" I barked.

But it was melancholy to see, on the far side of the field, vanishing into the woods, Harry and his tiny train, off on a hike, out of harm's way.

3.

Dave Werner, the head-counsellor and brother of my pal Husky, caught up to me on the way out.

"You're staying over with us, aren't you, Matt?" he asked.

"Over?"

"Over the week-end."

"Staying?"—I stared at him.

"Yes, ten or eleven of us are staying. We're counting on you," he said.

"No, I'm not staying," I said. "What the devil does he want?" I thought. "Why ten or eleven?"

"Some of the girls are staying," he said, aggrieved. "I think Maitabel is staying."

"No, I'm not staying," I said.

"They'll all be gone," he said.

4.

The masquerade was wearing off. It was becoming nature. Far across the baseball field Harry and his tiny train were vanishing among the trees.

I joined Mike, going down to the shore. It did not seem to me that I had any function in this place.

The Break-Up of Camp

On our way down, a dark kid of fourteen passed us, coming up. "Hi, Mike, Matt," he mumbled, hurrying past.

"Hey! mad dog! where in hell do you think *you're* going? out of bounds!"

"Mr. T. sent for me," he lied.

We let him go. On all sides the campers were streaming past, howling their howl. I had the impression that, going downhill, one was lapsing into confusion. But if one went uphill—in the direction that the dark boy had taken—the matter would become clear. . . . I stopped hard in my tracks.

"*Who is he?*"

"Who?"

"The dark one who went up, who lied to us?"

"Oh. Bayer. Julie Bayer. Free-style medal, junior division."

"*Has he been around all summer?*"

"For years. He's one of the Canucks. They leave early in the morning."

We went out on the dock. The boatman was satisfied. The boats were beautifully decommissioned. So far as he was responsible, there was not a lethal weapon in existence.

"Look," I said, "you called him a 'mad dog' . . . "

"Who?"

"The boy—the one who went up. Before, I heard somebody else use that expression. Has that expression been common this summer? I'm interested in such things."

"*Common? . . .* Are you *well?*"

"Do you think he knew Mr. T. was gone, and that maybe we didn't know it?"

"He knew that we knew that he knew."

I faltered—"Don't—don't you think he's an interesting-looking boy?"

We went into my theater.

—Too late! too late! It was too late to stage the legend of Almonds the canoeist, to show the kids indeed—and this was my sense of my chief function as their counsellor—to show them that there is poetry, all the poetry that there is, in our common incidents; that the poetry springs from

229

their own fantasies and helps us live on a little, considering what our camp life was worth. Too late to stage the delicious little comedy of Mr. T., roping on the trunk and skipping out half a minute ahead of the sheriffs—his farewell gesture with the left hand, fingers outspread, as if to ward off the answering look. *Leaving the camp to us*, to ten or eleven—all the rest would be gone; was not this just the condition for a romantic comedy, genre of *Twelfth Night* or *As I Like It?*

But it was, is, too late to fall in love with the boy, myself, just because my world has fallen into chaos. Desperately longing for immortality.

I was painting my name in red on the back wall of the stage:

MATHEW WAS IN CHARGE
OF THE STORIES

1932 - 1933 - 1934 - 1935

"Fuffski Huffski Puffski!" said Mike, as if out of a dream. "Somebody is on the water!" he hissed, and rushed out.

Two hundred yards out, on the glassy lake, Red and Ba Ba were in a canoe settling up to the gunwale.

"Bring that boat in."

"We can't. It's full up."

The voices came thin and clear across the water, followed by the echo from the Cove, Full up! full up!

Bluuuuues! Snoooooze!

The two kids, splashing in the sunlight, swam slowly toward the shore.

5.

"We only went out to play Almonds. But he got mad and we sunk."

"Why should Almonds want to sink the boats?" I fished.

"He's mad, because we drove him away and he was drownded," said Ba Ba.

"No no, the opposite. He don't want us to stay here, he busts everything 'cause he's an anti-semite!"

The Lonely Stranger came by water out of the north,

230

looking to establish himself at some campfire or other, instead of wandering any more. Fighting for this happiness, as he regarded it, he became a demon of Persistence, wherever the slightest occasion offered.

We, however, took our situation for granted.

He happened to come to our camp on a special night, Campfire. We were off our guard and temporarily made him welcome. Then by his charms and stories he cast a brief spell over all, a spell that lasted for one night and one day. But how soon the true canoeist was revealed to us, trying to oust Mike, the waterman, and to become *too friendly* with the girls. The spell was broken and now, in great fear, we drew back from any contact with him. And while we of the camp went to our religious services, he had to paddle forth into the storm. He was drowned.

But his spirit, freed from the body but fixed by the longing that had governed him when alive, returned to haunt our camp. It appeared among the girls when they were stripping for gymnastic dances; it appeared to little Sonny Benjamin on the outer baseball diamond; it appeared to Matt backstage. But at the words *Ma Tovu*—"how goodly are thy tents, O Jacob!"—he had to paddle away again.

From camp-site to camp-site he went, this stranger, creating unease, discomfiture, dissatisfaction with our lot; causing doubt in the evidence of our senses, by preternatural pranks; spoiling present fun by alluring tales of *other* places. Woe to him who would be seduced! To be swallowed in the lake. Even while he paddled away he was heard to laugh out loud. Tho he was gone, he was not forgotten; no one in our camp would ever be satisfied. The Senior boys wanted to go on a long canoe-trip; the women counsellors did not respond to the men's caresses. Besides, he acted like a kind of *Polter Geist*, he tipped trays of dishes in the dining-room, and he stove in the canoes.

Also he was Kwee-Kwee, the Algonquin that first founded our camp, long ago.

He came from the water as a man is born; he departed on a journey as a man dies. And in-between—stopped at our camp for three days; just as we were all stopping, just as we were all stopping for three days; just as we were all stopping at our camp for three days.

But with an effort of the will I dismissed this afterthought for another time, and I went up the hill to look for Julie Bayer.

6.

The sheriffs were still hanging around. Farmers with starred vests, they were just the outposts of the reinvading countryside, with which, despite many efforts, we had never established an easy relation.

There was a new functionary in the office, a Burlington accountant going through the books (he would skin them all, natives and foreigners both). He and Miss K., the secretary, were in the office; and Ostoric! apparently in a position of confidential importance.

"Well, soon the Jew-camp won't be here any more," said one of the policemen affably.

—All the same! all the same! I persisted in telling myself, the interesting thing was not this concrete little drama at all, but the abstract phenomena of the break-up. That the slogans were corrupted, the morals relaxed; the rhythm of the songs syncopated and quarter-intervals permitted. The owner ran away, the scholars delved into the legends, archaic institutions had a vogue. The moralists prayed for the destruction of the instruments of production before some irreparable damage was done. . . . By such reflections I was carrying on the interior persuasion that would keep me here a few days longer, because of the boy (who would be gone). "I think it is nothing but rolling heels over head downhill into confusion," I told myself, "and all the while we are really recovering our natures, *instead of what we have!*"—when all the while we were passing into the Very Last Times, and the boy was the Angel of Death.

Miss K. came out of the office, shaking her head.

"I'm sorry for you boys," she said to Mike. "There's no

train-ticket for you and Matt. You'll have to get home the best way you can."

"Please. Just how do we get home the best way we can?"

"Don't shout at me. It's not my fault."

"What's Ostoric doing in the office?" I hissed.

"Why, he's Mr. T's nephew; they need him for information."

"*He's* got a ticket!" I groaned, not otherwise than Macduff in the play says, "*He* has no children."

"No, he hasn't got a ticket either."

"It's O.K., Mike. We'll stay here, you and I, with Dave and Husky Werner and the rest, and we can drive to New York in Dave's car."

"*Stay?!*"—Mike looked at me with genuine awe.

"So Ostoric is T's nephew. At last I have something impersonal against him."

7.

We spent the time with Julie Bayer and his pals. I had no function in this place, and now, as it turned out, I had of course the one function that alone I ever carry out: to love, and praise, and lose, and wail. (This function has gotten me little credit.)

With perfect confidence I dispossessed from their table the counsellor who did not realize—but who could fail to realize it?—that he had the four jewels of the world. But four, so bright! how had *I* failed to notice them together? (They had never gone together.)

In the afternoon a light rain began to fall, the elements themselves turning to my advantage, for it assured our proximity. On piled-up trunks we played chess and contract-bridge. Julie had a brilliant card-sense and made a psychic bid, but Tony excelled at chess. It was now too late, but I dressed Teddy to be Malcolm in the play. We went swimming in the drizzle. We drove an overturned canoe out into the lake, and Mike and I, treading water, watched the four bronzen figures clamber onto this whale, and dive.

233

And during this happiness there was death in my heart—such death as we erotics have—because it was the end. Nor am I ignorant of the truth that that happiness was only a cunning forepleasure for the releasing of that grief much sought for—yet still not deep enough for tears. That I praise the object in order to bewail myself. That I love and praise the future peace of the world in order to lament the present state of the world. Because we *still,* as Franz said, do not eat of the fruit of the Tree of Life; *therefore* we are not in Paradise.

The rain stopped, and gave way again to an unusual sunset. On the indigo clouds stood a granite rainbow, whose colors were

> turbilous, pearl, and dizimal,
> the colors of September brilliance

—urging us to hope forever (after our fashion).

In the west, the light fell down in striped rays, then when the fiery ball itself appeared, setting, half-set, the bronzen clouds in the pallid sky lay in horizontal tiers of cirrus to the pole.

Husky Werner confronted me.

"You *are* staying with us over the week-end."

"Why?" I looked at him frankly. "Why ten or eleven?"

"We need ten men for a *minyan* for Kaddish. Otherwise Dave and I can't stay."

The brothers had lost their mother, and now morning and evening they said the mourner's prayer—but in the orthodox rite ten men are needed to make a congregation of Jews.

Yes, I was going to stay because I had fallen in love with our dead camp. What luck!

What luck for *them!*

"If Maitabel stays, I'll stay," I said.

8. *Manifestations of the Very Last Times*

Even before breakfast one father, who had driven since midnight from Toronto, took away his son. This boy, C.

234

Haskell, is remarkable as the first one to have left.

The meal was eaten in silence and in great haste, by even the New Yorkers, who were not to leave till the evening. We who were *not* leaving found ourselves still eating, disregarded, when the others had walked out. It was remarkable that we, who were staying on and still possessed and used the property of our camp, no longer belonged to the actual world. In this apparent world, the dining room where the head-counsellor was making his announcements, we fitfully passed in and out of the actuality. Dave had many announcements to make, but when he was talking of anything connected with our camp, of where to pile the mattresses or where to return the equipment, it was as though he were not saying a word, his remarks vanished on the wind. But if he mentioned the word "train" or said "those leaving this morning," his speech glowed with communication; and when he read off the list of the Montreallers, the room was bathed in light. There was a suppressed excitement.

During the night, Ostoric had committed the expected act of vandalism, the excessive act that would survive as a memorial of, no doubt, our vices. On the side of the theater, in red letters a foot high, were painted the words

FUFFSKI YUFFSKI

Dave, who was responsible to Mr. T., flew into a towering rage about it. *"No one will be allowed to go home until the damage is paid for!"* he shouted; but this foolish boast vanished on the wind.

In a flash were made manifest the relations of brothers and cousins, of neighbors in the city who shared a common trunk but who all the summer had seemed barely acquainted. The older brother who had sedulously avoided the younger now sought him out to check the tag on a valise, and at once you could see that they were brothers, the family features, speech, manners. These were the relations among us not made in this camp, not made for the camp, but recollected in the crisis, for the crisis. The stress of the last day brought us to the recognition of the real families, and real natures, overlooked in the distractions of the life of our camp. The counsellor who had promised mama that he would carefully watch her boy, to see that he took a certain medicine, now frantically sought him out; but the boy had grown three inches and was unrecognizable—and the counsellor sweated with anxiety.

We others, I say, were rejected, or had elected ourselves to be out of it (it comes to the same thing). Yet we were assigned certain auxiliary roles *in* it, and we hung around. That is, we were in the position of devils. A devil is one who takes part without sharing the common aim and drift; he has his own aim.

My job was to certify the baggage-tags. And so I noticed that Tony was the cousin of Rosalie; but *she* was Maitabel's tent-mate. So! If Maitabel was staying because I was staying, I schemed, and then why not Rosalie, then there would be grounds for Tony also to stay; but Tony, Julie, etc. were the four bright jewels! To be sure it was not Tony that I was interested in.

But scheming was hopeless, for we who were not in it were not in touch with the real tendency; by contriving one could successfully be neither in it nor against it. We should have drifted off by ourselves, retired; this would have spared us plenty of resentment and impotent rage. But we hung around.

I followed Julie Bayer with my eyes, but without determination. There was no common ground to move across to him. Was I not waiting—to strike? To serve!

Unstudied textbooks were discovered in the cobwebs, and newspapers dated June 28 blew up and down Company Street.

They began to give away their belongings. Everything was considered too troublesome to pack at the last moment: sweaters, comic-books, candy-bars, the things that had been invaluable. Tony offered me a silver-plated pencil, which I accepted. "These gifts are souvenirs," I told myself. But they were not souvenirs, because, although the thought of home was so powerfully influencing them in camp, it was not the case that they thought of the

thought of camp influencing them at home. But we counsellors, who had no past, present or future, were eager to
have souvenirs.

Or again seeing their friends continually going away,
they were *binding* them by generous gifts.

Mike's opinion was: "No kid any longer has a bunk of
his own; no one has a responsibility for his belongings,
because it is only when one has a bunk of his own that he
has property. But the sweaters, the cameras, the blankets,
the tennis-racquets, the silver pencils, have all reverted
back to their parents. Some of them are going to be held
responsible for the things they are now giving away.—

"And there are also those!" he cried, "who all summer
have been *careless* with their belongings, and now they are
frantically searching for everything that has been lost,
because it is their fathers'."

9.

Well! in their desperate haste to be ready in time, so that
many of them omitted breakfast and were now hungry,
the Canucks now had time heavy on their hands. It was an
hour and a half to train time, and the New Yorkers had the
whole day before them. The truck did not come, the horn
did not blow. There spread an intolerable ennui.

Hereupon (it was the moment I had been waiting for) we
manfully took up again our duties as counsellors, and I set
to entertaining the Canadians with a great police-
investigation: *"Who painted the name on the theater?"*

"Maybe it was the Greek (the chef)?" I suggested. "He
had it in for Mr. T."

"No," said Tony. "How would he have known the name
Fuffski Yuffski?"

We stood in front of the red painting.

"It's good printing," said Irving. "Maybe Huey Ostoric
did it, he can print."

"Look, here is the paintcan underneath the steps."

(He had broken into my paint-box! It was *still* my
paint-box.)

237

"It's paint from the theater," cried Irving, the actor, excitedly. "He took it from behind the stage. I'll show you where."

We went backstage. (At this moment had not my camp again come to life?)

"What won't Dave Werner do to the character when we find him out!"

The chest had been jimmied open.

"Maybe I did it," I said. "I knew where the paints were."

(I did it. It was I that broke into my paint-box.)

"No, you would've had the keys."

"*What time is it?*" said Julie Bayer, asking with keenest cruelty the crucial question.

"*It's a quarter of ten,*" I said. I could not take my eyes from the face and body of Julie Bayer.

"No proof," Mike went on—even though some one had already asked the crucial question. "Maybe Matty didn't use the keys in order to divert suspicion. Isn't that possible?"

"No. Matt would have used the paint and put it back. I know him."

"That wouldn't help. Anybody'd know the paint came from here. Where else is there paint except backstage."

"There's paint in the arts-and-crafts shack," said Julie Bayer.

"Well, anyway, Huey Ostoric did do it," said Irving, " 'cause I saw him."

"Look, Tony," I said, "would you like to stay on a few days with your cousin Rosalie, if she says you may?"

"Yes!" he cried. "Gee! Maybe. I don't know. I'll ask her when she comes to say good-bye."

A horn sounded. A whistle blew. With a grinding of brakes the truck from the station came slowly down the hill.

10.

The Montreal boys climbed up into the truck. They were near to tears. Blinding tears came into the eyes of some of the smaller boys and they had to be helped up. At this moment, being hurried off, they saw in a flash that the summer was over; their vacation had come to an end while they were thinking of something else. *Once in, it was forbidden to get down from the truck.* So lively and promising now seemed the visible camp, spreading all ways in its almost limitless grounds. But what was the use of their staying if they were *not* staying?—

Still Rosalie did not come. Tony was near to tears, because she had promised—and he wanted to ask her the question. "Can't you find her?" he kept asking me. I ran through the covered bridge and searched the girls' camp. But I could not find her.

"Good bye, Red," said Ba Ba of Manhasset. And the next moment this truck rolled away, this truckload of Julie Bayer and his pals. This company of angels—but we were only flesh and blood.

I grew slowly into a cold fury: that all summer I had never known Julie Bayer and his pals (to be sure I had known them all summer; Julie had acted in the first show of the season). That never had we acted out the legend of Armand and his canoe. That they were taking away from me forever my beautiful stage and my actors with their ringing throats. That my time of life was slipping away, it was slipped away. And what was the use of this desert camp-site?

Rosalie came. "You might have been on time," I choked. "The kid was crying.

"All summer you have been late to everything! And now you have to be late to this!"

I spoke so bitterly that she soon began to cry.

"Why don't you 'phone the station and have him sent back here to spend the weekend with you at least? Or are you too selfish for that?"

She 'phoned, but the truck had not yet arrived.

Finally Tony called: No, he didn't want to return; since he'd come this far he might as well go all the way home. No, he was not unhappy, he said, and hung up.

When I heard this, that my last connection with Julie Bayer was cut off, I called Rosalie a damned bitch.

Worst of all was the prospect of the intolerable boredom of the rest of the day, of the rest of the days, until, as Dave had said it, "they would all be gone," but *all!*

That the dining-room was raging like a game, and framed in the window the owner roped on the trunk and fled, as the starred farmers arrived; and Arky was only a college ball-player, and the small ones were vanishing in the woods; streaming, streaming past us on the hill, and the two I caught out of the corner of my eye; the red letters forever on the wall and old newspapers blowing up the street and the truckload rolling away; all scenes of dissolving into reality, and the meaning of it escaping out behind the vanishing-point—

They say that at the point of death we re-live all our lives; but it is likely that even then we remember only such wishes as need no longer be repressed.

III: A Congregation of Jews

I.

The red light of the caboose rapidly diminished down the starlit tracks, carrying away the children of our camp. The Great Bear hung already a little northward, at the end of summer.

"Matty! Mike!" Husky, the brother of the head-counsellor, called us to the circle near the truck. Gathered in a close ring were we men who had stayed over: Aaron, Leo, Dave, Husky, Artie, Harry, eight of us, counting Mike and myself. (A ninth was Mr. Tobias, the silent partner, who had stayed to supervise the closing up, for Mr. T., the owner, had fled ahead of the sheriff.) And there also, standing uneasily behind Husky, as if looking to squeeze into the circle—but there was no place—was a tenth man, Ostoric, the despised counsellor of arts-and-crafts. We were all ex-counsellors now.

When Mike and I came, a place opened for us in the ring, but Ostoric still hovered outside.

"For Chrissake," said Husky in a tense voice, "how do we get rid of Ostoric? Nobody asked *him* to stay over."

The stout untidy fellow heard this, blanched, and stepped back away. And I saw it and broke up the group.

On the way back to camp, Husky rode in his car with his brother and Mr. Tobias and Sweeney the caretaker and Ella, who was Husky's girl. That car had five seats. Ostoric rode with us in the back of the truck, with Mike and me and Rosalie and Maitabel, and Harry and Leo and three other girls. I am telling all these numbers because it takes ten men to make a congregation of Jews, and Ostoric

241

happened to be the tenth man.

It was cold and we clung together for warmth, but Ostoric was offended and sat by himself sucking noisily on a dirty pipe. As we bounded along on the stony road, Rosalie began to moan the song-hits of that time, and we all, also Ostoric, joined in the joyous choruses. "Violate me in violet time in the vilest way that you can!" Mike sang in a surprisingly loud and happy voice; it did not occur to me that he was feverish.

Sweeney who had got back ahead of us, came running down the road with a lantern, shouting that the farmers were everywhere like cockroaches.

No one had remained behind to watch over the deserted camp.

"Half go over to the girls' camp and I'll go with the rest to the boys'. Pile up the cots and mattresses. I'll have the truck along. When we got here there was ten farmers with flashlights carrying things off."

We got down, numb with cold.

Ostoric did not join either group, but went into the lounge to go to bed. He had made up his mind to leave in the morning and he did not intend to be more helpful than was necessary.

In the girls' camp the flashlights went out. Some one could be heard moving in the underbrush. We were afraid. It was dark. The hundred thousand stars and the Milky Way shed no light below. Our flashlights cast a gray illumination on the street and on the bungalows. A mattress, a book, a hat-box, a paddle, vestiges of those who had left. On the backroad a car rattled off; there was a loud report.

We had left for our city; why should not the natives come back and take possession? But we few had unaccountably stayed on.

Some of us had allowed ourselves to be persuaded (and we persuaded the others) to make up the ten men needed by Dave and Husky for a *minyan*. But why were they staying? It is not in a particular place that one has to mourn a mother. We were staying by inertia—absence of another force.

242

A Congregation of Jews

The girls' trunks, the duffle-bags, the valises had not yet
gone to the station. All this was to be called for next day!
What a badly planned departure, when half the things
were left for the next day! The porches and rooms were
piled with baggage tagged and labeled to New York and
Montreal. And there was camp-property too.

We dragged out the fifty trunks from the black rooms,
and the flashlights held in our armpits cast swift shadows
on the walls. Bent under servile loads of bags and boxes,
because unwillingly and unreasonably. We sweated and
then stepped into the chilling night.

No. It is reasonable for one to do this if he is here, on
behalf of those who are not here.

At last came Sweeney with the truck, the headlights
shooting long beams on the towering piles of bedding and
baggage. He blew his bass horn more than once till we
collected.

"Listen, Husky," I said spitefully, "Mike and I expect a
lift to New York Monday in your car."

Husky stopped loading. "It's tough," he said, "you're
the fifth person asked me. There's only three empty seats,
so I sold them five dollars apiece to Aaron, Artie and Ella.
Why didn't you ask first?"

"*Sold?*" I cried bitterly; "why do you think Mike and I
stayed, but just so you and Dave could have a *minyan* to
say Kaddish?"

"Do you need any money?" said Husky.

"No, I don't need any money; no, I don't have any
money. Skip it," I said. The cry "Sold!" held a moment in
my ear; and then, suddenly, I began, intermittently, to
take pleasure in these things.

"Skip it," I said, "skip it."—As for me, when the day
came I was going to hitch-hike home, alone, taking my
chances on the road; and the prospect of it already gave me
almost perfect pleasure.

By midnight, two hours after our return from the station, where we had bade good bye forever to our camp,
everything was in safe-keeping. The baggage was piled to
the ceiling in the lobby; in the music-room, which was

243

furnished with wicker sofas and a broken piano, were the heaps of old mattresses.

We began to laugh boisterously. We laughed at the trunk we had stoven in. The thought of Ostoric, provoked by a gesture up the stairs, made us choke.

Halfway down the stairs, warily creeping, were a pair of fat little twins, Melvin and Phyllis Kalman. Their father had arranged to drive them to Montreal, but he had failed to appear; and we also forgot them when we went off to the station. They had run upstairs to hide and cried themselves to sleep. Now here their round red faces, roused by our thunderous laughter, shone like twin suns—and it was, of course, the peak of everything funny: that from this Adam and Eve our camp itself should spring alive again (such as it was).

The telephone rang.

It was Sam Tobias, the brother of our Mr. Tobias. He had been expected to arrive from Montreal early in the morning, but he was phoning to say that he could not make it. This news was indifferent to us—nevertheless we had counted on Sam Tobias of Montreal to be the tenth man.

Our friend Mike, meanwhile, was pale, and trembling in every limb. Maitabel and I went into the kitchen to brew him some tea.—

We turned away sick. The unpaid kitchen-help had left without cleaning up. The garbage of several days lay on the floor; the unwashed dishes in the sinks were clouded with flies that swarmed in our faces as we turned on the light. There was a fearful stink. On the stove stood a great cauldron of cocoa, made for the last meal, still tepid, but with a thick scum on the surface and many flies already drowned. In the adjoining dining-room the tables were not cleared. Pieces of lettuce lay on the floor, a tomato squashed under my heel. On each table a milk-jug was overturned and the streams of spilled milk, swelled by slow drippings from the oilcloths, united on the floor in a gray network. The flies awoke with a cry.

This camp, where we returned after the time for it, was spread like a dirty body, in the room of the hotel of passage, when the illusory desire is spent.

244

A Congregation of Jews

In the morning (a Friday) Mike was very ill. Despite the appalling color of our room, with its crimson and gold wallpaper and the bedstead of tarnished brass, he had about made up his mind to remain in bed. But the sunlight outside was warm and moist, and the wasps buzzed angrily against the windowpane trying to escape.

A call from below decided it. "Matty and Mike, downstairs please!" Downstairs our *presence* was needed to make up ten men for morning-prayers. Mike put on his shoes, for is it not comforting to be useful by one's mere presence?

We came into the music-room where the prayers were to be said amid the five heaps of mattresses. We made ourselves hats out of newspaper.

Dave called for Mr. Tobias on the porch. The old man, six and a half feet tall, his gaunt jaw covered with white stubble, came into the room cramming an old felt on his head.

Now as soon as he entered, being the tenth man, there was a congregation of Jews; and at once Aaron, who was our Reader, faced to the Orient and took up the hum, the mumble, in which the orthodox hasten thru their lengthy prayers: from time to time it is punctuated by a sentence clearly uttered, either by way of a period at the end of the psalm, or when the person praying is suddenly moved by the meaning of what he is saying and so pauses a moment, or when he pauses for breath.

These sounds of prayer rose from all corners of the mattress-filled room lit by the moist sunlight. Yet only four or five were praying. I allowed my eyes and my attention to wander from the blue-covered Siddur in my hand: to take in all ten of us, those praying and those not praying. Whatever unity there was present amongst us was not the unity of morning-prayers.

"Ribon kal ha'olamim," said Aaron.

"*Sovereign of all worlds! Not because of our righteous*

245

acts do we dare lay our supplication before Thee, but because of Thy great mercy . . . What is our life? what our piety? what our strength? what shall we say before Thee, O Lord our God and God of our fathers?"

Sprawled in a wicker chair, Mr. Tobias lit a cigar and was reading a week old copy of the Montreal *Star*.

Leo, Husky, Dave and Georgie had put on the phylacteries, the little boxes on the brow and biceps and the leather thong wound seven times around the forearm and thrice around the middle finger.

Artie, at the piano, sounded three crashing chords.

"Shh."

Aval Anachnu Amcha—

"Nevertheless, we are Thy people," continued Aaron, *"the sons of Thy covenant, of Abraham Thy beloved to whom Thou didst swear on Mount Moriah."*

My eyes fell on Ostoric.

He was unrecognizable. So clean! Washed and combed and without the whiskers of a summertime. He was wearing a polka-dot bowtie, gray flannel trousers with a knife-edge crease (where did he get them pressed?) and black and white shoes. His blue jacket was carefully folded on the piano. All summer long he had kept this finery in hiding. Now helter-skelter, each thing jammed where it would fit, ties wrapped around shoes, he was cramming a small valise—preparing to leave.

Icy death gripped me. He was our tenth man. (Each one of us was indeed the tenth man.)

It was not the time to leave. In the dining room, with brooms and a pail, the girls were restoring a little decency.

Artie climbed on the mattresses to lie down.

"Get down! you'll knock them down!" said Mr. T. crossly.

"Hear O Israel, the Lord our God, the Lord is One!" said Aaron in a loud voice.

The moist sunlight poured into the room, impartially, among those standing and those not standing and the heaps of mattresses, and on the black letters of my book.

Mr. T. began to count the mattresses.

I anxiously watched Ostoric. Every other moment he

246

would step outside to knock his pipe against the porchrail. At such moments, was there or was there not a *minyan?* Did the congregation come to be and cease to be, moment by moment, as one would switch an electric-light?

With fearful eyes, the white showing, Dave Werner kept looking at Ostoric and the progress of his preparations to depart.

"Thirty-eight, thirty-nine, forty," muttered Mr. Tobias.

So we came to the great prayer of the Eighteen Blessings, of which Nachmanides once wrote to his son:

> During the prayer of the Eighteen Blessings, remove all the affairs of this world from thy breast; think of no other matter but that of fixing thy mind on this prayer with perfect devotion; prepare and purify thy heart and mind unto God, blessed be He—*thereby* will thy prayer be pure and untainted, devout, and acceptable before the Holy One, blessed be His name.

. . . "Lord, *open* Thou my lips, and my mouth shall utter Thy praise." So we began.

Open *Thou* them, for obviously I cannot.

"Will you sit on this valise," said Ostoric, "so I can lock it."

"Now wait till the prayer is over."

"Eighty-four, eighty-five, eighty-six," said Mr. Tobias.

Happy and dancing, washed and comforted, the twins descended from above. But in their haste to be out in the open world, they stumbled on the last step and fell prone.

V'l'yerushalaim ircha—

"*And to Jerusalem Thy City, return in mercy,*" read Aaron in a flat voice, for it is a hard passage for the Jews. "*Dwell there as Thou hast promised it; rebuild it soon, even in our days—an eternal building. Set up there again the Throne of David!*"

Dave and Husky repeated the Mourners' Prayer and the service was over.

3.

"You aren't going *away*, Eli?" cried Husky. For the first time all summer he called Ostoric by his first name, which was Elihu; but he refined the affectation too far, because as a nickname Ostoric preferred to be called not "Eli" but "Huey."

The ex-arts-and-crafts man said that he was leaving.

"Why are you leaving?" said Dave in an aggrieved tone. "There's nothing in the city. The best part of camp is after the kids go. Now is the time to take a rest."

Ostoric carefully explained that he had to get to Stroudsburg in Pennsylvania where his fiancée (as he said) had also finished a camp season, and then they were going to the World's Fair in Chicago. It was clear that he was really going to leave.

"Why didn't you go yesterday then, with the others, if you're in such a hurry?" said Husky bitterly.

"I don't want to get to Stroudsburg before tomorrow, because then I'll have to help Margot pack. She always leaves it for me."

"How are you going?"

"Hitch," said Ostoric. "That's why I'm all dressed up. Looks sharp, no?"

"Listen, you're the tenth man," said Dave, the head-counsellor. "If you go there is no *minyan*. We expected Mr. Tobias' brother from Montreal, but he can't make it till Sunday."

"Ostoric!" pleaded Husky, "stay over the weekend. Tuesday morning I'll take you all the way to New York by car."

"What about us?" I cried. Mike and I were also the tenth man.

But then I remembered—and the thought of it brought me almost perfect peace—that when the day came I was going to leave this place, alone. So I did not protest. I said nothing. I smiled with inward joy and esthetical contemplation. Lo, Ostoric!

Last night Husky was itching to be rid of him; now he

248

offered him the coveted prize of the place in the automobile. The stone that the builders rejected was become the capital of the pillar.

"Will you drive me all the way to New York?" said Ostoric, pretending to hesitate.

"Yes, what do you think?"

"I think—I'll think it over. Now supposing you drive me into Burlington now," he suggested blandly, "and I'll think it over on the way. Maybe I'll change my mind and come back with you."

As for me, I *loved* this Ostoric and could spend with him the eons apportioned to us in Paradise. Even Mike, who was ill and pale, spread his lips in a thin smile.

"O. K.," said Husky, almost with a sob, "you think it over." But he took the keys out of his pocket and brought the car around in front of the Lodge. Dave climbed in with Ostoric's valise.

"Good bye, fellows," said Ostoric warmly, and insisted on shaking hands with each one. "Maybe I'll be back; and if not maybe I'll see you next summer at some other camp. Who knows?"

He got into the car and they drove off.

"Let me wash my hands," said Leo, "to get the feel of that lizard off my hands. Let's shave," he suggested.

It was Friday, and we were accustomed, all except Ostoric, to clean up for the Sabbath Eve.

But when we went to fetch our shaving-kits, we made a curious, a frightening discovery. The holders of all our safety-razors had been robbed of their blades, and the spare blades were likewise gone, though the little boxes seemed untouched. We looked at each other, the whites showing in our eyes.

It was a practical joke of Ostoric's.

4.

To get away from the others, I took the twins for a walk. We went down to the boys' camp along the lake.

John Wells, a farmer from up the lake, was stripping the

torn canvas from the tentalows. "Morning," he said, continuing.

"Good morning," I said.

On the beach the wrecked canoes and rowboats, parched and warped, seemed a hundred thousand years older than yesterday. The pink war-canoe with its broken back lay like the skeleton of an ichthyosaur. Our camp had been bankrupt and badly equipped this last summer; but now today, the day after, the effect was not of decay, nor even of abandonment, but of absolute reversion to the natural environment. Ossification, petrifaction. Not as if the Jew-camp had ceased to exist, but as if it had never existed, in these late days.

"There are some good bulbs in the footlights on my stage," I said to Wells. "You can get in the back way by forcing the latch."

"Got 'em," he said.

The twins cried out in horror and seized me by the hand. It was Rollo, the little alligator, escaped from his tank and crawling away down the middle of the dusty street. "It's only Rollo; he was part of the museum," I reassured them; "don't you remember him any more?"

"What kind of thing is that?" said the farmer, paling a little. "No lizards grow round here as big at that."

"No they don't. He's an alligator, from the South. A vital principle."

The little beast (alas, no dragon!) proceeded slowly between the shacks down toward the lake.

"Good-bye, Rollo!"

"What will happen to him if we let him go?" asked Melvin.

"He'll jump in and drown," I said, turning up the hill.

"Bye," said Wells, holding out his hand. "Shan't see you again."

"Oh, we'll be around a day or two yet," I said acidly.

5.

Late in the afternoon the brothers returned from Burlington. They were not speaking to each other. At the last moment both had neglected to punch Ostoric in the nose and the pent-up aggression turned against each other. There was no longer a congregation of Jews at our camp.

"We called on a rabbi in Burlington," said Dave. "He said that in a pinch you could count in a boy not yet *Bar-mitzvah*, so long as he's circumcised."

"If you're thinking of Melvin Kalman, the father called for them an hour ago."

Now a bitter wrangle arose between Aaron, who was a rigorist, and Leo, who began to remember things just convenient to our case. "So long as there are 9 Jews it is sufficient, for Elijah can be counted in," said Leo. "Besides, there is a difference between a servant in the household and an ordinary *goy*; so Sweeney can be counted in. For that matter, why not count in one of the girls? In our times the status of women is not like what it was in the days of the Tannaim; isn't their religious status different too?"

"Sure!" cried Aaron. "Why not have one Jew present by telephone and make use of all modern technology. If you're trying to be funny you're old enough to go on the vaudeville stage."

"Don't be so sure of yourself," said Leo bitterly. "If Hillel were alive, who knows what he would say about it all?"

But there was one memory of Leo's that even Aaron conceded to have the earmarks of an opinion. In case one man is missing, it is permissible to regard an open *Siddur* as symbolic of an absent reader.

Dave too remembered it! "Yes—yes—" he said, trying hard to remember it. He remembered, twenty years ago, when he was just *Bar-mitzvah*, he had been part of a *minyan*—they called him from the street—and there for some reason that he did not understand at the time, but now it was all clear!—they called him away from a hockey game—an extra prayer-book was propped on a table, and somebody turned the leaves.

"Maybe for mama's sake we ought to leave," said Husky.

When he said it, my girl Maitabel uttered a wild laugh.

251

She stuffed a handkerchief in her mouth and rushed outside.

I followed her in anger. "What are *you* laughing at?" I cried.

—Where now were Julie Bayer and our boys? where were my actors and actresses? the three roarers of *Daniel*, and the little midget girls who danced the Dance?

For our summer-camp was *indeed* over. Where *now* was I going to direct the plays of the talented adolescents and the children whose every gesture and ringing tone is vital expression itself—but they are suggestible and plastic so that I could steal from their lives a body for my thought? Why should I lie? I am an artist; but I have never in long art had a happy moment except when arranging the plays, the choreography, of our children, *they* suggesting it to me. Never yet did the tears flow down my cheeks except when on the night I touched the head of the kid onstage and signalled for the curtain to rise; but they flood my eyes as I write of it.

It was not for Husky Werner's sake that we stayed on here. Unwilling, the last year, just to go away and not cling, just a weekend more, to that dreamy camp-life, such as it was.

"What are you *laughing* at?" I said with tears in my eyes.

"What are they haggling about? What difference does it make whether there is a minyam or not?"

"The word is *minyan*."

"Every time they open their mouths it's more ridiculous."

"Don't be so sure of yourself!" I was repeating the anguished phrase of Leo. "What you would save is a little trouble; you are afraid of making a fool of yourself. What *they* would save"—I did not say *we*, because it did not make any difference to me—"what they would save is the principle by which a person can make possible the acts of life day by day. If he can. Sleeping, eating, dying and having mama die. They all become possible.—

"To hell with it," I said. We kissed and made up. I do not mean that this contact was an answer to any problem, but at least it was the bedrock of contact on which all social

community is founded. If we stayed on another weekend
at this camp, it was to be with our girls, in the country, in
the pleasant season, beside the lake.

6.

We prayed in a third floor bedroom where Maitabel, who
was a registered nurse, had forbade Mike to get out of bed.
The tired overhead light on the crimson and brass was not
like one's home, one's home. My friend's head, at once
pale and burnt, lay nobly on the pillow, but except that his
fever was down you would have thought that he was going
to die.

Open to the Friday evening service, a book was propped
against a wash-pitcher. As we progressed, Leo turned the
leaves for the absent tenth man. It was not to be seen that
the Prophet Elijah turned them, nor that the Son of David
sat anywhere, anywhere, on any throne of glory. It was not
to be seen that the Son of David sat on any throne of glory.

So the brothers came once more to their Kaddish, saying
Yisgadal V'yiskadash—

*"Great and Holy be His immense name in the world
that He created according to His will!"*

What!

What is this thing that we say at the opened grave, when
they have let down my mama's body there? The place is
strange to me and I am not loosed to tears here. Let me be
more glad in the mutual aid of love and labor, then I'll cry
bitterly for dear loss. But to say, *"Blissful! Famous! Glorious! Uplifted!"*—encouraging ourselves with a proud
identification, not otherwise than unhappy children fan-
tasy that they are the heirs of a prince, but they were
kidnapped by gypsies.

The prayer itself forbids it. *"Although,"* so we say, *"although indeed! He is beyond all the blessings and hymns,
the celebrations and the consolations that are uttered in
the world."* What does it mean? Consider it, draw it to its
conclusions, perhaps it is not false. It means first, of
course, that we are not to worship idols; this goes without

253

saying. It means then that we are *not* to make the proud identification, but to be humble; and it is likely that the author (the Aramaic indicates a desperate period) meant most of all to urge this humility. No no! there is a further conclusion, implied in the prayer, to be explicated by us—if not by us, by whom? and if not now, when?—it means that we are to look to the things that *can* applicably be uttered in the world. I do not mean that we are to rely, to rely on our strength, for it is quite unknown to me for any good thing to come of my own will and plan without better help; but that we should look to it.

(Now it is again in Hebrew): Oseh Shalom—

"He who makes peace in His heights will make peace also among us, and all Israel. Let us say, Amen."

So we were all collected in Michael's sickroom, boisterously entertaining ourselves and him, making him laugh, and raising his fever, into the Sabbath morning.

IV: Ostoric

I have since come to ask myself about Huey Ostoric. The meaning of the rest of it I understand well enough—in a history that I have drawn from experience only in the sense that I willed the experience for that history; but wouldn't Ostoric have the right to say of me, like that canoeist long ago, "This dramatics-man doesn't know what he wants; I've met that type before"?

Let us suppose that Ostoric stole the razor-blades, carefully abstracting them from their boxes and touching nothing else besides. It was immediately before the Sabbath Eve, and we must say that his intention was that on this Sabbath at least, after the camp had departed, we would be unkempt, as unkempt as he used to be on *every* decent Sabbath at our camp. What then? Did not also I speak of the "service that I had said once too often," in the "camp that I was tired of," among the "friends of whom I had seen enough"? What if he perhaps felt a certain—disgust, that on this especial Sabbath, after the camp had departed, we were *still*, just as if nothing had happened, prepared and in readiness,

> prepared and in readiness

as the hymn says? This disgust he expressed in a practical joke.

All summer he carried on such a practical joke, slovenly, unshaven, unkempt, unpunctual, letting me down and not trying to be any more helpful than was necessary. In this way he cut a figure in the camp, in our camp, not in his camp. No no! it was also his camp, but he was not enthusiastic about his and our camp; likely he was not so

255

enthusiastic about us; certainly we were not so enthusiastic about him! Then why not show that? why not act that? The *fact* was that if one looked at the broken boats and the ripped canvas, and then looked *quickly*, before the illusion grew, at Huey Ostoric in his dirty sweatshirt and canvas pants matching pebbles on the shore, one saw a natural and proper scene, not so highly colored by mere ideas. And was *I* so enthusiastic about their camp that had broken up long before the first of September? and about my childish theater? But I used to be betrayed by a certain curiosity as to what these people wanted, and I expressed this by punctilious attention to my job.

What if all summer Huey Ostoric went in dirty clothes because he had no change of clothes? I do not mean that he had no clean clothes at all, but that they were packed in his valise. Throughout the summer he did not unpack his valise. Then when the rest of us put on blue polo-shirts and white ducks for the Sabbath, Ostoric, who also possessed those things, could not wear them because he did not want to unpack them. Nevertheless, *he had not come to camp with the intention of behaving in that way.* (I wonder if I could say as much.)

Mr. T. was not open-handed with the salaries of any of the staff; so far as I was concerned, he was even willing to leave me stranded, without a railway-ticket home. But Huey Ostoric was his relative, so it was unnecessary to pay him a salary at all. The rest of us, of course, had an advance, and for better or worse we were established; but to Huey, on the contrary, Huffski Puffski made it clear that he was "on trial," he was really just enjoying a vacation and might have to go home at any moment when the "regular" arts-and-crafts man arrived. (There was no such person.) At the same time, being a relative, Ostoric was more or less in his uncle's confidence and he knew, when the rest of us did not, that the camp was bankrupt. For the same salary he helped Miss K. with the books and he saw what was going on.

In these circumstances there was not a single day during the entire summer that the stout young man thought that he was justified in unpacking his little satchel. But when the camp was over! we saw that Huey Ostoric had a blue polka-dot tie and flannel trousers with a knife-edge crease.

It was easy!—I see it now—it was easy for me to identify myself with that Canadian canoeist, and to follow him with my heart when he paddled away, silhouetted by an orange flash of lightning. That canoeist with his three day disgust was a mere *idea*, and such an idea has always been easy for me, for persons like me. But Ostoric was *always* there and, in my case at least, I was supposed to work with him. He was the arts-and-crafts man, and I was promised that he would help me backstage with the carpentry and the electricity. What did I expect? that the *real* expression of my alienated heart would not *annoy* me, and that he would be there conveniently day by day as a reminder and not *offend* me? but thank God, when he dealt our Congregation its death blow, merely by going away—in the glory of a straw hat and a polka-dot tie—I was able to watch it with a certain—joy! for I too had made up my mind to travel on my own.

In my remembrance, Huey never said a resentful word to any of us. (But I enjoyed plenty of resentment, and that canoeist was burning with resentment.) Huey was friendly by disposition and he tried to be easy-going with us at the very same time as he was not cooperating on the stage and was not enthusiastic about the War—as if to say, "We are all fellows of the camp—such as it is." He was disturbed to learn that we relied on him to be the tenth man, for it had never occurred to him that just by his existence he was necessary, he was one of the *minyan*. He went away anyway, of course. Was it *his* fault that just by absenting himself he became the all-powerful judge of the congregation and condemned it to dissolution?

V: A Hitch-Hike

A rolling stone gathers no moss.
"It means," said the refugee professor, "that he does not become stodgy or as you say mossy."
"No. We use it to mean that he doesn't make any money."

I.

The farmer called for us at sunrise and drove us to the station.

No more days of vacation!
Off to the railway station!

No more days? On the contrary, it was just the beginning of my sweet and hard vacation. For to those of us who have lapsed into, or achieved (it comes to the same thing), a careless and unscheduled way of work and love, it is the times of general vacation, the weekends, the summers, that are painful. From our habitual distraction, that occasionally yields a good fruit, we are distracted by the demands of the others who are bent merely on distraction. There is nothing so tiresome as a person concentrating on having a good time. Till all men are clockless, I prefer to serve as a waiter during their leisure meals or as a crewman on the excursion boats.

With passionate eagerness I put my sick friend on the train, so eager to be rid of them *all*, and my old friend the last of them, that his bad luck was my good luck. "Goodbye and good luck," he called from the moving window. The noise and the vapor of the engine engulfed us, and his goodbye rapidly rang and diminished into the thousands of goodbyes that constitute, I guess, the ringing in my ears

258

that I hear when I lie relaxed, before the sadness rises in my gorge. The tail-end of the train diminished, it was swallowed by the hungry present, bloated and empty all about me, as again the tail-end of a dream vanishes on awaking: into the free, beautiful and senseless present moment that thrives on the lie that I have no past.

As the young man once I saw, at the top of the steps of a gray-painted house, carefully closed the door and threw wide his arms and cried "Freedom!" (I had my doubts), so almost—having disembarrassed myself of an old friend—I threw wide my arms; but I was holding a valise.

I crossed the street to the store and mailed the bag ahead of me. It would be odd when my clothes arrived home without me. As I thought it, the stout matron behind the counter looked at me candidly. I dismissed the afterthought—for another time! and scooped up the change from the counter. Then again, I reopened the valise and took out a pencil and my little pad. (Like the rest of us, I have paid for my immortality with my death.)

It was the beginning of the fall. The sun shone clear and bright, but not hot or brilliant. It served rather to give adequate illumination, to "put things in their proper light," than to attract attention to itself—yet I was attending just to it! as we watch a smiling prestidigitator whose gestures have a wonderful appearance of naturalness. Even so! everywhere, on all the apple trees and pear trees was edible fruit; by stepping momentarily off the highroad I could enjoy a piece of fruit. Was it not the ideal weather for seeing New England from side to side? and why shouldn't I poke into Massachusetts and New Hampshire for a day or two? New York one could always reach, for everybody went there. Only, provided it didn't rain! . . . Struggling to keep hold of the present, I could see only, through the dusty window-pane, Armand in his canoe struggling in the teeth of the wind and the rain, forced back three-quarters of a length for each length of advance, his double-paddle almost vainly rising and falling on either side; the orange lightning drew the outline of his figure, and they burst into the marching song:

If not now,
when!

—Well! I'd wanted to get away, and now I was away! The
recollection of the canoeist and of all that camp, vanished
from the gay morning.

I took my stand on the south side of the highway, Route
Thirteen of my country, and began to signal to the high-
powered automobiles flying past. They were coming at the
rate that one vanished in one extreme as another appeared
in the other, so they seemed to draw each other elastically
from the infinite poles. The notion, my notion, was for one
of them to stop at my gesture and give me a lift on *my* way
as far as *it* was bound. Then by the accretion of these short
and long rides, by the interplay of our contrary purposes, *I*
should eventually reach my destination! There was a post
of signs by the roadside:

100,000 years	THE GREAT STONE AGE	
1,000 years	THE DAY THAT I WAS BORN	
400 years	THE FOUNDING OF OUR CAMP BY KWEE-KWEE	
0 years	THE CREATION OF THE HEAVENS	
	AND THE EARTH	0
	THE REVOLUTION	?
	THE DAY I RECOVER CONFIDENCE	??
	A FREE SOCIETY	???
	THE TIME OF THE MESSIAH	????

The bright day, the flashing motorcars by-roaring, the
unending highway: these roused in me a calm excitement.
Who would stop? And how far would I go?

I was at the whim, but willingly, of whatever vehicle
might choose me. Each car of these hurrying along, with
anonymous exteriors of flashing glass, had some private
career that I, with my lifted right, was willing temporarily
to share, entering into the contract beforehand. It was very
different from being at our camp.

"*Dreams* are the royal road to the unconscious," said
the father of the psychoanalytic movement. The *King's*

A Hitch-Hike

Highway to the Dare-Not-Know—With mounting despair I watched flash by these uncommunicative images, manifest reflections of the stupid daytime, not yielding up their inner secret.

2.

With a startling hiss of air-brakes, a great red oil-tanker ground to a stop on the gravel twenty yards beyond. The driver thrust out his red head—Apollyon up from Hell, as Hawthorne would say it, his hair still full of smoke and fire. But I hastened to clamber aboard.

"We ain't supposed to pick up anybody," said the driver as we gathered speed. His thick forefinger touched a legend on the windshield,

ИО ᴙIDƎᴙƧ

"Who knows? You pick up a character who pulls a blackjack and throws you in the ditch. *You* look harmless."

There was an equal risk for those within the flying engines?

"But it gets lonesome on the road and a fellow likes to have somebody to talk to. Other day a character fell asleep at the wheel."

"How far down are you going? I'm going all the way to—" I whispered the name.

"You come a long way from there!" he said admiringly. "But I turn east this side of Burlington."

"Maybe I'll ride along," I said in a high voice. "Why shouldn't I see it all, from side to side?"

"Nothing to see," said the driver bitterly. "What's to see?" he said (I thought). "I've travelled the other routes as well, and it's all the same, boring! boring!"

"Not if you're a hitch-hiker," I stoutly maintained (I thought). "Trouble with you is you always have a sure ride, eight feet above the road, you giant!"

261

"Is that so? Let me tell you, young fellow, it's only human society that has an interest continually renewed."

"Ha! I can see that you've never been a counsellor at a summer-camp!" I cried triumphantly and refuted him.

He bit his lips.

Meantime we were steadily eating up the road, and for several minutes we exchanged no word. Suddenly, without turning his face from the road, he said to me between his teeth: "The chain! the chain! Do you hear the chain rattling on the road in back? They wouldn't let me remove it. Why not? Why in hell do I got to have this chain? *That's* why I picked you up; you looked like *you* would know."

"Sure!" said I cheerfully. "Sure I know. That's because the oil is swishing around in your big can and generating static. And if you don't keep continually grounding it, the whole works might blow up sky high."

"This they never told me," he hissed. . . . He jammed the brakes. "You get out. I don't like you. I never liked you from the beginning."

"O.K., O.K.," I sang. "I'm sick and bored with this concrete roadbed anyway. And thanks for nothing."

A moment later I was flying into the sun, up a less traveled road, with a trio of blonde girls in a two-seater roadster that made eighty without a purr. The white posts of the road formed a continuous blur. The hair of the girls was whipped by the wind. One head was copper blonde, one golden blonde and one ashen. Now this last, black blonde, is the color of hair that I love most; and I was seated beside her in the rumble-seat. At my remarks the girls burst into fits of giggling; and soon they began to tell jokes which, I must confess, were excellent.

"What is it, Matt," said the copper girl at the wheel, "that men have but don't carry and women carry but don't have?"

"It's not dirty!" cried the other two.

"Repeat it," I said.

"What is it that men have but don't carry—men have it but don't carry it—and women carry it but don't have it?"

"Well, I can think of some things—"

"Yes, but they're all dirty. And it's not dirty!"

A Hitch-Hike

"I give up."

"Hemophilia," cried the girl at the wheel.

An added spurt, up to eighty-five, and we zipped through Little Giddy.

"Do you want to guess another riddle?" asked Eleanor, the black blonde.

"Yes," I said eagerly, knowing that my friends would appreciate these fine riddles.

"What is it—listen carefully—what is it whose shape belies the function—what is it whose shape belies the function of one of its nicknames?"

"Well, what is it whose shape belies the function of one of its nicknames?"

"A doughnut!"

"Why a doughnut?"

"Because it looks like a life-saver, but it's called a sinker."

It was so pleasant, and joyous, touring the countryside on so bright a day with such vivacious girls—there hovered on their faces, as those in front or the beauty beside me turned momentarily toward me and away, their moist teeth in the wind and wisps of hair in their eyes, many other lovely faces, recalled, in this one's smile and that one's laughter, while the greenery flickered by and the white blur of the posts stood still and the copper girl stepped on the gas. I had a joyful anticipation. The dampness of that summer camp was dissipated on the wind. Was I not becoming my real self again, untired,

—Beginning over! beginning over!

back to a time before I could remember anything at all?

With a roar, that seemed much like a warning shout, our car came to a stop at a little side road turning up into the hills.

"Duxbury: here's where we turn in," said the driver. "I hope you have lots of luck exploring New England from side to side," said the ashen girl.

I would have said, "I'll go up this little road with you as well," but my tongue clove to the roof of my mouth.

263

Because my tongue clove to the roof of my mouth, I could not tell even myself (and cannot now) what it was that simple happiness was, and what forbade, nor what it was that had occurred long ago.

But I know, in *general*, that much of the misery made amongst us is avoidable.

I was standing alone, and thunderstruck, by the roadside, whether for a short or a long time I cannot tell, when a black frock-coated bespectacled grandfather in a yellow calash, driving a smart dappled nag at a brisk pace, said "Whoa!" and stopped beside me.

He said, "Hop in, sonny."

Mechanically I climbed up beside him, and for a good while in dead silence we rolled on at the new pace.

On the left, as if belonging to a different order of things, for we rolled on the gravel shoulder of the road, flew the high-powered automobiles, passing us by.

The old gentleman was a schoolmaster.

—Now once, when I was a child, as punishment for a hair-raising misdeed (that I would gladly repeat, that I would gladly repeat), I was put back to a far lower class in school; I was made to sit, humiliated, in a seat too small for me. In my dreams this wished for punishment recurs—except that, worse, I am lost and cannot find the room at all. Avoiding the room of the punishment; looking for the punishment; willing to endure the punishment again and again in order to have repeated the childish crime.—

We came, on the other side of Middlesex, to a traffic jam on the road, with scores of autos and farmers gathered to look on. It was a railroad crossing. During the night, just at the crossing, a big locomotive had jumped the rails, and it lay, half-over, with its nose off the track. Two of the great wheels were bent on a rock and the searchlight was shattered.

It had monstrously turned to confront us, in the night, with its violent force and the light blazing to the back corners of the soul.

What a rare spectacle! The great iron animal was hurrying through the night, darting along the endless track the long beam of its eye, and drawing on a copious store of energy in its forward rush, while the lengthening plume of smoke stood suspended for miles in the calm air. But it turned. Without *even* a warning shout, the engine was lying in the ditch.

"How many were hurt? how many were hurt?"—The automobiles kept continually augmenting, mingling their raucous voices. The farmers were in high spirits, lighting their pipes.

On all sides streaming past with their howls. *Bluuuues! Lose! Mad! Dogs!*—"Who is *he?*" I said to Mike. "Who? who?" said Mike (I thought)—"*Who?* WHO?"

Surely it was *somebody, somewhen.* But I cannot recall it. And what if it was nobody, but only the projection of my character? Then, why? For nothing comes from nothing.

A haywagon was waddling into the side road. I leaped onto it and buried my head. I had hit on a methodical scheme—choosing always the less traveled road of the fork, and the less traveled of the next fork—to come to a pause.

3.

The middle of the afternoon of the next day I was sitting, stranded among the daisies, beside a back road not marked on any maps. I was munching violet sickle-pears that I had gathered from the field. A little brook trickled through a clay pipe under the road. And to while the time, I was making parables and poems.

It was not probable that I should progress further, so long as I remained on this back road.

In the meadow, a dark-haired man was mowing with a busy, horse-drawn machine, but so far off that the noise of it was softer than the brook's.

Supposing I dropped a twig into this brook. Now this water ran into a stream and the stream into another and this into another that would eventually become the River Thames flowing into the ocean past New London. It did not follow that the twig would float all that way, because it might be snagged anywhere along the way. Indeed, with the keenest agitation one would see it being snagged and hope for it to break free, perhaps unsnag it (though that was cheating), to float further. Yet supposing the twig finally did break free and floated to the end!—then all that anxiety, and release from anxiety, would have been for a senseless twig in the sea.

The September sun was again a little golden, a little warming, not a featureless illumination. The solitude was not so lonesome, not so menacing with lonesomeness, but that I could relax my midriff and, ceasing to deceive myself, cry for my condition and the condition of injured people (they being not close by). Also recognizing the salient fact that it had not taken many rides to bring me to a relieving pause, here, now; that, in general, the moment—each moment—was the end result of the long process of time.

My midriff, I say, was loosed; but my face—I could not see my face—was watchfully waiting.

The declining sun cast a hue of bronze on the grass. A fish slipped through the long moss of a rock and fled downstream. From the distance rang the cry of the reaper, to whom had occurred a sudden thought: "Leonard!" The time of day was between four and five. And a white cloud, flying freely on the left, moved just beyond where I could glimpse it out the corner of my eye. I blinked. And when I opened my eyes, the world as a whole had passed on to a new configuration.

The *King's Highway* to the Dare-Not-Know!
—but I beg my rides, and well I know

these boring roads where hundreds and hundreds
of cars fade by in hundred-hundreds

of flashing windows too bright too fast
to see my face. I am steadfast

A Hitch-Hike

long hours o' the morning. I am so sad.
An old-time trap, an ancient sad

horse and his master stop by the way,
they'll take me one mile on my way
—out of my way—is this the Way?

I used to think I used to be happy,
but is it possible to be happy?

What is it like?—like Plato oh
we'll copy it at large and oh

plan a city where all the distances
(where? where?) are walking distances.

Towards evening, a large dark touring-car appeared on the hill against me and rapidly approached. A startling sight. The shadows of trees had gotten hundreds of yards long, the red sun was touching the horizon, and the reaper had left the field. There was an edge of chill in the air and my jaw began to chatter, loosening my fixed stare. As the car approached I got to my feet.

"Take me far as the main road," I shouted.

For I would not get far, even out of my way, if I did not get back to some kind of highway. Further I became aware of the expression that had been fixed on my face, the while I thought that I was breathing easy—anxious waiting.

With a quiet click of the brakes, as though it were a matter of course, by appointment, the dark-colored car stopped and the door flew open. I heaved a strong sigh of relief as I stepped in.

4.

It was Ostoric.
"For God's sake!"
—"Get in. Got to keep going."
"Where'd you steal the car?"

—"Sure I stole it. Those fat greasy slugs, going by by by."

"How long've you been on the back roads?"

—"Third day."

"I thought you had to get to—where was it?—Scranton?"

—"Stroudsburg."

I finally took courage to look at him. He was not so natty as last we saw him.

—"Too late!" he cried. "Too late for everything! If you're not there at the moment, nobody waits. There is a tide in the affairs of men which taken at the flood leads on to fortune! Got to keep going. Mustn't let people down! They don't forget."

"It's O.K. by me," I said. "I'm glad to see you," I said frankly.

—"I know what you're thinking! 'That lazy son of a bitch never did a stroke for me all summer, and now he says, "Got to keep going!" It's a joke!' What the hell do you know? I came five minutes late the first time."

I did not pursue this puzzling line. Also I was afraid to say what came to my mind, "Poor kid—" But I said, "Did you pick the car up by the road, or did you—"

—"Right! I shoved him out on his ass, into the ditch."

"But *he* was the one who gave you a ride, not like the others."

—"Saaay! Do you want to ride 'long with me or don't you? 'How sharper than a serpent's tooth!' Ha! *that's* what you're thinking!"

"Stop telling me what I'm thinking. You don't know anything about it. How long do you expect to cruise these fields before they catch up to you?"

—"Never never never never never."

"What do you mean, never?"

—"I still got bucks for gas."

He fell silent, while we tore the rubber off our wheels on the rocks. I felt that his silence was a bad sign.

—"All summer Nuncle lied to me. There never *was* going to be a regular arts-and-crafts man. All for a hundred lousy bucks, when I trusted him. He said he didn't send the wire because I *begged* him so. What do you know about it! . . . Oh God, I'm so sick and tired of begging, begging, rubbing up against your leg just to gain a little admittance. . . . Then he skips off anyway in his fat greasy car. *I* was supposed to drive him to the city."

"Well, he didn't really have much time," I said to mollify him.

> Poverty who lately made
> more wholesome the common diet,
> now has cast me in the dark,
> for I cannot pay the Company,
> the giant that turns switches on
> and floods our rooms with light.—

I was eerily moved. It was a poem of my own that he was quoting, a poem of so long ago that I could never have remembered it, so I heard it not with my present ears, but surprised, into the emotions of *those* times, before I had perfected every defense against hope and gratitude. Then the tears started into my eyes.

It was now nearly dark. I reached to switch on the lights. He jammed the brakes so suddenly that I cracked my head on the shield.

—"Hand over the $200," said Ostoric.

The bowie-knife was pricking my ribs, as I had feared it all summer.

"What $200?"

—"You know what. The August pay."

"*What* August pay?" I cried.

I emptied my pocket of a dollar and a quarter. "Here's what I have and you can't have it, because I need it for supper and breakfast.

"Snap out of it, Huey Ostoric. Put that pig-sticker away. You saw the books, you know who got paid and who didn't get paid."

His reaction to this was absolutely terrifying.

—"Poor Nuncle Ben!" he blubbered. "He *wrote* down in the books that he paid you. He was ashamed for me to think it otherwise. He was ashamed. And now, you weren't superior ones after all, shouting there with your

269

authoritative voices: pointing with your thumb to the switchboard script, and the other one, the admiral o' the ocean. Silent! silent upon a peak in Darien.—I never knew it. You're right. I never knew it at all. I only wanted to be able to share in." He burst into deep sobs, saying, "Poor Uncle Ben—poor Huffski Puffski."

I switched on the lights, calling into being the beautiful sylvan world. The knife dropped to the floor. He threw in the clutch and we rapidly accelerated.

"You're *lying!*" he cried, reaching his hands high.

I gave the wheel a smart spin, and we crashed.

5.

It was gray among the trees. A runnel of water was flowing into my collar and out through the sleeves; and this emerged from my last dream. The rain was loudly pelting the woods. I was stretched on a blanket in the shelter of a tree. I had a headache. I reached for my pipe and tobacco, to suck a little security: everywhere there were dolorous twinges—in the spreading continents and the rivers of water and the mountain ranges, but especially in the skyey dome—yet nothing excruciating, nor unresponsive to the soul. But the matches were wet.

There was a flame. Ostoric was offering the flame of his lighter and I got a light. I noticed that the stem of my pipe bore many tooth-marks of suppressed rage, and it was (I think) this observation more than the draught of smoke that brought the electric spirits tingling back into the torpor.

—"Are you all right?"

"I think so." I squirmed some more.

—"Why did you do it? why did you do it?" he said, weakly wringing his hands.

An answer slipped out of me, like a thunderbolt: "I'm bewildered too." It was the hardest admission I ever yet had to make in my adult life, more than to confess the envy or cowardice that take from me the savor of the world.

270

I got to my feet. The headache made me sick and I leaned against the tree. But it passed, it passed. It was simply suppressed bewilderment, and I cried out—not for the pain, there was no pain—but because my eyes did not focus and I was frightened.

—"Are you all right?" he kept saying, hopping about. The place, the road, was much more rough and sylvan than when I had gotten into that cursed car. The road gleamed with yellow puddles in which the raindrops were bouncing, through the overhanging trees. I stepped gingerly through the mud, from island to island, though I was soaked through and through anyway. "Come along," I said to Ostoric, though at the same time dissociating myself from him.

—"Yes! got to get going!"

To my astonishment I emerged (that is, we emerged) almost immediately onto a through way, a broad route of the Commonwealth whose marking I easily found on my rain-soaked map. This macadam road was not, to be sure, one of the great national ways, nor one of the international ways, yet even this road was traveled, even in this weather, by many cars, darting their yellow flares feebly in the dawn, through the rain; and it boasted many promising signs on the post, as well as the warning words

Out of the fog and rain, ever so fast, swished the high-powered cars, breaking the law moment by moment. We cowered on the side, almost invisible.

Every minute or so the noise of a car grew louder, and we stepped out from the shelter of an oak-tree to signal it. But

271

no car was willing to stop. The yellow lights briefly illumined us as each sped by.

"Trouble with this begging," I said bitterly, feeling terrible and losing my sense of humor, "is that we turn to each blow *after* it has struck."

In the teeming rain must not every car stop and pick us up? How could they not, seeing us with the water flowing in runnels into our ears and eyes?

"They don't like the idea of our wet clothes and muddy shoes soiling the upholstery," said Ostoric apologetically.

I looked at him in blank disgust.

"If I had a car," I said, "I shouldn't pass by *anybody* in such weather—even you."

VI: A Memorial Synagogue

It is not incumbent on you to complete the work; but neither are
you free to withdraw from it.
—RABBI TARFON

We willingly commit some folly, just to live on a little.
—GOETHE

I.

We three came to the city where, despite much busyness, there was little useful work; despite much art and entertainment, little joy; despite many physical comforts, almost no sexual happiness; where among thousands of thousands there was almost not one person exercising most of his human powers, but every one pursued with earnest concentration some object not really to his advantage and which, perhaps fortunately for himself and us, he could not achieve. Yet such as it was! so I remembered my city from early childhood and I shared its ways; and Lord! I was glad to come back to it, as each time I come back.

Yet for conversation, we three exchanged only sighs. There were many fine things here and many distractions, but as it turned out, it was not possible for us to turn our minds to anything but recent disasters, unfinished disasters, wreck of our happiness both by our own stupidity and by compulsion, inextricably involved, both by commission and omission, with the many disasters of other people. The suggestion of any distraction decayed on our lips, but heaving each his own sighs we communicated with each other—the Canadian and Ostoric and I.

273

2.

Also we—and I think many many others at this time—were simply *floundering*. (One cannot help saying that the young persons of the end of the first half of the century, those who have intellectual energy, are floundering.) Floundering: that is, willing to give ourselves, and *giving* ourselves, to what we *know* to be unlikely. It is not even a matter of faith, or of misplaced faith. But what would *you* do—just to live on a little?

3.

We came to a crowded part of the city and at once began distributing our handbills.

The proposal of these bills was neither daring nor modest, but in the middle; it was what seemed appropriate to us in the circumstance that we could not succeed in turning our minds from the recent disasters. The fact is that one *cannot* do nothing but sigh, without a more athletic and social exercise. But if the reader's response to our proposal is just to heave a tired sigh, that is not inappropriate.—

A PROJECTION,
IN HEAVY MATERIALS,
OF OUR GRIEF
The Jews ought to make, of heavy materials, of medium size, embellished by great artists, a synagogue dedicated to Grief for their own recent disasters and the disasters of all peoples.

On corners of a busy intersection, we stood giving out these bills.

4.

There are some persons who, when offered a free handbill, harden their jaws and stare stonily ahead, and will not take it. Sometimes they jam their hands defensively in

274

their pockets, for the hand is naturally apt to give and take. The reasons for this behavior are obvious: those that spring from fear are contemptible, but those that spring from wounded dignity are not (in our city) contemptible. But what is disheartening is to see a young person behave in this way.

Other persons accept the bill by an absent-minded reflex or out of courtesy, but they at once repent and angrily throw the offending paper into the mud.

Now still others courteously put the paper in their pocket, unread, perhaps carefully folding it. This delaying behavior creates a relation of complicity, almost of conspiracy. The moment will come—one may imagine in what dramatic circumstances! a man after the fourth ineffectual drink gives in to the distraction of emptying his pocket, to escape from the personal problem he is faced with across the table—and *out* of his pocket emerges this forgotten message, that he holds up unbelievingly to the light.

The man who has stonily declined a bill on the other corner stoops in the gutter to pick up the bill thrown away, now he is no longer face to face.

There are those who read and laugh nervously or snarl—for most handbills contain unpleasant matter; or who stand stock still, screw up their faces and seem to be spelling out the letters; or who, the experts in the kind of matters treated in free political handbills, give a cursory glance and at once engage you in argument.

5.

Before long fellows of mine (I am an anarchist) came by. They gave the bill a cursory glance.

"What's this!" they cried. "Have you taken leave of your senses? War-memorials! Do you think that war-memorials stop wars?"

"No, I don't," I said.

"Why the Jews? And *why* a synagogue? Have you suddenly become religious?"

"No, I haven't. But the city is full of Jews."

"The city is full of *people*," they corrected me.

"Look, Matt," one of them said, troubled. "What's the use of grieving and making Yom Kippur? The thing to do is to prevent a recurrence."

"You're right, you're right," I said wearily. "There's no use crying over spilled milk; the thing to do is to make a change for the better. But when I try to do it, the *fact* is that when I try to do it, it comes to nothing but sighing."

My friends respected me enough not to greet this remark with a hoot. But, a small knot of people having gathered around us, they at once began to harangue them about more hair-raising immediate and long-range action than we were proposing.

"I think," said a little old woman to me, "that the idea of a war-memorial is beautiful; there should be a great war-memorial. But it ought to be something useful, not statues. Many people are proposing that we build a great community-center, with social activities and sports for boys and girls."

"No no," I said stubbornly, "it has to be something heavy, of hard materials like stone and bronze, because there is a heavy place in my breast that I want to get rid of, out there."

6.

A man who had been listening to the harangue cried out, "The speaker is right! But he's too god-damned reasonable. We don't need so much sweetness and light; we need more anger."

I touched him on the sleeve. "Not anger. Not just now. Let me tell you something I remember. I remember when the war was just breaking out in Europe, that Toscanini gave a concert, they were playing the *Eroica* symphony; and in the performance, in the performance by Toscanini, there was an edge of anger—even in the last movement— of anger. What do you think?"

Another man read the leaflet carefully. "You boys are floundering," he said.

A policeman dispersed the crowd.

7.

"You Jews ought to grieve for yourselves," said a woman. "You had enough trouble without grieving for other people's trouble too."

"That's just what the Canadian said!" I cried, "—my friend on the other corner. But he was wrong. Because we have a saying: *Im ein ani li, mi li? Aval im ani l'otzmi, ma ani?* It means: *If I'm not for myself, who is for me? But if I'm only for myself, what am I?—*"

I stopped short.

The saying had a third part. But when the third part came to my tongue, I stopped short and the tears flooded my eyes. *V'im lo achshav,* is the third part, *eimatai?—*

And if not now, WHEN?

When this third question, this crucial question, came to my tongue, my tongue stuck to the roof of my mouth and I stopped short.

Next moment I burst into heavy sobs and stood on the corner with the tears streaming down my face, not even handing out the bills.

Hereupon (such is our city), whereas previously a knot of people had gathered, now they gave me a wide berth and a space opened around me.

8.

The oxen that drew the Ark brought it, without a guide, to Beth-Shemesh, singing.

The sculptor who had chosen himself to embellish the building (as we had all chosen ourselves, for so comes into being the project that people only potentially want: it is forced upon them)—the sculptor said:

"The chief object of embellishment must be the Ark, the box where the scrolls of the Law are kept, because this is the chief center of attention.

"Now for the right and left sides of the Ark I have designed two Cherubim, and they are these: Violence and Nature. But—but—"

He began to stammer, and then he began to weep.

"What's the matter, sculptor?"

"When I look at my designs," he said, "I can no longer remember, I can no longer distinguish, which is Nature and which is Violence.

"Once it was clear to me—if indeed it ever was.

"See, this one. His wings are spread across the top of the box, his hair is streaming: he is going aloft, from it, or with it—

"Ach! if I meant him to be an *ideal* motion, then he's Violence; ideas are *violence* to the nature of things: raising, raping, tearing by the roots, it's all one. But maybe I meant him to be soaring and spreading wide, like growing Nature.

"Well, the other Angel has his feet firmly planted, that's clear. He's standing in the live rock, and that's how we'll build it, too! But isn't he dragging the structure down, like a terrible wrestler? Good!—between us, I don't believe in that Law.

"I see that the two are fighting for the box—I didn't consciously mean this—the raised wings are trying to cover it, the wrestler is wresting it away. Maybe they aren't Nature and Violence at all. No matter!" he cried.

"Don't worry, sculptor; these are only designs. When you come to the execution and can think with your hands again, it will come back to you which is Nature and which is Violence."

"They aren't fighting at all. They're trying to embrace each other. But the box is in the way. Ha! I can fix that."

His face had a crafty look.

"I have planned the box as a movable furniture, according to the ancient way. It's a box of books in a dead language. If I—remove out this box—a bit—or *push* it back out of the way! won't they fall into each other's arms?"

"What! will they move?"

"Certainly they'll move!" said the sculptor arrogantly. "When my dolls move, you'll cry out, and the musician will blow the horn!"

He laughed raucously. "They're a pair of brawny movingmen," he said contemptuously, "tugging that little box as tho it were as heavy as a safe."

9.

The Painter had a different personality. A tiny Polish Jew, he was famous as a creator of wonderful whimsical animals. He said:

"For my part I wanted to use stained glass. But the architect says we must have white light for reading. Why must they read so much when they can look at my pictures? O.K. I can tell the story on the walls."

"What story?"

"A fable I heard in the old country, unless it came to me in a dream. It goes like this:

"God said to Noah, 'Build the ark, three stories high; then the animals, two of each kind, will go up in it and be saved from the flood.' This was the arrangement and Noah set to work and did his part. But when the animals heard about it they called a world Congress. (Maybe some of the finest animals didn't even come to the Congress.) They chattered and jabbered; finally it came down to two factions. The first faction was superstitious and they thought they'd better do as they were told. But the other faction was indignant and didn't trust the arrangement at all.

" 'Since when,' said they, 'have these men been so good to us that now we should put our trust in them and, to be quite frank, walk like boobies into a trap. I for my part have a lively memory of Nimrod, that mighty hunter. Ha! you turn pale. So.

" 'And what do you think of the accommodations? We go by twos; but Noah! he doesn't go alone with his wife, but he also takes with him those three fat boys, of whom I need say no further. *And* their wives. Include us out.'

"The others only said, 'We'd better go.'

"So the day came and Noah blew on his shofar a loud blast—"

"Excuse me," said Armand, "what's a shofar?"

"A shofar—is a shofar."

"Yes, but what is it? Noah blew a blast on his shofar; what's a shofar?"

"A shofar is a shofar, dummy," said the painter angrily.

"What is it, a kind of bugle?"

"Yes, it's a bugle. Noah blew a blast on his bugle!"

"What's to get angry about? How should I know? Why didn't you say it was a bugle in the first place?"

"Please—" the painter screwed up his face in pain and turned to us appealingly, *"is* a shofar a bugle?

"—He blew a blast and some of the animals came, and then came the rain and the flood. But the others *didn't* come, and they *drowned. Ach!*—So perished from the earth the wonderful snodorgus and the kafooziopus, and klippy, and Petya, and the marmape, and Sadie—"

It was impossible to believe one's eyes and ears, for suddenly the little man began to bawl in strange little sobs at the top of his chest, for his fantastic animals whose names he was making up as he went along.

"So died," he screamed, "the loveliest and the shrewdest. Petya! Petya! And my sister's little girls, and my brothers, and long ago my friend Apollinaire, who had the alivest voice.

"But I shall paint these beauties into existence again, on every wall in the world!"

10.

The architect said:

"In a building of this kind the chief thing to communicate is the sense of the Congregation. The sense of itself *by* the Congregation. Therefore we must be careful about the sight-lines."

280

A Memorial Synagogue

He hesitated. "The sight-lines. I arrange the seats in two banks, facing each other across a plain. The Ark is at the eastern end of the plain. See, the sight-lines: everybody is in full view."

He hesitated and began to draw lines on the tracing-paper.

"They flash across the space! Sometimes they get tangled in mid-air. What does *that* mean? It means that a man gets the impression he is being stared at.

"Don't misunderstand me," he apologized. "I'm not saying that it's embarrassing to be looked at; if that were so it would be the end of architecture; but—not just now.

"Strictly speaking there is nothing else to see in the Jewish service except the Congregation itself. There is no sacrificial act.

"A few men are called up to bless the passage; that's all the service consists of. That's what we have to keep in full view. Here they open the scroll to read it, and quidam is called on to bless the passage. Ach! *everybody* is suddenly looking at him, a fine representative figure of a man!

"Suppose with an angry flush on his face, he turns and stares at *you!*

"Maybe the visible Congregation is not such a good idea after all and something is to be said for the stained glass.

"The old men cover their heads with their prayer-shawls, but you could never get the young ones to do it. They are ashamed to be ashamed."

He began to slash the paper with heavy lines, as if the sight-lines were clashing in the space like knives.

He hesitated. The hesitation endured, but there was no moment at which you could say he fell silent.

Finally some one prompted him. "What about the sight-lines? What do they see?"

"The people are crying," he said.

He heaved a sigh of relief. "That solves the problem!" he said more cheerfully. "Each one is hiding behind a shiny wall of tears; they can't see each other anyway."

New York City
1935-1947

Textual Note

Goodman published four collections of stories during his lifetime, *The Facts of Life, The Break-Up of Our Camp, Our Visit to Niagara,* and *Adam and His Works.* The last was a collected edition and included most of the stories in the other three as well as a few "new" ones. Many other stories appeared only in magazines, and still others were never published at all. When he reprinted a story in a collection, he usually revised it, often extensively. Others were tailored to the needs of novels in which they were to be inserted.

In preparing this complete edition of all of Goodman's stories and sketches, I have returned to the earliest printed versions for my texts. Much of Goodman's revising was done twenty, even thirty years after first writing, and his style had changed enough to put his revisions at odds with his original conceptions. The general effect was to make all the stories, early and late, share a diction and syntax that is mere patina, spread thin over the variety of literary voices and manners he explored during a long career. His last and fullest revisions—for the majority of stories in *Adam and His Works*—were undertaken years after he had stopped writing fiction altogether, and after his style had undergone a journalistic refurbishing for his mass audience as a social critic.

I think that in every case his original stories are better than these later revisions. Moreover, since this is to be the definitive edition of his short fiction, there is good reason to represent his career as accurately as possible in its range

283

and its development. The revised versions mask and blur the relevant distinctions. And in any case they are already widely available in *Adam and His Works*, whereas the original texts are scattered among dozens of ephemeral magazines, and in books published in tiny editions, long out of print. Moreover, it would make little sense to print side by side stories written in the same year, one as it first appeared, the other as it was altered after decades had elapsed. Many of Goodman's stories did not find their way into any collection, and so were never revised. This edition includes twenty previously uncollected stories, nineteen never before published, and two dozen others that have appeared only in the special issue of *New Letters* magazine I edited in 1976. The establishment of an historical canon for all of these will make it possible to study the unfolding of Goodman's career by bringing together works that although written in the same period, repeating the same motifs, and even referring to one another, have never been available within the covers of a single volume.

(In the case of *The Break-Up of Our Camp*, I have used the text of the first publication of the entire work, rather than of the individual stories, to preserve its overall unity. In order to sustain similar values in *Johnson*, I have accepted the manuscript version as my basic text. Only two of the *Johnson* stories were published at the time of composition, and while retaining the substantive changes— not many—of those, I have emended the spelling and punctuation of the published versions to conform to the manuscripts. Still another chapter, "Martin, or The Work of Art," was published many years later, greatly altered, and since the original manuscript no longer exists, it has been treated here as an appendix.)

One further principle of selection needs to be mentioned. As the title of this collection suggests, it includes a number of works that are not strictly speaking stories, though they are not quite essays either but something in-between. A comparison of "The Father of the Psychoanalytic Movement" and "Golden Age" (see the edition of Goodman's psychological essays, *Nature Heals*, Free Life Editions, 1977), will illustrate the shading of one genre into the other, and my cut-off point: the former I include here among his fictions, but not the latter. On a slightly different basis I have excluded "The Diggers in 1984," a political tract disguised as fiction; Goodman himself so regarded it, and did not include it in *Adam and His Works*. I have also excluded separately published chapters of novels unless there is good evidence that they were originally intended as stories. Thus there is nothing here from *Parents' Day*, although some of it was first published in a magazine, as if a story; contrariwise, "Eagle's Bridge" and "The Continuum of the Libido" are included because they were conceived as separate works. The two adventures of St. Wayward and the Laughing Laddy, from the abortive fifth volume of *The Empire City*, represent still another category, works that were intended as parts of a novel but became short stories instead—as indicated by Goodman's including one of them in *Adam*. And of course I have included his two novels-in-stories, *Johnson* and *The Break-Up of Our Camp*.

Of the unpublished stories I have printed all that cannot be classed as unfinished or juvenilia. This is a matter of judgment. My own conviction is that Goodman's maturity came at a normal age for writers of fiction, about his twenty-fifth year. Anything written after *The Break-Up of Our Camp*, his first major novel, I have regarded as mature work even if Goodman never published it; stories written before 1936 have been considered on their merits. A few pieces published in high school and college periodicals have been omitted, but otherwise I have included everything of his apprenticeship that saw print, as well as several that he tried to publish, unsuccessfully. The manuscripts for a couple of dozen others, chiefly exercises of his undergraduate days, survive among his papers.

In editing this large body of work, I have tried to preserve Goodman's original intentions so far as they could be determined. Publishers took various liberties with his texts, and where I am sure Goodman preferred some other reading, I have adopted it. Thus I have restored "obscenities" censored by cautious editors, and have rescued the ending of "A Prayer for Dew" from the hell-box where its first printers dumped it when it would not fit the page.

Goodman's spelling and punctuation were somewhat idiosyncratic, especially during the first two decades of his career. Some publishers made his prose conform to their own style-books, others did not. I have not attempted to sort out his usage from theirs, for there is nothing to go by, case by case; he usually discarded his manuscripts as soon as a work had appeared in print. In most of the early stories "though" is written as "tho," "through" is "thru," etc., according to Goodman's habit. Exceptions probably represent editorial changes, to which he may or may not have agreed. Punctuation is even more difficult to deal with, for his own practice was sometimes inconsistent and careless, sometimes purposeful if eccentric. I have regularized a few recurrent patterns according to the modern usage that he himself sometimes followed, changing the old-fashioned "such-and-such,—" and "so-and-so;—" to "such-and-such—" or "so-and-so—" and sometimes "so-and-so;" depending on the sense. And I have made the use of quotation marks consistent, dispensing with them entirely for passages already marked as quotation by indenting. I have printed such indented passages in the roman font, even though Goodman often set them off by italics. (In making such emendations I have been instructed by particular instances of regularization in *Adam and His Works*.) Aside from these, and the correction of obvious typographical errors, the texts are as they first appeared.

Goodman ordinarily entered the place and date of composition at the end of each story. I have included these whenever I could find them appended to any version of the text, and I have supplied them in brackets for those stories that must be dated by extrinsic means. The order is intended to be strictly chronological, but there are a few cases where it has not been possible to discover which of several stories was written first in a given year.

The following is the publishing history of the stories included in this volume; reprints in magazines or anthologies are not listed unless of special interest. I wish to thank those publishers below who have given their permission, or otherwise facilitated the publication of stories which first appeared under their imprint. Admirers of Goodman's work should be grateful to David Ray, editor of *New Letters*, for first making so many of the unpublished stories available. I also want to thank my co-literary executors Sally Goodman, George Dennison, and Jason Epstein for their help, and my friend John Dings, and my wife Ruth Perry.

Collections

The Facts of Life (New York: Vanguard, 1945).
The Break-Up of Our Camp and Other Stories (Norfolk, Conn.: New Directions, 1949).
Our Visit to Niagara (New York: Horizon, 1960).
Adam and His Works (New York: Vintage, 1968).
The Writings of Paul Goodman, ed. Taylor Stoehr, *New Letters*, XLII (Winter-Spring 1976).

Publishing History

"A Study of Johnson" [1932], *New Letters*, 1976.

"Johnson and the Total Good" [1932], *New Letters*, 1976.

"The Mirrors (1932), *New Letters*, 1976.

"The Moon" [1932], *New Letters*, 1976.

"Dialogue of the Clock and Cat" (1933), *New Letters*, 1976.

"The Rivers" (1932), *New Letters*, 1976.

"The Tennis-Game" (1932), *Lavender* [City College literary magazine] (May 1933); *New Letters*, 1976.

"Out of Love" (1933), *Columbia Review*, XVII (May-June 1936); *New Letters*, 1976.

"Martin, or The Work of Art" (1933-1951), *Adam*, 1968.

"The Wandering Boys" (1933), *Symposium*, IV (July 1933).

"Pictures of Things Moving Toward their Goals" (1933), *New Letters*, 1976 (in part).

"The Propriety of St. Francis" (1933), *Mosaic*, I (Spring 1935).

"Dresses, Architecture and Church Services" (1933), *New Letters*, 1976.

"Iddings Clark" (1933), *Horizon*, IX (February 1944); *Facts of Life*, 1945; *Adam*, 1968.

"The Fight in the Museum" (January 4, 1934), *Tomorrow*, VI (June 1947).

"Phaëthon, Myth" (March-April 1934), unpublished.

"Gamblers" (1934), *Break-Up of Our Camp*, 1949.

"The Detective Story" (1934-1935), *New Directions in Prose and Poetry 8* (ed. James Laughlin, Norfolk, Conn.: New Directions, 1944); *Facts of Life*, 1945; *Adam*, 1968.

"The Joke" (1935), *Tomorrow*, V (January 1946); *Break-Up of Our Camp*, 1949; *Adam*, 1968.

"A Prayer for Dew" (1935), *The Reform Advocate*, XCIII (May 14, 1937); *Commentary*, I (November 1945); *Break-Up of Our Camp*, 1949; *Adam*, 1968.

288

"The Canoeist" (1935), *Facts of Life*, 1945; *Break-Up of Our Camp*, 1949; *Adam*, 1968.

"The Break-Up of Camp" [1935], *Break-Up of Our Camp*, 1949; *Adam*, 1968.

"A Congregation of Jews" [1935], *Jewish Frontier*, XIV (April 1947); *Break-Up of Our Camp*, 1949; *Adam*, 1968.

"Ostoric" [1935], *Break-Up of Our Camp*, 1949; *Adam*, 1968.

"A Hitch-Hike" [1935], *Break-Up of Our Camp*, 1949; *Adam*, 1968.

"A Memorial Synagogue" [1947], *Break-Up of Our Camp*, 1949; *Adam*, 1968.

Printed February 1978 in Santa Barbara & Ann Arbor for the Black Sparrow Press by Mackintosh and Young & Edwards Brothers Inc. Design by Barbara Martin. This edition is published in paper wrappers; there are 750 hardcover trade copies; & 200 special copies have been handbound in boards by Earle Gray.

Paul Goodman (1911-1972) the well-known social critic (*Growing Up Absurd, Compulsory Mis-education, People or Personnel, The New Reformation,* and many other books) had several careers before his fame in the Sixties. He was trained as a philosopher at the University of Chicago, taught literature in various colleges, became an expert on community planning with his architect brother Percival Goodman, taught ninth-graders in a progressive school, founded with Fritz Perls the Gestalt Therapy Institute and practiced psychotherapy, married and raised three children—all while living on an average income about that of a Southern sharecropper (when he started doing therapy in the early Fifties, his income jumped to $2,000 for the first time in his life). But these were really just his sidelines, and the reason that he lived in voluntary poverty rather than following one of the more lucrative callings open to him was that he regarded his work as a creative artist his true vocation. Among his thirty-odd books his novels, plays, short stories, and poems would fill a shelf by themselves. His masterpiece is *The Empire City,* a comic epic written in the tradition and with the zest of *Don Quixote.* His *Collected Poems* contain, among hundreds of fine poems, the extraordinary sequence he wrote in mourning for his son Mathew, *North Percy,* probably the most moving elegy in American letters. Even though they never made much stir during his lifetime, Goodman knew the worth of these works, and yet he himself spoke of his short stories as his personal favorites. He gave one of his volumes of stories to a friend in the mid-Sixties, and wrote in it that it was his best book. When asked why he preferred it, he said, "That's the book I think is lovely—*Our Visit to Niagara*—I just like it, everything in it. That last story—'The Galley to Mytilene'—it's enchanting, I love to read it."

The present four-volume edition of *The Collected Stories and Sketches* includes all of Goodman's previously collected stories, plus dozens that have never appeared in book form, and twenty new pieces, written during every stage of his literary career and published here for the first time.